Co

MW01235472

A SECOND CHANCE AT GOODBYE

BOOK ONE
A COMING HOME SERIES

TORI BAILEY

Tori Bailey

TURNIP PRESS PUBLISHING

Tori Bailey

ISBN-978-0692572740

Third Edition
Originally Published As
Coming Home

Cover and Interior Design
pdkingdesign.com

REVIEWS

"A very captivating book to read. The characters are real, and you become engrossed in the story line. The Dew recommends it."

—Idgie@Dew on The Kudzu

"Tori Bailey knows how to spin a Southern tale that is universal to all readers."

—Barbara Barth, author *Danger in Her Words*

DEDICATION

E.H.S.

PROLOGUE

Athens, Georgia

Mac walked through the old World War II hangar. The airport had a certain tranquillity to it at night. Everywhere he looked was a symbol of his years of hard work. He had built a successful business doing the one thing he enjoyed, flying.

It had not been easy, but he'd built a reputation as a pilot and a mechanic, one that was as solid as the old wooden railroad desk in his office. Piles of flying magazines, stacks of papers, and parts manuals littered the top. He took a bottle of Drambuie from the old Barrister bookcase. Never one for the hard stuff, he liked the taste of the liqueur. Late nights at his desk were the only time he indulged himself.

Mac pulled on the bottom desk drawer and reached inside for the folder he'd stashed earlier. The echo of a police radio against the stillness of the hangar's interior indicated the arrival of a long time customer and friend.

"Sorry, I'm a bit late getting here. I had to go to a robbery scene at the Iron Triangle." Paul Carroll leaned against the doorframe.

"Must have been important if the Captain of Investigations had to respond."

"Yeah, someone decided to rob the stop–n–go and put a

bullet in the store clerk." Paul reached to his side and turn down the volume of the radio. "So, what's on your mind?"

"Look at these and tell me what you think." Mac handed Paul the folder. "Notice I've circled any entries related to DE Aviation on the bank statements."

"Why's that?" Paul took the pages from Mac and sat on the sofa.

"Because I've never heard of them. Also, notice how there's no mention of DE Aviation on Lynda's financial reports."

"What made you suspicious?" Paul continued to scrutinize each item.

"I called Cooper Aviation last week to order some parts and was referred to their collections department. Imagine my surprise when I found my account was on hold due to non-payment."

"You think Lynda's stealing from you?"

"At this moment, yes." Mac paused to take a drink. "I tried to get into the files in her office. She keeps everything locked, including her desk."

"You say anything to her?"

"No." Mac swallowed, hoping the burning in his chest would ease. He wished he had not eaten the second piece of Ethel's lemon meringue pie at dinner. It was hard to stop when it came to his sister-in-law's cooking.

"Ummm, how much do you know about her?"

"Not much. Nick was the one who recommended her to me. Said she moved up here from Florida and needed a job. I was trying to handle everything by myself without Maggie."

"Aren't she and Dennis living together?"

"I think she moved in with him a few months ago."

"What about Keegan?"

"Why do you ask? He's a good kid and a damn good

mechanic. Keeps to himself." Keegan had shown up six months ago asking if Mac was hiring. Mac remembered the man from his trips to St. Simons. He heard about the incident in St. Simons. As a recipient of rabid airport gossip and innuendos, Mac understood all too well and empathized with Keegan. He judged people by their character and did not hesitate to give Keegan a job.

"Just thinking." Paul laid the pages to the side. "Let me do some checking."

"I appreciate this. When you going flying again?"

"I was thinking about taking the one-seventy-two down to the Keys to do some scuba diving. I've got some vacation coming up next month."

"Let me know, and I'll make sure she's ready."

"Thanks." Paul felt his pager vibrating and gazed down at the digital display, "That's dispatch looking for me. I'll catch you later."

Mac opened a bottle of antacids and popped a few of the chalky tablets in his mouth. The burning sensation in his chest continued to grow. He leaned back in his chair, his attention resting on two pictures. He took the one with a young woman standing next to the faded turquoise and white Cessna one-fifty. Her hand rested on the wing's strut. Mac studied her image. He could smell the sweet scent of her perfume, hear the lilt of her laughter, and feel the warmth of her touch. Even though a pair of aviator sunglasses hid her eyes, he could envision their shade of brown with flecks of green. His gaze rested on her mouth. The countless times he'd kissed it, taking for granted that those kisses would always be his to steal. Maybe he was wrong to have pushed her away. Mac put the picture of Maggie back in its spot.

He studied the second picture of a teenage girl. It was the only one he had of his daughter, Anne. Freckles dotted the bridge of an upturned nose pressed against the face of a grayish white horse. She had grown into a beautiful woman. He wished the divide in their relationship did not exist.

"Hello, old friend."

Startled by the baritone voice, Mac dropped the picture. A crack formed across the glass from the impact with the floor. "You use the term old friend loosely." The man drew from his cigar and exhaled before entering the office. He stopped in front of the desk and picked up the bottle of Drambuie. "You still drink this cough syrup? Personally, I like a good single malt. Now that stuff will put fire in your belly."

"I'm sure you didn't come all this way to talk about my drinking habits."

The man's potbelly shook from laughter. "Never said you were dumb, Harris."

"Never implied you did. What's the occasion that brings you here?"

"Just thought it was time to tie up some loose ends."

"Not sure what you mean."

"Guess what they say about age and memory is true, how time erases things." Ashes from the man's cigar fell to the floor. "My memory is clear as a bell though."

"Is that what this is about?" Mac did not break eye contact with the man.

The man leaned back and took another draw from the cigar. Not a muscle flinched in his aged-etched face. Gray-ish-white smoke billowed like a smoke-stack with the long exhale. "Despite everything, I've done well for myself. Shame the same can't be said for you."

"Don't know what you mean." The stench of the cigar robbed Mac of his breath.

"Word's gotten around you are about to go bankrupt. So I thought I'd come and help an old friend by offering to buy his business."

"It's not for sale."

"Can't say it's up to my normal standards of places I like to acquire, but for you, I'm willing not to consider how antiquated this place looks. How's that mechanic of yours working out?"

"None of your business." Mac tried to ignore the tingling sensation in his left arm.

"Touchy now. You always did have a soft spot for helping others. I guess your legacy should read Saint Mac…oh, that's right; you don't have much of a religious foundation. Guess you depend on that sister-in-law of yours to pray for your soul. How is Ethel?"

"Fine."

"Sure didn't take her long to move in and sit up house after Diane's death."

Mac did not like the man's insinuations about Ethel. "Look, I've said the place ain't for sale."

"Come on, Harris. Everyone knows you can't pay your debts. It's also no secret you're having problem with the local Airport Authority about this dinosaur of a hangar." The man gestured toward the picture of Maggie. "She sure was a looker then. I never figured you would have had the guts to let her go like you did."

Mac eyes dilated with surprise. "How would you know about Maggie?"

"I've kept up with you through the years." The man reached down and picked up the broken picture frame from the floor. "Sure does look like her ma. Shame she had to lose her like she did. Understand she's just as easy as her ma was." He continued to study the image. "You know she could've been mine. What is the saying, you always know your momma, but your daddy's questionable."

Mac lunged for the man. The picture of Maggie teetered before landing on the floor. Mac grabbed his left arm. The tingling turned into throbbing pain. The man dusted cigar ash from his black trousers and stood over Mac. "Bet you sure are upset she's been fooling around with that fly boy of yours, Nick Masden. Must stick in your craw to see a trusted friend take advantage of those you love."

The pain from Mac's left arm radiated into his back and up to his jaw. His heart felt as if it was in a vice. His body became lighter with each gasping breath. The man placed one of the snake-skinned boots in the center of Mac's chest and applied pressure. "Harris, you don't look so well. Wish there was something I could do for you." The picture of Anne dropped from his hand and landed on the floor beside Maggie's.

Thoughts and images swirled in Mac's mind, but one thought prevailed. He was dying. He fought to make sense of what he knew were his last moments. A lifetime of hard-headedness compelled him to take control of these fleeting seconds. His last conscious act was to once again study the photos of two beautiful young women who had defined his life.

ONE

nne felt like a stranger in the home she'd known since childhood. Most of the people were unfamiliar to her. She focused her attention to the man standing next to her. What she needed was a distraction and he was just the cure she needed. "I swear if another person comes up to me saying how great my father was I will have a conniption right here. There's more people here than at visitation last night. All of them with nothing but glowing comments and funny little stories of their encounters with the late Mac Harris."

The outburst coming from his late friend's daughter did not surprise Nick. It was no secret that Mac did not have a warm father-daughter relationship with Anne. "I have to admit it is overwhelming the number of people Mac knew." Nick scanned the room looking for a familiar face he was sure would have been among the crowd.

"You seem to be looking for someone specific."

"What do you mean?" Nick wished Anne was not so observant.

"Every time someone enters a room, you look to see who they are. What did you think? SHE would have the audacity to show up at his funeral. Wouldn't it be a little too late to try to make amends with a dead person?"

"One can never tell. The death of someone once held dear can make people do strange things. You can't help but be a little on the curious side to see if she would be here."

"I wouldn't hold my breath. She got what she wanted from my father." Anne concentrated on the three employees of Mac's Flying Service. The only one she knew was Dennis. Mac had brought him home for supper at times. He had been flight instructing at her dad's business since he graduated high school. She guessed Dennis to be about thirty. "I know I can depend on you to help me run the business until a buyer can be found."

Nick smiled at Anne's statement. "Hey your wishes are always my command. I spoke with Jared and Kyle. They were receptive to me flying for them until they can find a new pilot. Concerning a buyer, you let me worry about that. You have your hands full with the stables."

"Thanks Nick." Anne pressed against him. "I wonder what dear old dad would of thought if he'd known about us."

Nick took a sip from the watered down bourbon to wet his dry throat. "I haven't seen your Aunt Ethel. Usually she is like a social butterfly all around the place."

The mention of her aunt made her wonder where the woman had disappeared. She looked around the room and was met with a pair of disapproving eyes. Her Aunt Ethel was in the midst of giving their owner a hug.

"Isn't that dad's new mechanic talking to Aunt Ethel?" Anne remembered the man being introduced to her at the funeral. He had been sincere in offering his sympathies. The past two days had been a blur of people shaking her hand, giving her a hug, or placing a hand on her shoulder while the offered words of condolences or support.

"Yes. His name is Keegan O'Keefe." Nick followed Anne's gaze, "Why?"

"No reason, just curious." Anne did not like the way his

stare made her feel. She was tired of feeling judged by everyone in the room. She diverted her attention back to Nick. "Feel like slipping upstairs to my old room?"

"Anne Harris, shame on you. What would people think of the late Mac Harris's daughter consorting with such a cad like me?"

"When did you grow a sense of social etiquette and give a damn about what others thought of you?" Anne softened her voice to over emphasize her southern drawl. She lowered her gaze before looking back up at him through her long eyelashes. "Why Mister Masden, I's nevah known you to turn down a proposition, 'specially one full of risqué." Anne placed her hand on Nick's chest and allowed it to travel downward. "Or do you think you might have problems performing knowing Dad's room is just across the hall?" Anne blue eyes darkened to violet with devilment.

"Miss Harris, it seems that you have put me in quite a predicament." Nick played along with Anne. "I find myself in need to defend my manhood. I must do the honorable thing and accept your challenge."

"We can sneak up the back stairs." Anne smiled to herself what she needed was a distraction.

****

"Anne's behavior is nothing but disrespect for Mac's memory." Lynda snipped at Dennis.

Dennis tried to sound stern while chiding her. "Now Lynda, calm down. I didn't realize you held such deep feelings for Mac's memory. Or is it jealousy that she's with Nick."

"You know I am long over him. Nick Madsen has no loyalties except for himself." Lynda turned her golden eyes up to Dennis and smiled. It was getting tiring dealing with his insecurities. "Anyway, you should know by now you are who I want."

Dennis knew the words were meant to soothe him. He still could not wrap his brain around having a woman like Lynda. "Wonder where Keegan got lost."

"Not sure." Lynda was glad Keegan had not returned. "Have you had a chance to speak with Jared or Kyle?"

"I spoke with Jared last night at the funeral home. He expressed how he didn't feel right discussing business at the time."

"That's interesting, because I saw both of them with Nick outside the funeral home. The three of them were huddled together. They all shook hands before leaving. "

"Time will tell. They may have been sharing old times about Mac."

Lynda tried to curtail her impatience with Dennis. "Could have been."

"Like I said, time will tell."

"Time will tell what?" Keegan rejoined the group.

"About the future of Mac's Flying Service." Dennis replied. "I thought you had gotten lost."

"I stopped to speak with Aunt Ethel." Keegan took a sip of sweet tea. "The word from everyone is that Anne will get the business and sell it. Guess it's time to start updating my resume again."

"I guess all three of us need to be doing that." Lynda tried to ignore all the speculations of her job future. She was also tired of acting like she cared about Mac Harris being dead. "If you gentlemen will excuse me I need to find the powder room."

Both men stood in silence and watched Lynda's retreating

back. Keegan thought about how cool she seemed below the surface. He never understood the attraction between his two co-workers. Dennis seemed a little out of her league. "Do you know when the family plans to read the will?"

"From what Aunt Ethel told me, it'll be within the next day or two." Keegan sat the glass of tea on an end table. "She said Madison needed to make some contacts before everyone could get together."

"I wonder who they need to get together for the reading. It would seems like everyone involve is already here." Dennis's shoulders shook as he chuckled.

"Care to share your private joke?"

"Yeah, you know the kicker in this whole situation?" The more Dennis thought about the scenario the more it made sense. "What if Mac left his business to someone else."

"Couldn't think who that'd be."

Dennis thought of the one person who loved Mac's Flying Service more than Mac. "I was thinking more like a ghost from the past. Maggie Cosby."

In his short time at Mac's, Keegan felt like he knew her from the stories Mac would tell. "What makes you say that, considering she didn't even attend Mac's funeral?"

"Don't know." Dennis saw Lynda headed his way with her purse and his coat. "Looks like Lynda is ready. See you tomorrow."

****

"People never cease to amaze me." Paul watched Nick follow Anne.

"Yeah, know what you mean." Seth held little regard for Nick or Anne. Both struck him as selfish people. "You were on duty the other morning when Mac's body was found."

"I was on my way to headquarters when the call was dispatched." Paul thought about the sinking feeling he had when the patrol unit request for both the Coroner and an Investigator to a death scene. Although the officer had not given Mac's name across the police radio, the code for business owner had been used. "Things were pretty interesting when I arrived on scene. Dennis, Lynda and Keegan kept to themselves inside the hangar. The crime scene guys were busy in Mac's office."

Paul thought about how he was probably the last person to see Mac alive. On the surface, Mac's death appeared to be natural but it felt too convenient, considering their last conversation. He kept replaying every aspect of their meeting. There was one missing link that stood out in his mind since Mac's death. "I'm surprised Maggie is not here."

Seth recalled the tall slender woman with reddish auburn hair. He remembered how her brown eyes held flecks of green. "I wonder if she knows."

"I'm sure Madison contacted her. He still talks to her on occasion." Paul paused long enough to take a swig of the diluted sweet tea. "She was a hell of an instructor."

"Seeing her elbow deep in grease helping Mac work on one of the planes wasn't unusual. She never took any of our ribbing to heart." Seth thought of the early days when both of them were flight students. "Mac was hard on her in the beginning. There were times he pushed her to the point I felt sorry for her. She never complained about what he expected of her. "

"I felt the same way too."

Both men stood in silence each to their own thoughts. Paul scanned the room. Reading people's body language and expressions had become an essential tool for him. Ethel and Madison became the subjects of his people watching. The two had secluded themselves from the group. By Ethel's movements and facial expressions, it was easy to surmise the topic of conversation was intense. If Paul had to guess, it had to do with Anne. "Ethel and Madison seem to be in an intense conversation over there."

"They've been in the same spot for quite some time. Madison keeps looking at his watch."

****

"Her assistant said she would be back in her office around three." Madison mentally subtracted the hour from his watch to accommodate the difference in time zones.

"No time is going to be good." Ethel tried to sound strong. She placed a hand on his arm and gave it a squeeze. "You can make the call from the study. Do you want me there with you?"

"No, I just wish I didn't have to do this over the phone." Madison closed the door to the study. His fingers instinctively punched the familiar numbers to an old friend.

****

The throbbing headache continued to march through Maggie's temples. She leaned her head against the soft leather of her chair and stared at Nashville's skyline. In a few hours Briley Parkway would become a parking lot. She took in a deep breath and released it. She hated being enclosed in this office. The magnetic pull of a faraway place and time strengthen its grip on her memories and heart. Her mind drifted to the days she had spent in the World War II hangar with Mac.

The phone's ringing interrupted Maggie's thoughts. "General Aviation Operations, Inspector Cosby."

"Hello, Maggie." The image of Madison's tall athletic build

with salt and pepper hair came to her mind.

"Madison! How the hell are you? It's sooooo good to hear from you." The absence of a smart retort brought concern. The heavy breath followed with the nervous clearing of his throat made Maggie sit forward in her chair. She closed her eyes wishing she could close her ears and heart.

"Maggie, Mac passed away." There, he'd said it. He'd rehearsed different ways to say such a simple message. In the end, the words formed themselves.

The impact of Madison's word delivered a sucker punch to her emotions. She bent over and tried to control her breathing. The acid taste of bile burned the back of her throat. Maggie reached for the trash can and heaved.

"Maggie, Maggie you still there?" The thud of the phone hitting the floor brought Madison to his feet. He should have flown up and told her in person. Shoulda-woulda-and coulda wasn't going to help him now. "Maggie, please say something!" He shouted.

In a hushed breath, two words exhaled through the phone. "How, Madison?"

Madison's body sunk into the leather chair behind Ethel's desk. The racing heart that had threatened to escape his chest began to slow. "He was found in his office. They thinks it was a heart attack. Maggie, you okay?" As soon as the question was asked, Madison thought of its absurdity.

"I guess." Maggie focused on the picture of the Bonanza on her desk. A single thought whirled through Maggie's head. The man in the picture was gone, forever. "When's the funeral?"

"It was today. I tried several times to contact you. I wish I could have let you know sooner." He knew she was trying to keep a strong resolve.

"It's for the best that I was not there anyway. I would have been like a turd in the punch bowl, uninvited and unwanted." Maggie thought about Mac's daughter, Anne. The woman always seemed safety-wired in the pissed-off mode.

Madison cracked a smile and felt relief. "You have the most unique way of putting things." He paused at the small chuckle followed with a sniffle from the other end of the phone. He also recognized the truth in Maggie humour. "There is a meeting tomorrow concerning Mac's estate. I realize this is short notice but you need to be present."

"Madison, I'll be there, though I am not quite sure why I'd be needed." Maggie did not relish the idea of having to be in the same room with Anne. "I guess Anne will be there also."

"Yes, and Ethel. Will you fly down?"

"No, I'll drive. What time do I need to be at your office?"

"The meeting is at ten. You can come a little early to give us some time to visit."

"Then I'll see you in the morning." Maggie surveyed her office, the overflowing schedule of meetings on her calendar, and the stack of pending case files. Now it all seemed insignificant. All she wanted to do was to go home to Athens, the hangar and say goodbye to Mac.

TWO

tark white cumulus clouds floated against a cobalt sky. Maggie listened to the familiar voice that always guided her. "Use the right rudder to keep the nose straight with the cloud in front of you. Continue increasing back pressure and adding full throttle until you feel the airplane stall."

She hated stalls. The sensation of falling backwards became prevalent with the nose vertical to the horizon. The stall warning horn's loud shrill increased. With a shudder, the airplane's wings could no longer sustain the lift needed for flight.

Maggie released the back pressure on the control wheel. The nose of the plane did not drop to the horizon but rotated violently into a spin. The stall warning horn still shrieked of impending danger. She tried everything Mac had taught her to stop the spin to no avail. She looked over expecting to see Mac helping her stop the spin. His body was slumped against the door of the plane.

The sound of her voice screaming Mac's name ripped her from tormented sleep. The fog of the dream cleared. Reality that she was alone in a darkened hotel room began to settle upon her. A single tap silenced the obnoxious shrill of the alarm clock.

Out of habit and to clear the nightmare from her mind, Maggie pointed the remote control at the television. She flipped through the channels and settled for the cable weather channel. She and Mac had planned many of their days around the information provided by the morning's weather reports.

Days predicting bad weather meant working in the office. Sunny days meant back–to–back students with little time for a quick bite of lunch. Today's weather looked like it was going to be a sunny day.

The morning paper being dropped outside the room's door prompted Maggie to crawl out of bed. Reading the local paper had been another morning ritual. With it in hand, she started to sit on the edge of the bed. The headline made her almost land in the floor instead of the comfort of the mattress, "Airport Authority Considers Second Phase of Master Plan." She skimmed the first few paragraphs. The final comments of the article made her pulse quicken with anger.

The second phase of the Master Plan will include the removal of the old World War II Hangar, now used as Mac's Flying Service. According to one member of the Authority, "The recent passing of Mac Harris has left the future operation of his business uncertain. There has been an interest made in the lease of this property. All of us here on the Airport Authority have felt a sense of loss with the passing of Mac. His business helped shape the airport as it is today."

Pages of the newspaper floated to the floor around Maggie's feet. "The gall of them! Mac's not been dead a week." She kicked at the pages scattering them. "The damn buzzards are already circling, impatient to get their claws on what Mac had built from scratch."

****

Still angry from the article, Maggie decided to walk to Madison's office. She inhaled the autumn air filled with aromas from various restaurants, tainted with the overbearing sweet scent of yeast, and tinged with the stench of stale beer. This was Athens. This was her home.

She often told people that you could take the girl out of Georgia, but you couldn't take Georgia out of the girl. Tennessee fans in her office often teased her that she needed to learn to love the color of orange. Her retort was that her blood ran red and black with immunities against anything orange.

A gentle breeze moved through the Ginkgo trees lining College Avenue. Maggie enjoyed glancing in the windows of shops that had become institutions to the famous strip. Heery's Closet touted all of the latest fall fashions every college girl's closet had to have. The Grill had moved next to Barnett's News Stand from its tiny location on the corner. Flyers for the Forty Watt Club advertised bands coming to play. Remnants of the old church steeple where REM performed their first public show stood in the distance.

Maggie turned the corner and found herself standing outside Madison's office. She squared her shoulders, straightened her posture, and pushed open the door. Madison stopped in mid-sentence. He did not wait for Maggie to close the door. He encompassed her and gave her a tight hug. "Hey, girl."

Maggie sought comfort and strength in his embrace. It had been almost a year since she'd seen him. He often called her when he was in Nashville on a case. Sometimes, he stayed in her spare bedroom. Maggie stepped back and was not surprised to see the casual dress of the man in front of her. "What no suit and tie for the fancy new address? You've come a long way from the Victorian on Prince Avenue."

"Hey, just because the address changes doesn't mean I have. Only time I wear my monkey suit is when required. Come on into my office. We have a few minutes before the others arrive."

Maggie walked beside Madison. Everything about the

office's interior spoke of the essence of its occupant. Dark paneled walls with golden oak hardwood floors. It was cozy but not cramped. Maggie was sure Madison had hand selected every detail of this office. "Madison, why am I here?"

The announcement of Ethel's arrival helped Madison dodge Maggie's question. With arms open, she walked over and collected Maggie into a motherly hug "Let me get a good look at you...still skinny as ever. You need some of my cooking to get some meat on those bones of yours. Come on and tell me how you've been. Mac used to keep me up to date on how well you were doing with the FAA. He was so proud of you."

The older woman's revelation that Mac had kept up with her gave birth to dueling emotions. Part of Maggie found warmth by the thought while another part was angered. "I though he didn't care about what happened after I left the hangar."

"Hon that man never stopped loving you. I told him he was a fool for pushing you away. Still, Mac could be stubborn as a mule when he got a notion in his head." Ethel knew she'd been talking to a brick wall with Mac when it came to Maggie. Mac had surprised Ethel one night after dinner when he began to talk about Maggie. It was the first time since her departure that he broached the subject. The man she had considered to be as strong as an oak became old, tired, and lonely. For the second time in her life, she witnessed him weep. That night Ethel gave her solemn word to take care of Anne and Maggie. She did not realize that six weeks later she would have to honor her promise.

****

Anne stopped in the threshold of the office. Her eyes went straight to Maggie. Her body became rigid. Both hands balled into fists. "What the hell is she doing here? She has absolutely no right to be here."

"Listen here, I best suggest you get a civil tongue in that head of yours. She is here because this involves her too." Ethel's thick southern drawl had not been loud, but the impact of her words filled the room. "Now, act like you know some manners and not like a spoiled child."

Madison had expected Anne's reaction not to be a pleasant one. The open hostility in her eyes toward Maggie took him by surprise. He was thankful for Ethel's presence. Madison cleared his throat and began. "The purpose of this meeting is in regard to the last will and testament of the late Malcolm J. Harris. It was Mac's decision that I act as Executor of his estate." He directed his attention to Ethel and Anne. "I will be responsible for handling all of his funeral expenses and financial accounts until the will is probated. Ethel, Mac has deeded the house and rental property in White Hall to you. He also left you a sum of money in hopes that you start your catering business you have dreamed of having."

A muffled sob escaped from Ethel.

Madison paused and looked at Anne and Maggie. He never understood how Mac could let someone like Maggie walk out of his life. Then there was Anne. Mac had felt guilty for not being there for Anne after Diane's death. He hated seeing his daughter bounce from one casual affair to another. He often joked that if there was any way he could leave in his will a husband for Anne, he would. Mac often commented that the man would have to be as bullheaded as she was stubborn.

"Anne, your father loved you very much."

"Yeah, that's why he was such an attentive father and husband." Anne felt Ethel's hand squeeze her knee as a warning.

14

"Just get to the bottom line of things. What about that business of his?"

"Anne, your father left the farm to you, but the business is Maggie's."

Anne sprang from the sofa. Her momentum stopped with the placement of each hand on the arms of Maggie's chair. She hissed into Maggie's face. "That business does not belong to you, just like you don't belong here. I was so happy when you left. I thought good riddance."

Maggie felt the heat of Anne's breath in her face with all of its fire. She pushed herself up, making Anne take a step backwards. "What's wrong, Anne? Disappointed you are not going to get to destroy the one thing Mac cared about more than either of us." Maggie's emotions matched the anger and pain in Anne's eyes. "Here's a news flash for you. I didn't know about this."

Ethel feared that if she did not step between the two women, there would be more than hissing between them. "That is enough, Anne. You need to get a hold of yourself right now, young lady."

Shocked by the chastisement, Anne turned her venom toward Ethel. "You knew about this didn't you? That's why you and Madison were huddled up in the study yesterday." The one person she never believed would betray her had. This whole meeting had been a trap, and she'd strolled right into it. "How could you Aunt Ethel?"

Ethel's heart squeezed at the accusation of betrayal. "Anne, Mac did this for a reason. He knew you would sell the business."

"But why her?" Anne sounded child—like. She pointed at Maggie. "She abandoned him."

"No, Anne, she did not abandon him." Ethel continued to

speak to Anne but looked at Maggie. "He pushed her away." Ethel redirected her attention to Anne. In an attempt to offer comfort, Ethel placed a hand on Anne's arm. "But all this anger and hate ain't gonna change a thing."

Anne jerked back. In a flat cold voice she spoke. "You are right, Aunt Ethel, but a lawyer will." Anne turned on the heels of her boots and stomped out the office.

Madison started for the door.

"Let her go," Ethel advised. "Give her time to cool down. It would be a waste of effort to try and reason with her." Ethel grasped Maggie's hand. "Right now, Anne is angry with the world. Don't take to heart everything she says. Mac had his reasons for leaving you this business." She gave Maggie's hand a squeeze before releasing it.

"All these years. Nothing from him. Now this." Maggie could not formulate much logic to the past thirty minutes of her life. The discoveries, threats, and emotions all jumbled together.

Ethel turned to Madison. "Are you done with me?"

"For now." Madison could see why Mac referred to Ethel as the voice of reason.

"I'll close the door on the way out. Maggie, don't be a stranger. My house is open to you anytime." Ethel put her purse onto her arm.

Madison waited until Ethel closed the door behind her. "You may want to sit back down," he said as he took an envelope from his desk. "Maggie, this is for you."

She studied the handwriting on the envelope. Her fingers traced the script. She felt connected to Mac. Slowly, she opened the envelope. A small black velvet box fell into her lap followed by a set of keys. Another envelope slid into her lap. Maggie laid the contents to the side and focused on the black velvet box. Her hands trembled. The top snapped open from the pressure of her thumb. An oval cut London blue topaz ring with matching heart shaped accent stone sparkled. She shut the top and turned her head to the side away from Madison. With the weight of the box in her hand, more questions swirled in her mind. She placed the box and contents back of the envelope into her purse. "I don't understand any of this."

"Mac knew Anne would sell the business after his death. He wanted to leave it to someone he knew loved it as much as he had."

"Why, now? After all these years, why now?" Maggie paced the office. "You know what this is? It is just another example of Mac deciding how things should be. The hell with what the other person's opinions or feelings are."

She stopped in front of a window and watched people climb the Courthouse's massive granite steps. "He used his influence to get me hired with the FAA." Maggie turned to Madison. Her eyes brimmed with unshed tears. "I begged him to let me stay. Mac was great at throwing up brick walls when he didn't want to be pushed on an issue."

"Maggie, don't be too harsh in your judgment of him." Madison walked over to Maggie and wiped a renegade tear from her cheek with his thumb. "I know your relationship with Mac was complicated, but he loved you and always wanted what was best for you."

She gave a weak smile. "You know things never change, do they? Here I am, years later, standing in your office wailing away about something Mac has done to upset me. Tell me about the funeral."

"There were a lot of people who came to pay their last respects.

Anne and Ethel handled the arrangements. Phil Hardeman did the service."

"I'm glad that Phil did his service." Maggie recalled the Methodist minister. She'd taught both him and his son how to fly. "I take it he's buried next to Diane at Oconee Hills." Madison nodded. "I'm surprised Mac had a will. When did he do this?"

"A few weeks ago. He wanted to make it so you would get ownership of the business and be protected from any legal action that Anne could take."

"Something had to prompt Mac to do this." Maggie wiped her face with both hands and took a deep breath. "What about Dennis and the other two employees?" Maggie asked trying to remember their names.

"Lynda manages the office. She started not long after you left. Keegan works in the shop. Mac hired him about six months ago."

"I guess they are wondering about their future with the business."

"Rumors were already circulating before the funeral. Everyone was speculating Anne would get the business and sell it. Needless to say, yes, they are worried about their future. I told Dennis last night I'd get back to him today after the will was read."

"Now is as good a time as any to give him a call."

Madison dialed the number to the hangar. He mouthed the words, answering machine, to Maggie. He left a brief message for Dennis to call him. "What are your plans for now?"

"I'm not sure. Possibly going to the Frog Pond and having a stiff drink. Just kidding. " Maggie picked up her purse. "Give me a call on my cell when you hear from Dennis."

THREE

$\mathcal{A}$nne pressed and held the lighted button next to the door. She did not wait for an invitation to enter when the door opened. This was the only place that she could think to go after leaving Madison's office, its resident the one person she felt would share her feelings of betrayal.

"By the looks of your face and hair, I'd guessed you were at a fight and not a reading of a will." Nick had tried to ignore his watch. Several times he checked his phone for a text message. Anne's current state spoke louder than any text or voice mail.

"No one can call you short on observational skills." Anne tossed her keys onto the coffee table. "You might want to sit for this. Maggie Cosby was there." Nick's mouth dropped open in disbelief. "Seems like dear old Dad left the business to his ex-whore."

"You've got to be shitting me!" Nick's mind went into overdrive with the unexpected news. This was a ripple in his world he did not need.

"No joke, and it seems like Aunt Ethel knew of his intentions. She even had the audacity to defend him."

"What are you going to do?" Nick knew he had to handle this situation with a delicate balance.

"I told Madison that he would be hearing from an attorney."

"I'm sure one of the guys at the firm would help you." Nick walked over to Anne. "Baby, I'm…"

Nick was unable to finish his sentence. Anne gripped both sides of his head and kissed him. His body responded to the assault of the kiss. Impatient hands pulled and tugged at restrictive clothing. Half-naked bodies fell to the floor.

Anne rolled on top kissing and nipping her way down Nick's tight abdomen; she could feel his hardness against her. A blockade was placed on her thoughts and emotions. Who needed all the traps that came with the fantasy of love? Love was just an illusion. A hoax people played on their emotions.

Nick allowed Anne full command of his body until there was no need for him. Anne rolled to the floor, leaving him exposed. Neither person spoke their thoughts. Nick's traveled to a warm evening three months ago. He wasn't sure whether it was luck, fate, or a mixture of both that night. He'd walked into the Greek revival alone and searching for a new trophy. Lately, most of the women he pursued left him cold, making the catch hollow. Like any sportsman, he wanted a big trophy.

A tall blond standing among a group of men caught his attention. Her back to him, he felt something familiar about her. The toss of her honey colored mane exposed bare skin to the small of her back. His pulse quickened. His throat became parched. He felt like a bird dog on point.

Nick had found his prey.

His quarry turned. Violet-blue eyes challenged him. Nick swallowed hard. He knew those eyes. They had teased and played with him before. In a bold move, their owner began to close the gap. For a brief moment, Nick felt that the hunter had become the hunted. With each graceful step closer, Nick found himself entangled in his own snare. Reality rendered him speechless. His captor was Anne Harris.

Gone was the long single braid down her back. The silver lamé dress with a pair of heels replaced her normal attire of denim and boots. Thin material clung to womanly curves.

The bodice draped over mature peaks. Little Anne had grown up and filled out in all the right places.

Anne enjoyed the shocked expression on Nick's face. "Hello, Nick, what an enjoyable surprise to see you."

"Wow." Nick's face flushed red.

"I'll take that as a compliment."

"Does your daddy know you go out dressed like this?" Nick recovered from his shock.

"Daddy's opinion stopped mattering a long time ago." Anne controlled the venom in her voice. "How is Mac?"

"He's fine. I saw him earlier today at the hangar." Nick directed his gaze to the group Anne had left. "I never picked lawyers being your type of play dates."

"Henry is a pastime that is past his time." Anne had become bored with the overstuffed, pretentious man. At first, he'd been fun and someone who was good at scratching an itch. She had tired of his constant need to know her every movement.

"Too bad for him. You know, you and I are cut from the same cloth, never one for entanglements." Nick was pleased to hear of Anne's displeasure with her date. "I'm glad he's the reason for you being here tonight. Seeing you has definitely made this evening promising."

"Stop flirting. You forget I know all your secrets and schemes." Anne agreed she and Nick were of the same fabric. "Actually, Joan is one of my borders. Her daughters take lessons at the farm. I couldn't miss her birthday party. Anyway, it was a chance to feel girly and get dressed–up."

"There is nothing girly about the woman standing in front of me." Nick was already imagining the touch of her skin and the taste of her mouth.

"You're gonna make me blush." Anne enjoyed the game of cat

and mouse being played. "You here alone?"

"For now. Unless, you wanna ditch your date?" Nick did not miss Anne's hesitation to decline or accept the offer. "Maybe another time."

"Maybe." Anne put her hand on Nick's arm. "It was good seeing you."

Nick watched Anne disappear into the crowd. He turned and spotted a brunette sitting at the bar. The woman had been sending him 'come-hither' signals all night. With a shrug, Nick walked over to the bar.

****

Anne stepped onto the side porch and welcomed the solitude. The warm June air caressed her skin. Even in a crowded room full of people, she could not stop the loneliness that gnawed at her. She thought about her date and didn't care if he missed her company.

Thoughts of Nick preoccupied her mind. His reaction to her had ignited a fire of curiosity. She thought about the first time her father brought him home for supper. She'd been sixteen to his twenty-years. The way he looked at her, laughed, teased, and talked created an instant case of puppy love. While her friends fantasized about the latest teen heart-throbs, Nick filled hers.

"There's, you's are." Henry's slurred speech indicated his level of his intoxication. He grabbed Anne around the waist and pulled her close. Hot breath full of alcohol and cigar smoke assaulted the fresh air between them. Anne tried to push away, but Henry's grip tightened. "Come on, let's go somewhere we can get nekkid. You know you wanna ride the one-eyed bologna pony into tuna town."

"Henry, you've had too much to drink." Anne tried to

wiggle free. The crassness of his statement left her cold.

"Oh, don't goes acting all rigidity on me. I know what a hot little filly you can be. You been advertising all night in this skimpy dress. Come on now, give big daddy some lovin'." Henry leaned into kiss Anne.

Anne put all her weight into the shove against Henry's chest. Her attempt for freedom gained her more than what she bargained. A rush of air across her bare chest caressed her exposed bosom. Grabbing the thin fabric that once covered her chest, Anne looked up to see Nick's fist make contact with Henry's jaw.

Henry's mouth filled with the sweet, metallic taste of blood. "Hey, man, whys you do that for? Hell, if you wants the slut, yous can have her. Ain't gotta go hittin' a man." Henry turned and staggered back into the party. "I was finished with her anyway."

"Are you okay?" Nick removed his jacket and placed it around Anne's shoulders.

"Yeah."

"Guess you gonna need a lift home." He did not wait for Anne's response. "My car is parked around back. We can get to it without anyone seeing us."

*****

Luck, fate, or the combination of both, either way he had found his trophy. Anne Harris brought a lot to the table. Mac's decision about the business was an unexpected turn. Nick rolled to his side and looked into her face. "Feel better? 'Cause if not then…"

"Are you willing to help out?" Anne sat up and started dressing.

"Of course." Nick propped his head on his hand and

watched Anne. Her body was muscular but in a feminine way.

"I think you've gone beyond the expectations of friends with benefits." Anne pulled on her boots. She thought about how Nick had been by her side since her father's passing. Through the funeral, he'd held her hand. Afterwards, he had walked her to the car and kept her from seeing the casket being lowered into the ground. She thought about how Mac warned her that nothing good would come from a relationship with Nick. He loved Nick like a son, but knew Nick loved to chase skirts. He warned Anne that Nick was using her. Deep inside, she hoped that the warnings Mac had given were empty.

"Think nothing of it." Nick sat up unashamed of his natural state. "I'm flying Lou down to Panama City. Do you want me to mention anything to him?"

Anne looked at her watch. She had stayed longer than she should have. "No, Joan is bringing the girls down to the farm today for a lesson. I'll talk to her." Grabbing her keys from the coffee table, she admired the beauty of Nick's body. He had satisfied her physical needs. "Sorry, I barged in here. I didn't know where to go when I left Madison's office."

"Don't worry, we'll figure this out somehow. I want you to know that you are not alone." Nick made eye contact with Anne. "I understand how it feels to be betrayed by those we call family."

****

"How'd it go this morning?" Joan removed the bridle from Belle and slid a halter over the horse's head.

"Not the way I thought. My father had a few unexpected surprises for me." Anne loved the smell of leather and horse.

"How so?"

"He left me the farm." Anne brushed one side of Belle while Joan worked on the other side.

"What about the business?" Joan could tell by the tense expression on Anne's face that something was wrong. She had not expected the response to the questions.

"He left it to Maggie Cosby." The words were still hard to say, and Maggie's name stuck in Anne's craw.

"Are you okay with that?" Joan recognized the name from the past. "Never mind—that was a dumb question. What do you need me to do?"

"Help me contest it. I want that business."

"If you don't mind my asking, but what did he leave Ethel?"

"The house in White Hall and some money to start her catering business."

"What about his personal accounts?" Joan knew that Mac had multiple investments in local businesses. Their paths had crossed at some of the board meetings and functions.

"To be honest, I didn't know much about my father's personal finances."

"Let me make some phone calls and do some poking around. I saw where the Jensen's moved their horses, Buddy and Casey." Joan had noticed their tack missing and the vacant stalls. "I guess I don't have to ask how bad that hurt. Did they say why?"

"They said they had found a farm closer to them." Anne knew their reasons for moving the horses. It was the same as her last three clients. Their horses were not safe at her farm.

"Hang in there." Joan patted Anne on the shoulder.

"Thanks." Anne's words were drowned by the sound of a low flying plane.

"That must be Nick and Lou on their way to Panama City." Joan shielded her eyes and spotted the plane. "I told Lou I'd be down here this afternoon. That was sweet of Nick to buzz the farm. Let me get this lady put up. I plan to take advantage of an empty house tonight."

"Enjoy. I have a date with my office tonight." Anne looked over at the black barn cat lounging on a bale of hay. "Come on, Nails."

The black cat followed Anne. He wove himself between her legs and entered into the house. She passed her office and tried to ignore the pile of bills stacked in the center of her desk. Their presence was a reminder of how much she needed Mac's business.

FOUR

Soft ground cushioned Maggie's steps to the place where Mac had been laid to rest. An occasional dove's coo accompanied with the caw of a crow greeted her. The Middle Oconee River meandered through the trees. It reminded her that life continued. Death may rob the body of its breath, but the soul lived on through the lives that person touched.

She dropped to her knees next to the grave. With tear filled eyes, she laid a single red rose on the center. Her hand instinctively touched the blanket of sod. Rocking back and forth on her knees a primal scream ripped from her core, *Maaaac*.

All these years, Maggie thought to herself, she had allowed anger, fear, and pride rule her decisions regarding Mac. She wished with every fiber of her being that she could just see and talk to him one more time. "Mac, I'm sorry." There were so many unanswered questions. "What I would give just to hear your laugh and see your smile. Foolish, that is what both of us were, foolish, prideful, and obstinate fools."

The corner of the small white envelope tucked inside her purse caught her attention. She pulled it from her purse and began to read its contents.

Maggie,

How does one begin a letter like this? I find myself looking at your picture thinking of what beauty you brought into my life.

27

You made me feel alive and not just a shell of a man.

You should have found a small black velvet box along with this note. Its content was purchased at a time when I had convinced myself our love was stronger than my fears. Looking at the ring is reality that my fears prevailed. For that, I am angry with myself.

The most prominent of my thoughts right now is to say, "I love you." I don't think I ever spoke those simple words aloud to you. Even now, you have to read them. I guess if I had ever verbalized them, I would never have found the strength to let you go. The day you left, you took with you my heart and soul.

I am asking you to do what you pleaded for the last day in my office. Funny, I can already hear that sharp tongue of yours retorting back at me. I ask that you trust me one more time. Take care of this business, but also promise that you will not bury yourself in it and my memory.

Love Mac

Maggie kissed the pages before placing them into her purse. Her hand enclosed around the small velvet box. She removed the ring. It was a perfect fit on her left hand. She studied the ring and thought of Mac's words. "I promise, Mac. I'll protect the business."

****

The familiar black rounded roof of the World War II hangar stood tall among its modern counterparts. Maggie pulled into the same spot she'd parked many times before. Bold red letters painted on the cinder block side advertised *Mac's Flying Service*. A tin roof supported by white posts provided shelter to the entrance door and a small wooden porch. Maggie was not surprised to find the same old padlock on the blue metal door. Her key still worked, and the door still squeaked.

Maggie gave her eyes a moment to adjust to the dimness of the hangar. She could hear Mac's voice and laughter. His tool table remained in the same spot. It was not a stretch for her imagination to visualize him working on an engine.

She looked up to find the familiar chicken wire used to keep birds from roosting on the rafters. She thought about their hangar cat, Foots. Mac had given the gray and black tabby the name because of the extra toe on each of his front feet. Foots had disappeared one weekend. Both she and Mac had searched for him, but to no avail.

Maggie passed the old camper everyone called the Hilton. Maneuvering around the tail section of an airplane, she stopped at the lobby door. The words "final flight" were written beside Mac's name on the dry erase board. Her name had once filled a spot. She pushed the door to the lobby open and was not surprised to see nothing had changed. Mac was a creature of habit. The décor screamed seventies with its wood panel walls, orange carpet, and faded furniture. She stopped in front of a picture of a Corsair in flight. It had been a gift from her to Mac.

Maggie turned and walked through her old office. She ran her hand on top of the cold surface of the desk's top. It seemed sterile without any mementos to reflect the person that occupied it. Everything about the office seemed benign. Maggie continued her exploration of the offices; her final destination was Mac's office. His desk the chaotic mess it had always been. A bottle of Drambuie sat on the top shelf of the old barrister's bookcase. Maggie picked up the bottle and a cup.

She poured the honey colored liqueur and sat in the chair Mac had occupied. Her attention focused on the picture of her. She had struck the pose acting like a model. The young girl

29

seemed like a stranger to her. Mac had taken it. He teased that he wanted one for his desk.

"Seems like that was taken ages ago."

The male's voice startled Maggie. Her reflexes knocked over the cup of liqueur. "Nick."

"I didn't mean to scare you." Nick stood in the doorway. "Here let me help you."

Maggie pulled a handful of tissues from a box. "I've got it."

"I never understood how he could drink that stuff." Nick's voice quavered. He would miss his late night visits with Mac.

"Same here"

"It is still hard to believe that yesterday I attended his funeral." Nick pushed his hands in his coat pocket and leaned against the doorway.

Maggie did not miss the sadness in Nick's voice. "He was like a father to you."

"That is what makes all of this so surreal." Nick swallowed hard and looked at the last spot he'd seen Mac. "How'd you find out?"

"Madison called me."

"Sorry you didn't get here in time for the funeral."

"It was for the best. Nick, did Mac seem okay to you? I mean health wise."

"He seemed worried and tired, but you knew Mac as well as I did. If there was anything, he would not admit to it. How long are you planning to be in town? I'd love to take you out for old time's sake. Maybe Harry Bissets. There are a lot of memories in that place."

Maggie smiled at the memory of the place where she'd literally fell into Mac's and Nick's lives. "Maybe."

"So, how long are you going to be around?" Nick did not miss the dodge on his invitation.

"For a while."

"Where are you staying?"

"I haven't decided yet." Maggie hesitated on sharing the news of her being the new owner. She understood the strength of the airport gossip mill. Nick was often one of the chief correspondences for making sure the news traveled to the correct sources. She sighed and knew there was no way to keep this cat in the bag. "Mac left me the business, Nick."

"Well, I'll be damned. I guess congratulations are in order."

"Thanks."

"Maggie, I'm here to help you anyway I can. You just let me know."

"I appreciate that."

"Think I'm gonna head out." He embraced Maggie. The way her body stiffened did not surprise him. "Let's do that dinner soon."

"Sure." She did not have any intentions of accepting the dinner invitation or Nick's offer to help. She waited until the exit door's squeak announced Nick's departure before turning the lights off and closing the door to Mac's office. Technically it was her office, but in her heart it would always be Mac's. She listened to the hangar's usual pops and creaks.

Maggie stopped at the camper. Her hand reached for the door. The cool darkness of the interior enveloped her, but the smell of Mac's cologne warmed her. Instinct guided her hand to the interior light.

A blue oxford shirt hung on the door to the tiny bathroom. She removed the shirt and buried her face into the fabric. With each inhaled breath Mac became alive, awakening her senses to him and the longing for him. She removed her clothing and slipped the shirt over her body. The fabric caressed skin thirsty for his familiar touch. Arms wrapped around her mid-section and tightened their embrace.

Maggie's eyes closed, and her head fell backwards. Parted lips anticipated the succulent taste of forgotten kisses. Silence replaced the hangar's nightly chorus. Not a door creaked or rattled. The solitude of Mac's universe brought comfort to an aching soul.

FIVE

"I could have sworn I locked the door last night." Dennis' voice echoed through the hangar. "I'm also positive I turned the hangar lights off."

"You did because I had to wait on you," Lynda said before taking another sip of her coffee.

"Did either of you recognize the car in the parking lot?" Keegan asked. "Looks like it was there all night from the frost on it."

"Didn't pay it much attention." Dennis stopped abruptly, almost causing a collision.

"Hey man, what did you stop so sudden for...almost spilled my coffee all over..." His words evaporated as he spotted the reason for Dennis' abrupt halt.

"Maggie!" Dennis took in the appearance of the disheveled woman.

"Hi, Dennis." Maggie pulled at the hem of the blue shirt to try and cover her bare legs. The frigid concrete floor was turning her feet into ice cubes. Her teeth began to chatter despite the flush of embarrassment spreading its warmth across her face. She was on her way from using the lobby bathroom when the creak of the door stopped her in her tracks

"Hey, what are all of you standing out here in the cold for?" Madison saw the answer to his question. The sight of Maggie brought both amusement and concern. "This is why I couldn't find you last night."

"Yes." Maggie gave a polite smile.

"We'll see you in the lobby once you're more presentable." Madison wasn't surprised that she'd stayed at the hangar.

****

"If I still remember, you like yours with cream." Dennis offered Maggie a cup of coffee. "I guess you are in town because of Mac."

"Thanks, Dennis. I do and yes." Maggie graciously accepted the steaming mug of liquid vitality.

"It is nice to finally meet the infamous Maggie Cosby." Keegan offered his hand. "Feels like I already know you from all the stories Mac told about you and him."

"I'm quite sure he embellished a lot." Maggie was familiar at Mac's talent of spinning tall tales.

"He loved to talk about the days when you were here." Lynda pasted a polite smile on her face.

"That he did. I'm glad you got here to see the place before Anne sells it." Dennis turned to Madison. "I guess that's what you're here to tell us this morning."

"Not exactly." Madison cleared his throat. Three faces filled with dread stared at him. "Dennis, Lynda, Keegan, meet the new owner of Mac's Flying Service."

"Congratulations, Maggie." Dennis gathered her in a bear hug.

"Thanks." Maggie steadied herself. "I hope the two of you find this to be good news."

"The best. I did not relish the idea of having to look for employment." Keegan was sure Maggie surpassed the legend. "This place has become like a home to me."

"Mac's has a way of doing that to people," Maggie's voice soften with nostalgia.

34

"Guess you and Madison have a lot to go over this morning." Dennis refreshed his coffee.

"Damn phone. It is a necessary inconvenience." Madison pulled the cell phone from his pocket. "Be right back."

"Man, I'd hated to have been a fly on the wall yesterday at his office." Dennis took a sip from his coffee.

"Let's just say you would have gotten more than you bargained for." Maggie picked up her cup. "Anne didn't take the news very well."

"Speaking of Anne, she didn't waste any time finding herself an attorney." Madison returned. "That was Judge Meek's clerk. The Judge wants us in her office this afternoon at two."

"Nobody ever said Anne wasn't fast." Maggie looked at Madison and the rest of the group. "I guess we need to make sure there is a business worth fighting over.""

"I need to get going. See you at the courthouse." Madison left the foursome.

"I told Doc I'd start his annual today." Keegan followed behind Madison.

"Jared and Kyle wanted me to get their invoices ready." Lynda left Maggie and Dennis.

"Want to go into Mac's office?" Maggie picked up the powdered creamer and added more to her coffee. It wasn't the hazelnut flavored she preferred, but it served the purpose.

****

"I can't imagine how stressful it's been for all three of you." Maggie leaned back in the chair and propped her feet on the bottom desk drawer. She held her coffee mug between both hands. "I'm glad to see you are still around, although somewhat surprised."

"Yeah, just consider me part of the furniture around here."

Dennis patted the sofa cushion next to him. "Mom's health kept me close to home."

"I didn't realize she had been sick." Maggie knew Dennis was all his mother had left.

"She had a rough battle with the big 'C'." Dennis had been by his mother's side through her struggle. "It finally beat her last year."

"Dennis, I'm sorry to hear." There had been a time when she and Dennis were thick as thieves.

"She never quit fighting." Dennis gave a quick smile. "Anyway, looks like you got a fight on your hands."

"Seems like it." Maggie had expected Anne to keep her word. "Were you the one who found Mac?"

"No, it was Keegan."

"He seems to be nice."

"Yeah, everyone loves him."

"I'm glad he's willing to stay." Maggie took a sip of her coffee. "Where'd he work before here?"

"St. Simons. He and Mac became friends there."

"Mac never met a stranger. Why'd he come here?"

"Not sure. He showed up one day asking Mac if he was hiring."

"And Mac hired him, no questions asked."

"Pretty much."

"You and Lynda an item?"

Dennis almost strangled on his coffee. "Madison tell you?"

"No just guessing. I have to admit she's not your usual type."

"I'm not sure if I should be insulted or complimented."

"No harm intended. The main thing is, does she make you happy?"

"She does." Dennis still wasn't sure of the meaning behind Maggie's comment. "She does a helluva job running this office."

Maggie was sure Dennis' barb was in retaliation to her comment. "She keeps an immaculate office." Maggie felt the need to change the subject. "Dennis, did Mac seem okay to you the past couple of months?"

"He seemed preoccupied about something and stayed tired a lot. He started having me fly with him on trips, said he wanted to let me build some more twin time."

"How did Jared and Kyle react to that?"

"You know they never questioned Mac when it came to flying."

"What about the flight school and the rentals?"

"We have about twenty students. Matter of fact, I have a student that should be here any minute." Dennis stood and looked at Maggie. She seemed to be at home behind Mac's desk. "I'm here for you any way you need me to be."

"Thanks, Dennis." Maggie sat her empty cup on the desk and studied the chaotic mess in front of her. Mac always knew where everything was among the piles of papers. She was one for organization and lists, and abhorred clutter. Maggie moved stacks of papers until she was pleased with the blank space on the desk. She took a note pad and started making a list of priorities for the business. The top item was Jared and Kyle's account.

They were the bread and butter to business. Maintenance was second. Rentals and lessons were the fair haired stepchildren. First thing was first, Maggie put three stars beside Jared and Kyle's names. She needed to schedule a meeting with them.

The loud rumble of Maggie's empty stomach reminded her she'd not eaten since yesterday's lunch. She needed food, a hot shower, and clean clothes. Maggie stopped at Lynda's desk. "I'm going to the hotel and then over to the Courthouse.

Here's my cell number in case you need me."

****

Renewed from the shower and change of clothes, Maggie punched the elevator's button for the floor to the hotel's restaurant. She thought about the many times Mac had shared the same elevator with her. The ding of the elevator doors opening propelled her forward, but her thoughts remained in the past. The brute force of colliding into the solid wall of another person jolted her.

"Maggie." A familiar baritone voice spoke while strong hands steadied her.

Maggie's breath caught in her chest when she recognized the mature version of Seth Anderson. He had once been her nemesis with his constant teasing and practical jokes. There were times he infuriated her to the point of wanting to wring his neck. She could still see the light of devilment dancing in his brown eyes. Hints of gray formed at his temples. Everything about this man spoke of confident, male testosterone. "Oh my goodness, Seth, I am so sorry."

"No need to apologize. It's not often I get plowed over by a nice looking woman," Seth teased while he retrieved her room key from the floor. His heart dropped at the sight of the blue topaz ring on her left hand. Seth straightened and handed the room key back to her. "Guess you heard about Mac."

"Yeah." Maggie was unsettled by the electric jolt created by the touch of his fingers. "I heard you were one of the pall bearers at his funeral."

"I was." He searched for any reason to keep her talking to him. Over the years, he often visited the memories of her and the hangar. Giving respect that she belonged to another, he always felt he had to admire her from a distance. The ring on her hand warned him that nothing had changed. "Hey, I was on my way to lunch. Why don't you join me?"

"Sure." Maggie reached for her flight bag. Their hands collided. Again, electricity surged through her. The crisp scent of outdoors filled her senses. Even his cologne defined him. His stride was uniform and with purpose.

Seth stopped at the hostess stand. His voice spoke with request but his message carried the weight of a command. "Can you take care of this while we eat?"

"Sure, Mr. Anderson." The college-aged girl smiled at him. "Your usual spot, Mr. Anderson?"

"You must come here often." Maggie had not missed the young girl light up when he approached. She noticed how several women stopped their conversations or eating their lunches to glance his way.

"At least once a week." Seth met Mac each week for lunch. It had become a standing invitation with them. "I see you still travel light."

"I wasn't planning on being in town long."

"You on your way back to Nashville?"

"No. It seems like I'm going to be here a little longer than expected."

"Came home and decided you can't go back?"

"Something like that, but the decision was more or less made for me." Maggie took a sip of water. The blue topaz ring sparkled. "You still in the Marines?"

"No, I'm back living in Athens. I left the Marines a few years ago. Now I'm flying for one of the major carriers out of Atlanta. How's the FAA been treating you?"

"Fine. All I fly now a days is a desk."

"That's a bummer. I remember how much you loved being in the air." Seth did not miss her failure to mention anything personal. He wondered if there was someone else in her life. It had to be with a ring on the left hand. "Remember how Mac pushed you after you got your private license. It was like every other month you were getting a new rating or license."

"Those were some intense days. All the trips the three of us took in three-niner-hotel. You in the back seat as safety pilot while Mac tortured me."

"We had some fun though." Seth thought about how Maggie had never complained during long hours she spent flying under the "hood" simulating instrument conditions. He still carried the image of her curled up asleep, exhausted, on the tiny back seat of the plane while he flew the trip home.

"Yeah, we did. We also antagonized each other mercilessly. The practical jokes we pulled. There were times we had to have made Mac nuts with our sniping and antics."

"Don't fool yourself," Seth said. "Mac was the instigator at times. Man, believing he is gone is hard. I guess the place will be closed down soon."

"One can never tell."

"What makes you say that?"

"Because you are looking at the new owner of Mac's Flying Service."

"So that's what you meant earlier about the decision being made for you."

"Pretty much." Maggie checked her watch, "Matter of fact, I hate to be a lousy lunch date, but I have to be at the court-house in about fifteen minutes. Anne has decided to contest her daddy's will." Maggie reached for the check.

Seth grabbed the check from the table before she could.

"Here, lunch is on me. It's not often I get run over by a pretty female oblivious to her surroundings." The fire in Maggie's eyes was worth the price of lunch. "Good luck this afternoon. Maybe we can do dinner soon."

Maggie looked at Seth Anderson. He had become everything the military had taught him and what women longed for. "Thanks and we will. You know where to find me."

"That I do." Seth watched Maggie walk away. It seemed like that was what he always did with her. Watch her walk away.

****

Madison paced the sidewalk outside the courthouse. He checked his watch to see the hands had ticked off more valuable time. He did not like being late. The sight of Maggie strolling toward him brought some relief. "Do you ever answer your cell phone? I even called the hotel, and they said you checked out."

"Yeah, I decided I'm going to stay at the hangar." Maggie kept moving.

"Are you sure that's a good idea?" Madison took each one of the granite steps with ease.

"I've stayed in the *Hilton* before. It has everything I need right now, hot and cold running water, a stove to cook on, and its rates are like a sore dick; you just can't beat it." Maggie paused and waited for Madison to open the heavy wooden doors to the courthouse.

"You have a potty mouth sometimes." Madison knew Maggie's comment was meant to stop him from objecting to her decision. "Please, promise me you'll be a lady while we are in judge's chambers."

"Why, Mister Barfield, I do know how to behave properly in public." Maggie gave her best imitation of a southern belle accessorized with a pout.

"That's questionable at times." Madison opened the door marked Probate Judge. He held it while Maggie walked in front of him.

"I take it that is Anne's attorney sitting with her." Maggie whispered

"He's with the firm Nick flies for. His name's Lou Holsenbeck."

"By your tone, I can tell don't think highly of him." Before Madison could answer, they were all summoned into the Judge's chambers.

****

"The reason for this meeting is to discuss motions filed on behalf of Ms. Anne Harris concerning the estate of Malcolm J. Harris. Mr. Barfield, I show you on record as the executor of the estate."

"Yes, your honor."

"The part of the will that Ms. Harris is contesting concerns the deceased's business, which he left to a Ms. Maggie Cosby." The judge looked at Maggie, "That would be you, correct?"

"Yes, your Honor." Maggie felt like she had been summoned to the principle office.

"I have reviewed the will and documents drawn up by Mr. Barfield transferring ownership of the business to Ms. Cosby. I've also reviewed what Mr. Harris left to his daughter." The judge turned her attention to Anne. "Mr. Harris left you the farm and the residence in Farmington. You currently reside and operate your business at that location."

"Yes ma'am."

"Why do you want the business he left Ms. Cosby?"

"I am his daughter. That business should have been left to me." Anne paused allowing her voice to become soft with emotion. "I would hate to see his years of hard work and sacrifice destroyed, especially by someone who obviously does not care about the place except for what financial gain its sale would give them."

Maggie could not believe the words spilling from Anne's mouth. She began to move but felt Madison grab her knee and squeeze it hard.

"Mr. Barfield, you are currently allowing Ms. Cosby to manage the day-to-day operation of the business."

"Yes, your honor. We have agreed that she will report to me weekly on its status." Madison could already imagine Maggie's thoughts on the weekly meetings. He did not intend to follow through with them.

The judge sat for a moment and made notes before closing the folder. "It will take at least six months contingent upon no delays in probating the will. During that time, I am ruling that Ms. Harris is to be made party to all activities of the business. She is to be included in any meetings between Ms. Cosby and Mr. Barfield concerning Mac's Flying Service. Mr. Barfield, you will let Ms. Harris know of these meetings." Madison assured that he would. The Judge looked at Anne. "Before I adjourn, I wish to speak off the record with you Ms. Harris. I knew your father. He was a respected member of this community. I'm also aware of your lack of interest in this business in the past. I hope that your motives in this matter are sincere and not a waste of mine or this court's time."

****

"Lou, thanks for this." Anne extended her hand to Joan's husband. "Tell Joan I'm sorry she couldn't make it today. I hope she feels better."

"I'm sure she will." Lou smiled at the woman before him. "Looks like you at least have your foot in the door with the business."

"Yes, it does." Anne glanced over to where Madison and Maggie stood. "I guess I had better go and let Ms. Cosby know I plan to keep an eye on her."

Lou had to give Anne credit for her level of tenacity and grit. He watched her approach the opposing parties. It didn't take anyone with great wisdom to foresee the turbulent storm brewing between the two women. He would have loved to have stood around and watched, but other pressing matters needed his attention.

****

"You'd better get used to seeing me around that precious hangar of yours." Anne made direct eye contact with Maggie.

"Anne, it might do you some good to see what Mac worked so hard at building." Maggie had enough of the arrogant posturing of Mac's daughter. "All Mac wanted was to share his life with you. He wished for the day you'd ask him to learn to fly and become a part of the business. He wasn't the one that shut you out. It's a pity the only thing you care about is yourself and your anger." Maggie turned and walked out of the courthouse. She did not care that conversations around her had stopped and she had become the focus of attention.

"Hey, slow down." Madison tried to keep up with Maggie.

"She infuriates me to no end. I wanted to slap that smug, obnoxious smile off her face." Maggie fumbled around in her purse for her car keys. "Now, I have to endure her coming out to the hangar watching me. To add insult to injury, I also have to report to her about the status of the business."

"Maggie, she is like a kid with a new toy. She is going to be a nuisance for a while until the novelty wears off." Madison tried to reassure Maggie. "Anyway, she has her own business to run. I doubt she is going to be in the way that much. And you are not reporting to anyone about the business."

"I know. It's just the fact that for the next six months, I am in limbo. Will the judge decide to make Anne part owner of the business? Then there's the issue with the Airport Commission talking about tearing down the hangar. I have a meeting tomorrow with Jared and Kyle in hopes that they will allow me to step in as their pilot. I feel as if I am reliving history of falling in love with this place again to have it snatched away. Madison, I don't think I could handle leaving again."

"Look, you have the best attorney in town on your side, me." Madison put both hands on Maggie's shoulders. She dropped her head and stared at her shoes. Madison placed a finger under her chin, lifted her face, and looked into her eyes. "Look at me and listen. I don't think Judge Meeks is going to rule against the will. It is like she said, this whole process is going to take at least six months even if there wasn't anyone contesting it. So, why not let Anne get to know her father's business? Mac knew what he was doing when he did this. Trust him and trust me. Just promise me you will play nice when Anne is around."

"You mean I can't take her up three thousand feet and push her out of an airplane?"

"No, and no taking her up and pulling some of your stunts to scare her. PLAY NICE."

"You're no fun, Madison."

****

Anne tapped her finger on the steering wheel to the beat of the country song and sang along with the chorus. The number she'd dialed on her cell phone continued to ring. "Please don't go to voice mail...Hey, Nick, I was hoping to catch you..."

Nick rolled over and grabbed his cell phone from the nightstand. "Hey, Anne, you out of the meeting?" For a brief moment he was afraid she was on her way over to his house.

"Yeah"

"How'd it go?"

"The judge granted Lou's motion contesting dad's will. Madison has to include me in any meetings he has with Maggie. The judge said she would make her final ruling in six months."

"Why six months?"

"The judge said that's how long it'll take for all the legal crap to get finalized."

There was a pause on the other end of the line. "So what did Lou say?"

"Not much. I'm glad he was able to step in for Joan at the last minute."

"Yeah, it sounded like she took a nasty fall down their stairs." Nick had been with Lou when the news of Joan's accident was received. "You on your way over?"

"No, I gotta get back to the farm. You flying today?"

"No," Nick said, relieved at her answer.

"Why don't you come down to the farm this evening, maybe play around in the hayloft some?"

"You know I hate the smell of hay. I need to do some stuff with the plane today."

Anne felt like she was getting a brush-off. She had not missed the relief in Nick's voice earlier. "Sure, just give me a call later if you change your mind."

"I'll try." Nick laid the phone down and pulled the naked woman beside him closer, kissing the back of her neck.

"I guess the meeting is over." She rolled over and faced Nick, her hands moving to the places she knew would get the expected response.

"Yeah. It's gonna be six months before any final decisions." Nick enjoyed the feel of her hand on him.

"What about in the mean time."

"Anne's in on the business decisions." Nick did not want to continue talking. He wanted to act on the urgency her touch was creating.

"You know the old man isn't going to be happy when he hears about this. He's getting antsy about that place. You gonna call him or do you want me to?"

Nick groaned at the thought of the old man. Any intention of indulging in one more interlude with his bedmate was squelched. He rolled to his side and sat on the edge of the bed. "I'll take care of it."

SIX

*T*he weight of the groceries and her flight bag was forgotten when Maggie entered the hangar. The clanging of tools being tossed around and the sight of the man standing at the exposed engine made her knees weak and her legs jelly. She leaned against the door frame to steady herself

Keegan had heard the footsteps on the wooden porch. He turned to see Maggie transfixed in the doorway. He knew by the expression on her face it was not him that she was seeing. Grabbing a grease rag, Keegan wiped his hand and walked over to her. "Here let me take these."

Keegan's voice crashed the illusion Maggie had wanted to be real. It took a few seconds for her to comprehend the intent of Keegan's offer. "Thanks but I've got them."

"Sure." Keegan returned to his tasks. He thought about the woman moving around inside the camper and the lost look on her face when she realized he was not Mac. It was obvious that she was moving into the camper. He wasn't sure if that was a good idea, but he knew not to meddle in the decisions of others. The camper's screen door clicking followed by soft footsteps indicated she was approaching.

"Working late tonight?" Maggie stood next to him looking at the components of the engine.

"Doc wants to leave this weekend for Kentucky. I promised to have this annual finished."

"Have you removed the other inspection plates?" Maggie reached into the toolbox for a screw driver.

"No."

"I'll get started near the tail section."

"Thanks. Mac used to talk about how you preferred being out here instead of in the office."

"He used to get aggravated with me. Said he couldn't see what he was working on because I was in the way." Maggie used her best Mac imitation. "He'd say, 'Girl, don't you need to go run a vacuum cleaner or something?'"

"You have him down to a 'T'. I could hear him saying something like that." For the first time since finding Mac's body, Keegan found himself laughing.

"Mac was good at knowing what to say to get the reaction he wanted from people."

"But no one ever got upset with him and his teasing." Keegan moved to the next inspection plate. "He was always the center of the group. It didn't matter the age or background. Mac held everyone's attention."

"Because of the way the he dressed and spoke at times, some people misjudged Mac for the amount of intelligence he had." Maggie sat on the creeper and stared across the airfield. Daylight had surrendered to night. "He taught me to never judge a person by how they dress. Faded jeans, a work shirt, and grease on a person's hands are not indicators to their wealth or intelligence."

"That was Mac."

"How'd you meet him?" Maggie asked.

"I needed a job and he hired me." The casual air around Keegan dissipated. "Well, that's the last inspection plate on my side. How about yours?"

"Same here." Maggie felt like she was being dismissed. Keegan's shift in mood sparked her curiosity. It would take a few phone calls to check into the man's history. "Who's out in the one-seventy-two?"

"Seth Anderson."

"I thought I saw Dennis' car in the parking lot."

"He's with Nick on a trip."

"Oh." Maggie thought the combination was unusual.

"Nick called this afternoon and asked him to go with him." Keegan shared Maggie's surprise. Nick never had time for Dennis. "I'm gonna call it a night. You staying in the camper?"

"Yes, I don't like hotels, and it has everything I need."

"You're a brave girl considering the stories I've heard."

"I'm familiar with them. I think a lot of the encounters were just tales that both Nick and Mac spun to entertain their audience at the time."

Keegan walked over to the oversized, metal hangar doors. He pushed his shoulder against one like a linebacker. The high pitched noise of metal scrubbing against metal filled the hangar.

The sounds of the doors were like a favorite song to Maggie. These were the sounds of home. Maggie entered Lynda's office and sat at the desk in front of the large picture window. She watched the last hangar door close. Keegan gave a quick wave before disappearing through the exit door. In the quiet of the hangar, Maggie pulled on the desk drawers to find them locked. She wanted to start reviewing the financials. Maggie tried the filling cabinet only to find all the drawers in it locked too. Discouraged, she thought of the pile of papers on Mac's desk. At least, she could get a start on organizing the rest of his office.

After an hour of sorting, reading, and creating neat stacks, Maggie sat back and looked at her achievement. The waste basket was filled with dirty paper towels. The office gleamed and smelled fresh. Mac hated it when she'd sneak in his office and organize his things. He'd spend days grumbling about how he couldn't find anything. It amazed her how through chaos there was organization for him. Needing to stretch, Maggie walked over to the door that led to the back hangar. Darkness greeted her with slivers of artificial light from an exterior security lamp. The back hangar had been used to store clients' planes.

Maggie approached the side of Jared and Kyle's plane. She climbed the small steps into the plane and made her way to the cockpit. Her small frame slid easily into the pilot's seat. She leaned her head back and thought about the first trip she'd flown in the plane. It was to St. Simons. She'd rushed home to change out of her jeans and t-shirt when Mac invited her.

She'd worn the one dress she owned. The square neckline of the black dress exposed creamy white skin adorned with a single strand of pearls. The short hem line struck at the knee. Well shaped legs were set off with a pair of low heels. Maggie had pulled her hair into a twist exposing her delicate jaw line. Pearl studs had been her choice of earrings.

"Man, you know how to clean up nice." Mac stopped and stared at her. The girl that had entered into his life and hangar had changed into a beautiful woman.

Mac's comments were silenced by the arrival of a black sedan. She watched the vehicle's occupants exit. The air became fragrant with expensive perfume. Laughter and excited talk echoed between the hangars. Women dressed in designer clothes and sparkling jewels made her feel plain.

"Hey Mac, how's the weather tonight? You know Sheila here

won't fly if there's a cloud in the sky," one of the men commented.

"Sheila, you have nothing to worry about." Mac put his arm around the woman's shoulder. "The skies are clear and no weather on the radar to be concerned about. I specially ordered it for your birthday."

"Hey, who's the pretty lady here, Mac?" The second man approached.

"This is Maggie Cosby. She's helping me around here." Mac motioned for Maggie. "Maggie, this is Jared Willingham and his wife, Sheila" Mac turned to the other couple. "And this is Kyle Blackmon and his wife June."

"Hi Maggie." Jared offered his hand.

"Nice that you can come along." Kyle followed with a hand-shake.

"You flown before?" Sheila asked.

"No ma'am, this is my first time."

"Mac is the best around when it comes to flying." Kyle patted Mac on the back. "Jared nor I could get our wives on this thing if he wasn't"

"We better get going. Our reservation is at eight at the White Pelican."

Maggie was last of the three women to enter the plane. Mac whispered into her ear, "Take the right seat."

Maggie nodded and entered the cabin. She made her way through the narrow aisle and slid into the copilot seat. The many instruments and levers intrigued her.

Mac eased himself into the tight area of the cockpit and slid into the pilot's seat. Again, he found himself admiring the woman sitting next to him. He took his headset from its hook. "You can wear the one on your side. They'll make it possible for us to talk during the trip."

Maggie nodded. She watched in amazement at how Mac made the airplane come to life. The cockpit filled with the grinding sound of gyros beginning to spin and fuel pumps priming the engines. The dark faces of the radios now glowed with yellow-orange numbers. Both engines sputtered awake from their deep slumber.

The take-off had been exhilarating. She liked watching the plane accelerate down the runway, hearing the noise of the engines at full rpm, and feeling the pressure of being pushed into the seat during the lift-off. The sight of floating over the downtown Athens excited her. She'd not realized she had released a small gasp.

The small gasp in Mac's headset brought concern. "You okay?"

"This is incredible!" Maggie gushed.

"I'm glad you came along." Mac wanted this night to be special for Maggie. She had brightened the place with her warmth. Many times he caught himself watching her work in the office.

"Thanks for asking me." Mac's masculine voice coming through her headset tickled her eardrum and sent a chill down her spine. Goose bumps appeared on her arms.

"Are you cold?"

"No, I'm fine. I think it's just all the excitement of flying for the first time." Maggie stared at the altimeter. "Are we at seven thousand feet?"

"Yes." Mac was impressed with Maggie's interest in the plane. "You are over one mile from the ground."

"Cool beans. It's hard to believe you get to do something this exciting and get paid for it. How'd you get into flying?"

"When I was in my late teens, I'd hang out at the old airport. Got to know some of the pilots, and on occasion they'd take me up."

"What do you mean the old airport? I thought Ben-Epps was the only airport in Athens."

"No, the old one is now Baxter Street and Alps Road. The Navy used Ben-Epps as a training field during the second war. My hangar is the last remaining one from that era." Mac reached down between the seats and switched fuel tanks. "After high school, I went into the Army. When I got out, I used the GI Bill to become a mechanic. I went to school down in South Georgia. I stayed down there for a few years before coming back home to start my own place."

"My folks owned their own business. My dad loved driving trucks." Maggie thought about her parents and how much she missed both of them. "Mom ran the home front while he was on the road. He'd come in on Friday and be gone on Sunday. It got lonely for her."

"I think it was the same for Diane. In the beginning, she went with me on trips. Then Anne came along." Mac tried to not focus on the hard times in his marriage. Anne had been the one shining moment in his life with Diane. "Your dad doesn't drive anymore?"

"No, both of my parents were killed last year. Dad's truck slid on a patch of ice coming across Sam's Gap."

"Maggie, I'm sorry I asked. I hate it when people assume that Diane is still alive." Mac avoided talking about Diane's death. He felt connected to the young girl sitting next to him. "She and Anne had finished unloading the horses at the farm and were on their way home. An on-coming vehicle crossed the centerline. She died on the scene. Anne was alive but unconscious when the Sheriff's deputy arrived."

"What happened to the driver of the other vehicle?"

"No one knows. Whoever was driving did not stop. It

was late at night on a country road."

What Mac had not included was how that night robbed him of more than his wife, but also an unborn child. The news of Diane's pregnancy came along with the news of her death. Mac felt like he'd been dealt a double blow. The doctor stood in front of him saying both mother and child were lost. At first, he thought he'd lost both Diane and Anne until the doctor informed him that Anne had a concussion and broken arm, but she would be fine.

"Hey, Maggie." Seth was not prepared for the blood-curdling scream that responded to his question.

"Oh...dear...sweet Jesus...you scared the poop out of me." Maggie paused for a moment to gather her wits. "Don't you know how to let someone know you are around?"

"I called your name several times."

"What brought you back here anyway?" Maggie regretted the chastising tone in her voice.

"I saw your car in the parking lot and came back in to say hello to you. When I couldn't find you in the office...what does it matter anyway...seems like you don't need any company." Seth turned around and exited the plane.

"What's that suppose to mean?" The irritation in Seth's voice confused Maggie.

"Obviously you were too busy visiting the past to be aware of the present."

"Well, forgive me for wanting to reminisce a little."

Before Seth could respond, the roar of an airplane's engines filled the hangar. The noise turned a shouting match into a whisper. Maggie and Seth stood glaring at each other. The sounds of doors opening and voices echoed between the buildings. Maggie recognized the men's voices.

"Nick, thanks for being able to do this for us on short notice. Dennis, I'm glad you come along. It gave all of us a chance to talk tonight during the flight." Jared's baritone voice echoed.

"Thanks, Jared. I'm glad that we could come to an agreement on me flying for the two of you." Dennis knew he owed Nick for helping him convince Jared and Kyle to hire him.

"Mac's death and the uncertainty of his business have left us in a quandary. It's disheartening to know Anne plans to sell it." Kyle extended his hand to Dennis. "Dennis, we'll be looking forward to continuing to see you at the controls, but in the left seat for now on."

Seth saw the look of anger, hurt, and confusion on Maggie's face. It made him want to confront Dennis. "Maggie, I'm sorry."

"Sorry for what? That I am naïve enough to think I can walk back in this place several year later and expect everyone to be the same as when I left." Maggie turned away from him, "Maybe, I should just let Anne have this place."

Seth grabbed Maggie by the shoulders and spun her around. "Sorry that you have not let go of the past. Sorry that people you considered loyal employees and friends have their own agenda. Even though some of us have changed in our appearance by growing older and grayer, our respect for you remains the same. Most of all, sorry that the Maggie I remember would never give up so easily. She was not someone who would feel pity for herself, unlike the one standing in front of me now." Seth leaned down and kissed Maggie with full force on the mouth. The abrupt ending to the kiss and his release made Maggie step backward to gain her balance. Angry with himself for his lack of control, he began to apologize. "Maggie I shouldn't have done that considering you're engaged to someone else."

"What do you mean engaged to someone else?"

Seth lifted Maggie's left hand. "When a woman wears a ring on the left hand, it usually means she is committed to someone else. I have to say whoever he is has good taste."

"It was among the things Mac left me." Maggie whispered.

"Like I said, you belong to someone else." Seth released her hand and left her standing in the darkness.

The slamming of the side door caused her to jump. With a trembling hand, Maggie pressed her fingers against her lips. She could still taste Seth's kiss. The sting of his words echoed in her soul.

SEVEN

Daylight had not broken, but the barn's tenants were wide awake and ready for their morning feeding. A steady conversation of whinnies, neighs, and nickering greeted Anne. Nails stirred from his favorite spot. Front legs stretched followed by each individual back leg, the cat gave a wide yawn and hopped down from the bale of hay. He brushed against Anne's legs. "Let's get this crew fed."

This morning she felt optimism for the first time in several months. Today was the beginning of her getting her father's business. Anne sat the buckets on the ground and began to mix the feed for each of its owners: PJ, Girl, Angel's Glory, Chance, Mister, and Belle.

Nails followed like a dutiful assistant. He knew the barn's rituals. First each horse would get their morning feeding, and then there was the letting them out to pasture, followed by cleaning of stalls. Next came watching his owner and the farm's stallion work for an hour in the ring. It was his job to catch mice and any barn intruders.

The black stallion stuck his head over the stall door and blew. He knew he was the last to leave his stall every morning. Anne held her closed hand up to the warm breath coming from the flared nostrils. She turned her hand over and opened the palm to expose the expected treat. "You're a silly boy."

The stallion nodded his head up and down in agreement.

Anne opened the stall's door and gave way for the massive horse to exit. PJ was her pride and joy. Together, they had brought home a lot of blue ribbons and cash. The stallion stopped at the spot where she groomed him each morning. He turned his head and stomped his front foot.

"Bossy this morning, aren't we?" Anne began grooming PJ. Her hands did not need her attention to perform their tasks. She thought about the day ahead. Anne couldn't wait to see the look on Maggie's face. It was her every intention to start going through the business' books and finding the money she knew her father had hid from her.

****

Maggie wedged her body into the opening of the two center doors. Using all of her strength, she pushed against the doors. Heavy metal doors moving across the track echoed through the hangar, and morning sunlight began to fill the interior with its warmth. Pleased with herself, Maggie pushed the last door open. With a spring in her step, she started for the camper. The squeak of the front door brought a pause to her plans.

"Cosby, you look like shit. Isn't that one of my father's shirts?" Anne came primed for a fight and did not mind drawing first blood.

"At least, I don't smell like shit, mainly horse shit. It's none of your business whose shirt I am wearing." Maggie wanted to scratch the arrogance off Anne's face. "Why are you here?"

"To make sure you aren't squandering father's assets." Anne was pleasantly surprised by the moxie displayed by her opponent. So, Ms. Maggie Cosby had some fire to her sugary sweetness.

"You mean his bank accounts because I'm pretty sure you don't give a rat's ass about his planes except for their value."

"Cosby, I don't plan to find myself in one of those contraptions to worry about that. You're right. The balance sheet and bill of sales are all I care about."

"Wow, Harris might want to be careful throwing around terms your equine mind can't understand." Maggie was sure Anne Harris knew the importance of financial statements and bottom lines.

"At least, I'd rather be associated with the head of the horse and not its ass."

"Ladies, ladies, I can hear both of you out in the parking lot." The two women fell silent but continued to glare at each other. Both crossed their arms across their chests. Keegan wasn't sure if he wanted to get into the middle of the two, but he was certain the business' dirty laundry should not be aired for anyone to hear or see.

Anne found herself looking into the same pair of disapproving eyes she'd met the day of her father's funeral. Their color reminded her of a lush summer's pasture. She liked the way the sun played with the tints of red in his hair. The fabric of the chambray shirt molded to his broad shoulders and across his chest narrowing at his waist. For once, Anne found herself without a smart retort.

"What's wrong there, Harris? Cat got your tongue?" Maggie taunted.

Anne felt her cheeks warm. "No, I just don't appreciate being judged by strangers that don't know their place."

The muscle along Keegan's jaw twitched. "I'm not sure what you mean."

"The way you judged me at my father's wake and now." Anne dropped her arms to her side.

"Trust me I know my place. Unlike you, who provided

quite a show of disrespect to Mac with your display of inappropriate behavior."

"Keegan, Anne has decided to take an interest in her father's business." Maggie enjoyed watching Anne being put in her place. "What that means, Mr. O'Keefe, is that I will be around watching everyone."

Keegan was not sure whether he wanted to wipe the smirk off Anne's face or kiss her. "I have to get work on Doc's plane."

Anne enjoyed the sight of Keegan walking away. The denim jeans caressed his backside. His boots tapped a beat of confident steps. She verbalized her private thoughts. "Man, I bet he rides well."

Maggie caught the meaning of Anne's comment. "Harris, the last thing I need around here is you causing problems because you have an itch that you can't seem to get scratched right." Maggie opened the door to the camper and stepped inside.

Anne stood and watched Keegan work. She wanted to hate him for his arrogance, but she found herself drawn to him. Why did his opinion of her stick in her craw so badly? She had never been one to let other people's judgments define her. All that mattered was getting this business and getting rid of it. Anne looked around the interior of the hangar. The airplanes and the shanty looking structure that was the offices brought back memories. She'd forgotten the visits to the hangar with her mom. She had always been so excited to tell people her dad flew airplanes and that one day she would be a pilot just like him.

Everything changed; her parents began fighting. She heard her mother crying and yelling about the lack of time Mac spent with her. Anne thought about how she had lain in bed holding onto the stuffed horse she loved so much. Mac had brought it to her from one of his trips. Then the accident happened. It was this place her father buried himself in forgetting her.

Anne's anger rekindled, fueling her determination to destroy the one thing that robbed her of her father. She flipped on the light switch in her father's office, and was surprised to see pictures of her sitting on the old barrister book case behind the desk. Walking over, she recognized some of them from her horse shows. One particular picture caught her attention. Picking it up, she stood and studied the faces that were smiling at each other. The photo showed her parents in front of the sign advertising Mac's Flying Service. Her mom wore a pair of white capris and a sleeveless blue shirt, her hair pulled back in a ponytail tied with a scarf. One could not see her eyes for the big framed sunglasses. Her father wore jeans, a plaid shirt, and boots. They had their arms around each other and were smiling.

"I always admired that picture of your dad and mom. They both looked so happy."

Anne replaced the picture. "What would you know about my parents' happiness? Anyone can smile pretty for the camera."

"True happiness can't be faked with a plastered smile for a few seconds. You see it in their body language. The way they are holding each other close together. Their smiles are not tight, but relaxed, as if someone shared a funny joke with them before snapping the picture."

Anne looked away from Maggie to the stacks of papers in neat piles on the desk. She did not want to hear the truth in Maggie's words. Her eyes stopped on the picture of Maggie. Anne picked up the picture and studied it for a moment. "I guess he thought more of you than his own family."

"What do you mean?"

"Your picture sits on his desk instead of his family's."

"I don't think my picture on his desk made the one over there any less important. Mac loved all of us in his own way. Maybe he wasn't great at expressing it, but he did."

"Who are you to lecture me on my father and his inability to express his feelings?"

"Someone who loved him with all her heart and being. A person who is just as angry as you are with him in his lack of showing how much he felt for me…" Maggie paused. "Anne, as much as you would like to think you have the market cornered on feeling angry, hurt, and rejected by Mac, you are not alone."

Anne stood and stared at Maggie, not sure of what to say.

Maggie spoke in low tones to keep Lynda from overhearing. "Regardless of how much you dislike me and my being here, I have a business to manage with employees. I can't keep you from being here, but I do expect you to be civil to me." Maggie turned and left Anne standing behind Mac's desk.

Lynda sat her coffee on the desk. She looked up to see Maggie. "Sorry I'm running a bit late this morning."

"That's fine. This place has never had set hours." Maggie tried to ignore her thoughts of what Anne's next move would be. The closing of the door to the back hangar made her breathe a little easier. She hoped that maybe Anne had decided to take her high horse back to the farm.

"Thanks, I usually get here before nine. It gave me time to get Mac's coffee started." Lynda unlocked the filing cabinets. "Oh, Dennis said he wouldn't be in until after lunch. He doesn't have any students until late today."

"He must have had a late night with Nick last night." Maggie noticed Lynda's back stiffen. "Keegan said he went with Nick on a flight last night." Maggie began to sift through the stack of mail. "Is this today's mail?"

"I haven't gone through it." Lynda's abrupt turn made the folders in her hands slip. The last thing she needed was Maggie snooping through things in her office. The folders in her hands landed on the floor, spilling their contents.

"Oh, here let me help you." Maggie put the mail on the desk and stooped down.

"Really, you don't have to. I'm just clumsy this morning." Lynda's frantic hands tried to rake all the contents into a jumbled pile.

"I came in last night to look over the financial reports for the business." Maggie gathered stray pieces that had floated out of Lynda's reach. "But everything was locked."

"Mac suggested I started locking them at night." Lynda stood holding the disarray of papers close to her chest. "Since people are in and out at all times of the day and night."

"Now that I am staying in the camper, it isn't necessary for you to do that." Maggie placed her stack of papers on Lynda's desk. "Would you like me to help you sort through this mess?"

Lynda's lips thinned into a tight smile. Keegan's entrance was a welcomed reprieve for her. "Hey, Maggie, could you help me for a moment in the shop? I'm getting ready to do a compression check on Doc's engine."

"Sure, it's been a while." Maggie followed Keegan. She picked up the metal bar with two gauges from the tool table. "Can you see the gauges if I stand here. I don't want to get too close to the propeller."

"Yeah. That's perfect. Mac taught you well." Keegan held the plane's propeller with one hand and filled air into the cylinder. His attention focused on the gauges. From the corner of his eye, he caught the movement of blond hair near the propeller. He stopped the flow of air into the cylinder but continued to hold the propeller in place. "Get out of the way! This prop's like the ass end of a horse. You treat it with respect 'cause you never know when the damn thing is going to go off."

Anne's face turned bright red in response to Keegan's chastisement. "You don't have to be so nasty. I was just curious."

Keegan regretted the harshness of his words. "That's fine. I just don't want to see anyone getting hurt. Come over to this side if you want to watch."

"I thought you slinked off to the farm." Maggie muttered when Anne moved next to her.

"You wish." Anne was intrigued that Maggie knew what to do with the various tools and instruments. Her true surprise was the feeling of jealousy. She had watched the way Keegan and Maggie shared a common bond. The sudden surge of possessiveness for Keegan had been unexpected. "Shouldn't you be in the office instead of out here?"

"Yes as a matter of fact I do. I have a meeting with Jared and Kyle this afternoon." Maggie decided to turn the tables on Anne. She hoped Keegan would not hate her for her suggestion. "Are you offering to help Keegan finish up here?" Maggie didn't wait for an answer and extended the metal bar to Anne.

Anne didn't expect to find herself backed into the corner of working with Keegan. "I'm sure it doesn't take a lot of brain power to hold some gauges so he can read them."

"Then I'm sure you are well qualified for the position." Maggie ignored the exasperated look from Keegan.

"I'm sure we can put our newest employee to work with no problem." Keegan decided to make light of the situation.

"Let's get one fact straight. By no means am I an employee

or someone to be bossed by you. Don't get comfortable with the idea that Maggie is the owner of this place." Anne did not care if Maggie heard her or not.

"Maggie is my boss lady. Until that changes, I don't see the need to censor the content or manner I speak to you. Now, if you happen to know the difference between a wrench and a screw driver, hand me a Phillips head."

Anne, without hesitation, picked up the requested screw driver. She placed it in Keegan's waiting hand with the precision of a skilled surgical nurse. "How come you know so much about the ass end of a horse?"

"Just do."

"That's not an answer."

"I was raised on my grandparents' horse farm near Savannah."

"Then how did you end up working on planes?" Anne tried to sound casual.

"Sure are inquisitive? Are you sizing me up to see if I'd qualify as your next bed partner?" Keegan noticed the way she was drinking in his every movement.

"Only could you hope it was true." Anne averted any eye contact with him.

"Don't be so sure I would be willing. I prefer someone that doesn't see bedding men as a sporting event. Anyway, what would your current fling have to say? Oh, yeah we are talking about Nick. He wouldn't care." Keegan wondered why he was letting Anne get next to him. The thought of her with Nick Masden angered him. Why did he care who she let into her bed?

Maggie exited the office to see Anne's hasty retreat from the hangar. "Who put a burr under her saddle?"

"She probably didn't like what I said."

"Maybe today was enough to make her decide she doesn't want to be here. Anyway, I'm off to see Jared and Kyle."

"Don't worry. I'm sure everything will be fine." Keegan returned to the task at hand. Thoughts of Anne kept interrupting his concentration. He knew her type well. The last thing he needed was an attraction to Anne Harris.

****

The events at the hangar dissipated Anne's surge of optimism. She did not expect to encounter Keegan O'Keefe and the forgotten memories of happier days. The picture of her parents haunted her. Maggie's words about Mac echoed in her head.

She rested her back against the tack room's rough wooden walls. A bale of hay became her chair. Hopping up, Nails butted her arm with his head. Anne scratched the cat between the ears. Maybe she would try Nick one more time. Deep down, she knew that he wasn't the answer to the ache in her soul. When she closed her eyes, it was Keegan's face that appeared. Her imagination did not have to wander far to hear the Irish lilt of his voice. His words continued to echo. He had as much as called her a whore. For the first time, Anne felt shame for her actions. The cell phone interrupted her thoughts. Maybe it was Nick. The hell with what Keegan O'Keefe thought of her! She was her own woman!

Anne pulled the phone from her back pocket. Aunt Ethel's name appeared on the tiny display. She'd been dodging her Aunt's calls. "Hello."

"Anne, I'm glad I got you."

"Sorry, Aunt Ethel. I've been busy the past few days."

"So I've heard." Ethel was met with silence on the other end. "The reason I called was to see if you wanted to come over for dinner tonight?"

Anne knew she could not avoid her Aunt. "That's fine. What time?"

"How about six?"

"See you then."

****

Ethel laid a bouquet of fresh flowers on Diane's grave. The faded red rose on Mac's caught her attention. There was no question as to who had placed it. Looking back at Diane's grave, she spoke. "It is time your daughter knows the truth about the two of you. Out of respect for ya'll, I've kept my silence but not any longer."

CHAPTER 8

*K*yle could tell by the way Jared drummed his fingers on the desk the call was not going well. Their Project Manager in St. Simon's was a nervous Nellie and often required a lot of hand holding. He waited until Jared was finished with the call. "We need to get down there now and soothe him before he blows this deal."

"I know." Jared was already trying to find Nick or Dennis. Both phones went to voicemail. He left messages for them to call or text him.

"We've got that meeting with Maggie." Kyle's was surprised when Jared informed him of the meeting. Neither had heard from Maggie since she moved.

"It's almost three. Knowing Maggie, she'll be..." Jared's phone interrupted him. "Like I was about to say, she'll be here fifteen minutes early, and she is."

"Maggie, it is good to see you again." Kyle extended his hand. Her grip was firm but delicate.

"Thanks, Kyle, likewise." Maggie accepted the well-manicured hand. His once blond hair was now cotton white, well-trimmed, and groomed with no sign of a receding hairline. The tailored suit accentuated his tall muscular build.

"Guess you are in town because of Mac. Kyle and I are going to miss him." Jared admired the woman before them. "He was more than a pilot to us, a trusted friend."

"A lot of people are going to miss Mac." Maggie decided the best approach was a direct one. "I imagine you two are curious why I asked to meet."

"Yes." Jared appreciated her directness.

"Because I am the new owner of Mac's Flying Service." Maggie waited for the two men to digest the news. "I'm here about your plane and the pilot services agreement you had with Mac."

Both men exchanged a nervous look. Kyle was first to respond. "Maggie, we didn't know what Mac's plans were with the business. We always thought we would not have to think about our plane or a pilot for many years to come."

"That is understandable. Everyone has been taken by surprise by Mac's death."

"I guess what Jared is trying to say is that we have already made an offer to another pilot. I'm sorry, Maggie, but we didn't know."

"I understand that you flew with Nick and Dennis last night." Maggie enjoyed the look of surprise on the two men's faces.

Kyle strangled on his club soda. "I guess news travels fast around the airport."

"Not really. I was at the hangar last night. I heard all of you come in from your flight." Maggie made her next move. "Even the part where neither of them corrected the two of you about Anne selling the business. It is interesting how they misled you and didn't bother to tell you that Mac's had a new owner."

The color drained from Jared's face. "Maggie, I don't know what to say ."

"My question at this point, gentlemen, is would it have made a difference? Would you decide to hire someone that is blatantly dishonest or stay with someone that would not make you question their loyalty?"

Both men looked like deer caught in headlights. Jared, the first to recover from the awkward situation, smiled at Maggie. He spoke to her like he often did to his daughter. "To be honest we feel comfortable with having a male pilot. It keeps peace with the wives."

"You understand. Many of our trips are overnighters. We're gone for days at a time." Kyle jumped in to help his partner. The little twitch at the corner of Maggie's lips told him she was not buying their reason.

"I see." Maggie sat for a moment. "I'm sorry I forgot my manners earlier and didn't ask about your families. Kyle, how's your daughter?"

"She's fine. She's a surgeon." Shaking his head in confusion, he said, "I'm sorry but what does my daughter have to do with our business at hand?"

"Nothing, I just wondered. I'm surprised that you supported her in that profession, considering she is a woman. What if she had a patient's wife object to a life saving operation because she was a woman? Surgery can be an intimate procedure."

Jake spoke up. "I think you are mixing apples and oranges."

"No, I understand that in ya'lls eyes there are some careers fitting for women, but flying your plane isn't one." Maggie looked at both men. She'd fought this battle all of her career. "I'm surprised at the two of you. You speak of your confidence in Mac's abilities as a pilot. You know he taught me everything I know about flying. So I have to question the validity of your concerns. Let me leave you with this one thought: with me, I would be more than someone logging hours until an airline picked me up. I would give the same level of dedication and loyalty to the two of you that Mac did, something that you two don't have for him."

Maggie gathered her purse and left the two men in stunned silence. She knew she had burned a major bridge, but at that moment, she didn't care. Somehow, she would make Mac's work without their account.

"She's got a point." Kyle did not like that Dennis and Nick had not disclosed the news about Maggie.

"About what?" Jared was checking his voicemail.

"She is an extension of Mac. Don't get me wrong; Dennis is a good pilot."

"You don't like that he nor Nick told us about Maggie. You're also questioning how long before he leaves us for an airline job." Jared had heard Dennis mention several times how he wanted to get with the majors.

"That. And here we are needing him to fly us and can't find him." Kyle knew they were losing valuable time.

"Yeah, St Simon's has left me four more voice mails."

"Then I say let's get Maggie to fly us." Kyle was already out the office and walking across the landing. He leaned over the railing and looked into the lobby. "Maggie, hold up come back and let's talk some more." Kyle watched her hesitate before walking to the stairs. He waited at the top for her. "We don't want any bad feelings. Let's discuss this some more."

Maggie remained silent. She was afraid if she started speaking that she'd do more damage to the fragile situation.

"Maggie, we want to first apologize for our behavior." Kyle hoped she accepted the sincerity of his words. "A lot of what you said about loyalty to Mac and confidence in him is true.

The point about his dedication to our families was important also.

"The bottom line, Maggie, is we would like for you to be our pilot." Jared knew Kyle was floundering, and they did not have time to waste. "And we needed to be on our way to St. Simon's an hour ago. Can you fly us tonight?"

"Yes." Maggie managed to utter the affirmation. She was stunned, confused, and filled with a lot of questions. She also knew that she needed to grab the opportunity and worry about the consequences later. Another part of her was questioning why she felt like she owed an ounce of worry about Dennis' feelings. He had been dishonest to get the job offer and not given her any thought.

"There is one condition though. It's no reflection on you. In a way Mac has spoiled us. We prefer that there are two pilots on board."

"Was that the same condition you gave Dennis last night?" The avoidance of eye contact was all the answer Maggie needed. "That's fine."

"Could you have us in the air within the hour?" Jared's phone began to vibrate again. It was another call from the project manager.

"Yes, I can." Maggie exited the office and hurried down the stairs. She thought of another set of stairs that had changed her life.

****

"Hey, Keegan." Maggie eased her car into traffic.

"How'd it go?"

"A lot of turbulence. But, I need you to pull the four-four-teen out and get it gassed. I'm flying them to St. Simons. Do you know where Dennis is?" Maggie had no intentions of ask-

---

ing Dennis to fly with her. She wanted to be prepared if he was around for any confrontations.

"No, his student canceled so he went with Nick on a trip."

"Why? Did you need him to go with you?"

"No. Just curious. You wouldn't happen to have a multi-engine rating?"

"No, why?"

"I need a co-pilot." Maggie's mind searched for a possible solution to the need of a co-pilot. The idea of the stipulation stuck in her craw. The only name that came to mind was Seth. His branding kiss was still fresh in her memory. She had no choice but to ask and hope that they could get past the previous evening's tiff. Maggie merged her car into the flow of traffic on the north loop. "Do you have Seth's phone number?"

"Yes, but he's standing right here." Keegan had watched the man pace the hangar floor and check his watch with each passing minute.

"How'd it go?' Seth hoped that Maggie was able to convince Jared and Kyle that she would be better for them. He had no personal grief with Dennis as a pilot and until last night as a person. Maggie was a reasonable person and would have included Dennis on trips.

"They need me to take them to St. Simons." Maggie exited the loop and turned towards the airport. She tightened her grip on the steering wheel and momentarily bit her bottom lip. "I need a co-pilot. Would you be willing to fly right seat?

"It'll cost you," Seth teased to ease the tension. He could tell by the tremble and hesitancy in Maggie's voice that she was nervous about asking him. It was he that should have been nervous and hesitant.

"How about dinner at Emeline and Hessin in St. Simons?"

Maggie was relieved by the teasing tone in his voice. "Will that be payment enough?"

"You've got my attention. Keep talking." Seth would have accepted an offer to eat a peanut butter sandwich with her. "You know right seat is a demotion for me."

"Okay, you can order the most expensive thing they've got, and I'll even throw in dessert."

"You've got a deal. I'll go ahead and check the weather and file a flight plan."

"See you in about fifteen minutes. I'm exiting the loop now." Maggie put the cell phone back into her purse. She knew the first rumble of the plane's engines and sitting behind the controls Mac held would be emotional. Reflections of her accomplishments and the life she had brought a sense of deep gratitude. Mac had pushed her and demanded a lot, but he knew it was for her benefit.

New thoughts emerged surrounding Seth. He was interwoven into the fabric of her past as much as Mac.

****

Seth was on his way to his Jeep for his flight case when Maggie pulled into the parking lot. "I've checked the weather. Everything looks good for tonight. I also filed an IFR flight plan. Keegan is putting fuel into the plane."

"Good. Jared and Kyle should be here shortly." Maggie grabbed her purse and pushed her sunglasses on top of her head.

"I can do the preflight if you want to freshen up." Seth smiled at the familiar action that revealed her jaw line and neck. He thought about the previous night's kiss. It had looped in his dreams and greeted him with the morning light.

"Are you saying I look like a mess?" Maggie worried that

she looked frightful. She was sure her makeup had been washed away. Her hair felt like it needed brushing, and her slacks had wrinkles.

"No." Seth wanted to tell her that she looked beautiful the way she was at that moment.

"Good because that would cost you dessert." Maggie shut the door to her car. "I need to get some items out of Mac's office."

"You know that's your office now. It would be okay to refer to it as yours."

"It will always be Mac's office regardless of who sits in it." Maggie stepped onto the wooden porch and entered the hangar.

****

Maggie leveled the plane and adjusted the RPMs. She reached between the seats and switched the fuel tanks from main to tip tanks. It felt good to be flying for a reason and not as an observer. The moment of contentment became lost with the violent yaw of the plane. The propeller of the left engine slowed and began to windmill. Maggie moved with skill and efficiency in correcting the airplane's yaw. She applied all the pressure she could muster onto the right rudder. Her hands reached to the left fuel lever between the seats and turned it to the main tank position.

Jared and Kyle's deep discussion had become silent. They watched Maggie move with grace and confidence, her hands steady on the controls. Within minutes of losing the left engine, she brought it back to life.

Everyone gave a loud cheer when the engine sputtered, and the propeller gained speed. Kyle was the first to pat Maggie on her shoulder. "Girl, you were amazing. What happened?"

"It may have been some air in the line that interrupted the fuel flow."

Jared leaned into the cockpit. "You were right. Mac taught you well. We'll discuss the business of you taking over as our pilot tomorrow."

"Thanks." Maggie was glad no one could see how bad her legs were shaking.

"You were amazing." Seth's voice created an extra heartbeat. "Do you really think it was air in the line?"

"I'm not sure, but like Mac use to say, if you do something and you don't like the plane's response, then undo it. For now, let's hope the main tanks will get us to St. Simons." Maggie checked the fuel pressure gauges and was pleased that both were steady.

****

The wheels barked upon contact with the runway. A textbook perfect landing. Maggie inhaled the coastal air and could taste the brininess of salt water. St Simons would always hold a special place for her.

"Looks like Nick's here." Maggie recognized the blue and white twin parked next to them.

"Yeah, it does."

"Ya'll goin' to be need'n anything tonight?" The lineman asked.

"I need the main tanks topped off, and is your mechanic still around?"

"Yeah, Raymond's still around, why?"

"I just want him to take a quick look at something for me."

The lineman spoke into a radio. "Josh to base. The four-fourteen needs the mains topped off and for Raymond to meet them on the ramp."

A reply came across the radio with static. "He'll be right out."

The gas truck's brakes squealed as it stopped in front of the plane's nose. The driver of the truck hopped out like a young teenage boy despite his older years. "Hear ya'll need some fuel and a mechanic."

Maggie was taken with the jovial nature of the man. "We lost the left engine when I switched to the tip tank. Probably air or trash in the line. I'd like you to check it."

"If it ran fine on the main tanks, you're probably right."

"Thanks. When I get home Keegan can do a more thorough inspection."

The man stopped in mid-step. His jovial expression turned to stone, "You talk'n about Keegan O'Keefe?"

Maggie and Seth answered in unison. "Yeah"

"I told Mac not to hire that boy. He was nothing but trouble the day he started here. Moody, hardheaded, and rude." Raymond began to remove the bottom cowling off the left engine. "I was sure Mac listened to me 'cause he never mention hiring that boy."

Maggie was taken aback by the bitterness of Raymond's words. The Keegan she knew did not match the one Raymond described, but she'd known him for only two days. It was obvious that Keegan didn't like talking about his past. The way his demeanor changed during their conversation had made that evident. She would make it a point to get her assistant to run a background on him.

The stream of fuel against the bottom of the bucket made the remainder of Raymond's comment inaudible. He swirled the bucket before tilting it at an angle. With his finger tip, he touched the side of the bucket and examined the specks of black flakes. "Yeah, just like you thought; it was some trash. Why don't you fire her up and see how she runs on the tip tanks?"

Maggie climbed into the plane and started the engines. She switched both engines fuel flow to the tip tanks. Neither engine sputtered or hiccupped but continued to run in sync. Maggie kept the engines running for about five minutes just to be sure. Satisfied, she cut both engines.

"Looks like you should be fine."

"Thanks, Raymond," Maggie answered while exiting the plane. "Is there any way we could use a courtesy car to get a bite to eat?'

"Just go inside and see Ruby. She'll fix ya'll right up."

****

"Maggie Cosby, how the hell are you?" A bleached blond woman came from behind the counter with her arms wide. Her dark wrinkled skin told of too many years spent in the sun.

"I'm doing fine, Ruby. It is good to see you."

Ruby released her hold on Maggie. "When I saw that plane taxi up, I still expected to see Mac. It broke my heart when I heard about him. He could really make me laugh."

"He always loved seeing you." Maggie wiped the moisture from her eyes.

"He'd come through the door saying, 'You got any wheels we can use?'"

"You'd reply, 'Of course. You know I always have wheels for you.'"

Ruby reached into the front pocket of her tight blue jeans and pulled out a set of keys. "Speaking of wheels, here you go, sweetie. You and that nice look'n fella go and find ya'll some dinner.

"Thanks, Ruby." Maggie took the keys. "We're going over to Emmeline and Hessians."

79

****

"Let's see, I believe the agreement was I could order anything I want." Seth opened the menu and continued his thoughts on selecting a few of the menu items. "I'm thinking lobster. It pales in comparison to my hourly rate, but since you're a friend."

"Maybe you ought to get a piece of cow to go with that. I'd hate to be accused of making you slave labor."

"If that is what will make you happy, then by all means it is a sacrifice worth making just to see your pretty smile." Seth closed the leather bound menu. "So, what are you going to have tonight? I bet you haven't eaten all day."

"All I can afford are some crackers and a glass of water." Maggie did not look up from the menu but thought about how true Seth's statement had been.

"You might want to eat more than that. I'd hate to have you passing out on the flight home. It wouldn't look good to our passengers."

"Well, if you insist." Maggie put the menu down and waited for their waitress. "Why don't you order first? It will give a better idea of what my pocketbook will allow me."

Seth never took his eyes off Maggie while speaking to the young girl. "I'll have the Grouper blackened with steam vegetables, Caesar salad, and sweet tea, no lemon."

"I'll have the same except put lemon in my tea please."

"Copy cat." Seth teased. He didn't give Maggie a chance to reply and said. "Okay, I've been in suspense too long. What happened this afternoon, and why does Nick and Dennis being here have you nervous?"

"I just don't want any awkward situations." Maggie played with the paper wrapper from her straw. "He never returned Jared's or Kyle's calls to fly tonight. The only reason they asked me is because they were in a jam."

"That's what Jared meant by what he said in the plane about making you their pilot." Seth had thought the comment was odd.

"Yeah. They initially had no interest in entertaining the idea of me taking Mac's place in the left seat. Things got intense. I let my mouth get the best of me before I walked out of the meeting. Kyle stopped me and asked me to come back. Sugar couldn't drip from their mouths fast enough. They did some major back peddling."

"But they left you hanging on whether tonight was a one-time chance and put in that stupid requirement of having a second pilot." Seth leaned back to give the waitress room to place his salad on the table. "Please tell me you are not entertaining that idea of using Dennis as your co-pilot." Seth leaned toward Maggie. "He showed no loyalty to you last night. Why should you show any to him?"

"I know, and if he had been opened with them about me, I would not have an issue. However, at the same time Jared and Kyle were adamant about two pilots on board. They say Mac spoiled them. Let's face it, I got lucky tonight that you were around. You have your own life. I can't assume you are going to be around or willing to fly right seat on every trip with me."

"That's bullshit, Maggie. I sure didn't hear them make that a condition to Dennis last night. Why should it be any different for you? Secondly, you let me make my own decisions about my availability to help you."

"Sorry, I didn't mean to step on your toes. Look, I know this stipulation is asinine. Bottom line, Mac's Flying Service needs this account. Things have a way of working out without trying to force a solution."

"Maggie, I'm willing to do whatever you need to keep Mac's business going. I can afford to take a leave. Just know that I am in your corner and will help you anyway I can."

"Thanks, Seth." Maggie liked the thought of having Seth around the airport. "How much do you know about Keegan?"

"You thinking about what that mechanic said?"

"That and last night." Maggie saw the puzzled look on Seth's face. "I helped him on Doc's plane. The conversation was light and casual. We mostly talked about Mac. His whole persona changed when I asked about his past. It was obvious he didn't want to talk about it."

"The Keegan I know didn't match what that guy was saying." Seth felt confident in his judgment of people. "Mac wouldn't have hired him if he was trouble."

"I need to check in at the office tomorrow. I plan to ask my assistant to run a background on him." Maggie reached for the vinyl folder left by the waitress but did not get to it before Seth. "I said I would pay for tonight."

"I know what you said." Seth placed some bills in the folder. "Don't get me wrong. I'm all for equality, but when it comes to opening doors and paying for a good looking lady's meal, that's when I draw the line."

Maggie knew she was fighting a losing battle. She glanced at her watch. "You feel like rambling around for a while?"

"Sure, under one condition. You let me drive."

"By all means, I would hate to wound your male pride." Maggie dangled the keys in front of Seth.

****

Ocean waves accompanied with the wind and an occasional sea gull contributed to the relaxing coastal evening, which gave way to the night bringing a full moon. Its pale yellow light danced across the restless sea. Maggie lifted her face and enjoyed the ocean's salty fingers on her face. Memories of another time she'd stood on the pier washed over her. Mac had held her close and made her feel secure. With him, she felt like a grown woman with ambitions and not a kid with dreams or fantasies.

Seth knew he'd been left in the present. He envied the way the ocean breeze caressed her face and played with her hair. He could imagine the taste of salt on her lips and skin. The desire to kiss her grew, but the fact he would be a fill in for a memory stopped him.

The ringing of Maggie's cell phone broke the silence. "It must be Jared or Kyle." She reached inside her purse and answered, "Hello…sure we are on our way back to the airport now. No need to apologize. We will be waiting when ya'll get there." Maggie closed the phone. "Guess we'd better head back to the airport. Jared said they should be ready to go in an hour."

****

Maggie walked up to the counter and placed the keys on it. "Thanks for letting us use the car. Can you send me an invoice for the fuel?"

"Maggie, I'd love to but…we have to have cash for the fuel."

"I thought Mac had an account with ya'll"

"I'm sorry, Maggie, but his account is delinquent, and the new management froze his credit."

"That doesn't sound like Mac. He was particular about making sure his bills were paid."

"We kept sending him invoices and trying to get him. I always got that girl. She'd tell us she'd talk to him about it."

Maggie pulled a credit card from her wallet. "Put it on this."

"I'll just put your name on the invoice."

"Thanks, also how much does Mac owe?"

"Let me pull it up in the computer, and I can give you a print out of his account."

"That'd be helpful. I'll make sure you guys get paid."

"No problem, sug."

"Thanks, Ruby. Tell your boss this will be taken care of by the end of next week." Maggie took the papers and walked out to the plane.

"Everything okay in there?"

"Mac's credit isn't good here. Seems like he has a delinquent balance." A car pulled up before Seth could reply, and Jared and Kyle exited.

The flight home seemed faster despite the headwind. Maggie's mind was preoccupied with the three employees of Mac's Flying Service. She didn't know whom to trust among Dennis, Keegan, and Lynda. Each had given her reason to question their relationship with Mac and his business.

NINE

"You're going to have leftovers for a week." Anne could not take another bite of her aunt's cooking. It was obvious that the meal was meant as a peace offering. The table had been covered with all of her favorites: fried chicken, turnip greens, butter peas, mashed potatoes and gravy. She was sure she spotted a pound cake on the kitchen island.

"I thought you'd take some with you. I figured Maggie would appreciate some home cooking. I plan to run a care package to her later. Madison said she's staying in the Hilton. I can't imagine her in that tiny camper. I worry about her being at that place at night alone."

"I'm sure Maggie is grown enough to know how to take care of herself." Anne could feel the jealousy welling within her. Everyone seemed worried about poor, fragile Maggie.

"I am sure she can. I also worry about you being alone at that farm. And the choices you make at times." Aunt Ethel knew her last comment would ruffle Anne's feathers.

"Nick is not as bad as everyone makes him to be." Anne felt defensive of the one person who showed any genuine concern for her. Aunt Ethel was not one to harp on a subject, but occasionally got a jab in to remind Anne of her disapproval. Anne recognized this as one of those moments.

"I just wish you'd be careful with him, Anne."

"I get what I want from Nick."

"There's more to life than having casual affairs. Find

someone and settle down with them. Someone like Keegan O'Keefe, he's such a nice man."

"I can guarantee you one thing, Keegan O'Keefe is not for me. He's too judgmental and uptight." Anne wanted to continue to tell Aunt Ethel how this nice man had all but called her a whore. "Anyway, you have Dad to thank for my lack of interest in being committed. He's the one that taught me about abandonment. He wasn't there for Mom and me. It was you who stepped up and made sure I was taken care of."

"Don't be so hard on Mac. There are things that you don't understand about your parents' marriage." Ethel knew it was time to set Anne straight about her parents. "You have to remember I knew both of your parents long before you were born. You finished with your plate?"

"Yes ma'am."

"Good 'cause I made a lemon pound cake. You want coffee with your slice?"

"No ma'am, tea's fine."

"Let's go out on the back patio. The evening temperatures are getting pleasant for sitting outside."

"What about the table?"

"I'll get that later."

Anne picked up her glass of tea and cake. She knew that Aunt Ethel was not finished with their conversation about her parents. The patio was one of Aunt Ethel's prize sanctuaries around the house. Anne sat in an oversized rocker and took a bite from the slice of cake.

"I want you to listen to me before you speak. I figured the best way to fill that sharp mouth of yours was with some of my lemon pound cake." Ethel sat across from Anne. "For years, I've kept my silence about your parents out of respect for them.

Mac was too good hearted and loved you too much to tell you the truth. Mainly, because it involved destroying the image of your momma you've built in your mind. He felt that you'd lost enough and didn't need anyone doing more harm. Because of him, I promised to keep my peace. But now I'm afraid if you don't know the truth, you will continue on this road of self destruction. I love you too much for that."

Anne had never seen her aunt so serious before and apprehensive in her mannerism. Goose bumps appeared on her arms, and fear churned at the pit of her stomach.

"Your momma was always a bit grown for her age. She had big dreams of being more than the daughter of mill workers. She knew her beauty and how men reacted to it. There was a man, way too old for her, she began to fool around with him. Momma and Daddy sent her to one of our cousins down in Americus to stop her." Ethel continued to rock. "One of my cousins was a little bit older than Diane. He would go and hang out around the airport. Diane convinced everyone that she couldn't get into any trouble being chaperoned, so she went with him to the airport. That was how she met up with your dad and a buddy of his. She took a liking to your dad's buddy. One thing led to another, and she got herself pregnant. The man refused to take responsibility, said he wanted to marry someone with status and wealth, not some common laborer's daughter. Your dad stepped up and married Diane. He did it protect her and the baby. Back in my day, it wasn't popular for a girl to be pregnant out of wedlock. Single motherhood was not as acceptable. The whole incident caused a rift between him and his buddy."

"Was that child me? Are you saying Mac wasn't my father?"

"No, dear you are very much Mac's child."

"Shortly after your momma and daddy married, Diane had a miscarriage. Your daddy was a driven man with dreams. He worked hard while trying to take care of your momma, but she was a spoiled child, always demanding for more than what he could give. Mac took on a side job while finishing up his schooling. Money was tight, and Diane was insistent they rent a house Mac couldn't afford, but he wanted to please your momma. He came home early one day to find her in bed with his old friend. By that time, the old friend had married a local girl from a prominent family. See, that is why I don't care much for Nick. He reminds me of the type of men that Diane tended to be drawn to."

Anne remained quiet and leaned forward in her chair. She could not believe her mother could be this cold, selfish person. Guilt began to form a knot in the pit of her stomach of how she had misjudged her father. Her heart ripped with pain for him and the betrayal he must have felt.

"Not long after the incident, something bad happened involving the man's family and a plane crash. He walked away from the crash but blamed Mac for the death of his family. Mac had been the last to work on the plane. Mac and Diane moved back up here to get away from the accusations. He was cleared, of course, of any wrong doing." Ethel reached for her cup of coffee. "It wasn't long after that you were born. Initially, Mac had his doubts about you being his. It wasn't until your first riding accident that his doubts were put to rest. You needed blood."

The man her aunt was speaking of did not fit the image of the one she had resented all these years. He had married a woman he did not love to protect her. He continued to protect her after she had betrayed him with his best friend. He had loved her even when he had reason to doubt she was his daughter. What had she given him over the years?

"Your birth helped balance things between your parents. They both took their love and gave it to you. Mac would come home for dinner and tuck you in before going back to the hangar to work. If he had to be out of town, he called to check on you before he retired for the night. He loved it when Diane brought you out to the airport. You were his pride and joy. Diane loved that your dad's business was successful. She liked bragging about the people Mac flew.

"For a while, they were happy, but as the years progressed your dad's business grew, demanding more from him, and Diane settled back into her old selfish self. She began picking fights with Mac when he was home. She usually waited until you were in bed before she'd start. That is why he bought that camper. He'd make sure you were tucked in and then leave to stay at the airport. He'd return home in the morning to eat breakfast with you. It was important to him to protect you.

Tears streamed down Anne's face. In the distance, a whip-poor-will sang its solitary song for the night. "How do you know this?"

"I found your dad sitting outside with a bottle of bourbon after they'd had a fight. He was never one to drink to get drunk. He was at his wits end. I listened while all the years of unhappiness poured out of him." Aunt Ethel paused for a moment. "That night Mac said he suspected that Diane was seeing another man. What both of us didn't know was that she was pregnant again. It wasn't until Doc told us in the lobby the night of the accident that Diane was pregnant."

Anne looked up at Aunt Ethel as she digested the words. "Was it his?"

"No, Mac knew the child wasn't his. Again, Diane had managed to get herself caught in her own trap."

"Did he know who?"

"No."

Anne began to sob uncontrollably. The words she had spoken about how does one make amends with a dead person swirled in her head. She didn't realize how fast they were going to come home to roost.

Aunt Ethel stooped down in front of Anne and took her into her arms. "Sssh, now baby. Sssh now. I wish I could take your hurt away."

Anne wrapped her arms around her aunt. "He never said anything all these years. He just took all the crap I dished his way and never spoke up."

"He didn't want you to think less of your momma. It was easier for you to hate him than her."

"What have I done, Aunt Ethel? I threw away all those years because of my stupid anger and pride. I will never get the opportunity to be a true daughter to him." Anne leaned back and wiped her face with her hands. "The way I acted in front of everyone during and after dad's funeral. Everyone must think I am a cold hearted bitch like my momma."

"No, just angry and confused, someone who is very reckless with her life."

Aunt Ethel's tears brought more shame to Anne. She'd never seen her aunt cry. "I am so sorry for the way I acted and how hateful I was to you in Madison's office."

"I knew you were angry and upset, but now you know the truth"

"I guess I do, regardless of how painful it is."

"Why did Dad leave Maggie the business? Was it because

he was afraid I'd sell it."

"Partly, but not totally. It was his way of making up to her how much he'd hurt her. He knew she was unhappy in Nashville."

"What do you mean he hurt her?"

"Mac became concern about Maggie's safety around the airport. Remember Foots, the rescue cat he kept around the hangar."

Anne thought about the gray and black tabby polydactyl cat. "Yeah, the one with extra toes on his front paws."

"Foots went missing for a few days. Mac found his body in the tool room. A vulgar note was attached. It threatened Maggie's safety. He pulled some strings and got her hired with the FAA. Mac never found out who was responsible," Ethel said, noticing the odd expression on her niece's face. "You seem worried."

"I haven't said anything to you because I didn't want to worry you, but there have been some incidents at the farm. I've lost almost all my borders."

"Is that part of the reason why you want to sell the business?"

"The money would help give the farm some financial security. Until now, I didn't care about what happen to the place."

"I'm worried about you now. I hate you being so far out by yourself."

"I can take care of myself. I always have Buddy with me."

"I wish you'd talk to Paul." Aunt Ethel was familiar with her niece's pet name for her handgun. "Maybe he still has some connections with the Sheriff Department down there."

"I'll give him a call if it will make you feel better."

"It would."

TEN

*A*nne sat in the truck and studied the exterior of the hangar. The people who walked through the entrance were friends and not customers. That was evident at his funeral. Many seemed lost at the news of his death. Mac's Flying Service was a hang-out. A home. Her father's and Maggie's.

It was also a place Maggie had been banished without explanation. Anne tried to imagine suddenly being told she could not stay at the one place she loved and felt secure. It would have been scary and heartbreaking. That must have been how Maggie felt.

"Hey, what brought you back?" Keegan had not expected to see Anne. He'd assumed the footsteps on the porch belonged to Doc. They'd talked earlier about Doc stopping by to drop off the log books for the plane.

"Aunt Ethel wanted to send some food over for Maggie." Anne held the sack of food in front of her.

"She had to fly Jared and Kyle down to St. Simons."

"I take it the meeting went well then."

"I guess so. She didn't have time to say a whole lot when she got here." Keegan's stomach rumbled at the smell of the food. "Whatever your Aunt cooked smells good."

"Have you eaten?"

"No."

"Aunt Ethel sent enough to feed Pharaoh's army. You want some?"

"Sure." Keegan wiped the grease from his hands.

"Think Maggie would mind if we ate in the Hilton?"

"No." Keegan, shocked by the question, noticed Anne's red puffy eyes.

Anne entered the camper behind Keegan. She thought about the words her aunt had spoken in regard to the tiny camper, how it had become her father's refuge from a loveless marriage. The interior would fit in one of her stalls.

"You want me to get you a drink from the fridge?"

"Anything diet is fine."

Keegan could not get the image of Anne out of his head. The Anne that stood in the camper was not the one he'd met this morning. She seemed lost, scared, and sad. He closed the door to the refrigerator and returned to the camper. "Here is one diet drink for the lady."

"Thanks"

"Damn, this looks good. Your Aunt can put out a spread." Keegan removed containers and filled a plate. He took a bite of the potatoes with gravy. "This makes me miss my mammaw's cooking."

"Your mammaw?"

"Yeah, my grandmother. Every Sunday after church, all of us would pile around the table for dinner. She always made sure everyone's favorite item was present. It was the one day of the week that we stopped working on the farm and came together."

"Sounds like Aunt Ethel. We do the same every Sunday."

Anne was intrigued by the similarities in her life with those in Keegan's. "Did you and your parents live on the farm?"

Keegan stopped chewing and began to push the food around on his plate. "No, just me."He could sense the unasked questions, but he did not look up from his plate. "My parents died when I was seven years old. My dad's parents raised me."

"It must be hard not knowing your parents and who they were."

"I always felt like everyone pitied me and tried to overcompensate for me not having my parents."

"How many are there in your family?"

"I have two uncles and three aunts. Between them there are about twenty cousins." Keegan saw Anne's eyes widen. "My family is Irish Catholic, and we believe in populating the earth."

"I grew up with my two cousins, Aunt Ethel's boys, Thomas and Mathias. We were more like siblings. I sometimes wonder how Aunt Ethel kept her sanity."

"Same here. We were always at each other's houses."

"What type of horses did your family raise?"

"Mainly Tennessee Walkers, but we also had other breeds."

"What made you leave?"

"Stupidity and anger." Keegan not wanting to talk about that part of his life shifted the subject. "Did I see some pound cake in one of those containers?"

Anne, curious to know more, was disappointed at how fast Keegan closed the subject. "Lemon, I think Aunt Ethel sent half the cake." Anne reached behind her for the container.

The aluminum door rattled with a gentle knock. "Hey, you guys up for company?"

"Sure, Paul. Come on in and sit down."

Paul hid his surprise at seeing Anne sitting at the table. "Evening Anne."

"Hello, Paul. You want to sit here?" Anne slid over on the bench seat to make space.

"No thanks. I'm looking for Maggie."

Keegan answered between bites. "She's not here. She flew Jared and Kyle to St. Simons."

"I needed to talk to her about the business."

"If it is anything to do with dad and this place, you can tell me." Anne saw Paul's hesitation. "I would like to know."

The softness in Anne's voice caught Paul off guard. He had never known her to show humility. "Sure, can we talk alone?" Paul looked at Keegan. "No offense to you, man, but some of this I would prefer to tell Anne in private."

"No problem, I understand."

"Want to talk in dad's office?"

"That's fine."

Paul followed Anne into Mac's office. Images of the last time he stood in this room flashed through his memory. He still felt as if he was missing some important piece to the puzzle.

"What did you want to tell me?" Anne stood at the corner of the desk where Mac's body had been found.

"The night Mac died he asked if I could come by. He gave me this." Paul held the envelope to Anne.

"What is it?" Anne sat on the corner and opened the envelope.

"Mac felt someone was embezzling from the business. He asked me to check on Lynda's background."

"Did you find anything?"

"Not really. Except she left Florida after divorcing an abusive husband, who, by the way, has not been seen or heard from since her departure."

"How did she get here?"

"Nick Masden." Paul waited to see what type of reaction Anne had to his comment.

"I guess she is one of Nick's old flings." Anne held no jealousy toward the idea. She accepted Nick for the person he was and did not expect more from him.

"Pretty much. She and Dennis have also been an item for the past year." The coolness in Anne's response confirmed what he had suspected. He was familiar with her reputation and felt that she and Nick were well suited for each other.

"But why would she want to steal from Dad's business?"

"That's the big question right now."

"You said you came here the night dad died. Don't you think it's odd that circumstances happen the way they did?"

"One would have to wonder about the timing. That brings me to what I needed to talk to you about."

"What?"

"I spoke with Jim at the Coroner's office today. They are ruling Mac's death as natural causes."

Anne's gaze moved from the pages to the picture of her and her horse, Dapples. Goose bumps prickled her arms as a chill ran down her spine. Snipets of the accident flashed through her mind. She remembered being lifted and held close. "You were there the night my mother died."

Images of another crime scene flooded his memory. "Yeah, I was. That is a night that still haunts me." Paul had been a rookie with the sheriff department then. He'd been patrolling when he discovered the overturned truck. He had prepared himself for the worst when he shined his flash light into the carnage of the truck. As suspected, the driver was deceased. The beam of light moved to where the passenger side of the truck should have been. It took him a few minutes to focus on the body of a young girl. Paul reached across the driver and expected to find skin cold to the touch and lifeless. A small whimper followed by a moan responded to the contact.

"You carried me out of the truck."

"I lifted you through the truck's windshield and held you until the ambulance arrived." Paul did not know Mac. Only, that he felt the need to protect a young girl from the horror that had taken the life of her mother.

"Until now, I never have been able to remember anything about that night."

"There are times when lapse of memory is a blessing."

"Were you the one that got Mom's camera out of the truck?"

"What do you mean?"

Anne picked up the picture. "This was taken that day at the show. How did Dad get it? I searched through mom's things and never found her camera."

Paul took the picture from Anne. "Hon, I don't know. There wasn't any camera among the contents that was inventoried in the truck." Paul continued to look at the picture. He'd seen it dozens of times sitting on the desk. Something was different about it. "Do you mind if I keep it?"

"As long as I can get it back."

"I promise you will." Paul walked out of the office.

Anne took the picture of her parents and sat down on the sofa. She studied the images and thought about what Maggie had said earlier. They did look happy. The sound of Keegan's voice at the doorway startled her. "Sorry, didn't mean to scare you." Anne just smiled in return. "I'm closing up shop for the night. Are you planning to wait on Maggie? It might be a while."

"Probably not. I just want to sit here for a while."

"You gonna be around tomorrow?"

"I don't know." Anne was not sure of the intent of the question. "Why, are you trying to decide whether or not to come to work tomorrow?"

Keegan ignored the comment. "Thanks for sharing your Aunt's cooking with me tonight. I put the rest of the food back in the fridge."

"You're welcome."

"See you later."

"Night." Anne listened to Keegan's fading footsteps. The squeaking sound of the exit door announced her solitary status. Restless, she wandered through the offices and into the hangar. She walked around, touching and feeling the planes. Anne stopped at the work table covered with tools and parts. How many times had her dad touched these items? She took a wrench from the table.

Anne thought about the numerous times he had invited her to come with him. He offered to teach her to fly. The invitation to be a part of his world was there. All she had to do was accept. Like her mother, she had refused him.

She looked at the camper and thought of Maggie. She had accepted his invitation without hesitation. In return, she was pushed away without knowing why. Anne could understand how this place meant so much to Maggie. It was where she held memories of love and happiness.

Anne felt jealous that Maggie held memories of her dad when he was happy. She also recognized the cold hard fact she had no one else to blame but herself. The creaking sound of the entrance door startled Anne. The wrench in her hand fell to the concrete floor.

"Seems like I keep making you jump out of your skin tonight. I was almost to my trailer when I realized I didn't turn the air compressor off. It makes an ungodly sound when it comes on. I didn't want it to scare Maggie." Keegan stopped. "Anne?"

She turned her back to him. It was embarrassing that she could not control her tears. He was the last person she needed to see her vulnerable. The concern in his voice and the soft way he spoke her name made her cry more.

Keegan turned her around. He lifted her chin. The strands of blonde hair fell back. Her violet eyes brimmed with tears. She bit her lower lip. He took a clean shop rag from his back pocket and began to wipe the wayward tears.

He had once been where she was now. Keegan knew that time and love could heal the self-inflicted wounds. The defiant woman who had challenged him this morning was gone. The grief and sadness in her eyes pulled at him. He wanted to take her into his arms and protect her.

"That may be Maggie getting back." An airplane approached the hangar.

"It's Nick." Anne caught a glimpse of the plane before it turned behind the hangar.

"Maybe he can finish what I started." Keegan stepped away from Anne and replaced the shop rag in his back pocket.

"What's wrong, O'Keefe? Don't like being the teaser for the stallion? Anyway, thought you didn't like women who made bedding men a sport." Anne was confused by the sudden air of hostility between them. Moments earlier there had been compassion from Keegan. She wanted to be in his arms and feel his kiss.

"Glad we agree on something." Keegan did not allow Anne

99

a chance to respond. The heels of his boot echoed against the walls of the hangar. He yanked the exit door and allowed it to slam behind him.

Anne glared at the closed metal door before walking to the back section of the hangar. She squeezed her frame through the opening of the hangar doors. It was obvious Dennis was agitated in his conversation with Nick. Several times he pointed in the direction of the hangar.

"I'm not sure what this is going to be about. Talk to you tomorrow man." Nick was surprised to see Anne this late at the airport.

"Sure thing," Dennis said and walked away.

"What's got you out here and this late at night? Surely, you're not waiting on me."

"Kinda sorta. Haven't heard from you in a while. I was beginning to wonder if you've lost interest since I didn't get the business."

"That's not fair, Anne. You know the firm keeps me busy flying. One thing has nothing to do with the other."

"I just thought you would be around a little more. Have you heard anymore from that buyer that was interested?"

"Yeah, they're still interested. Are you still on track to get this place from its current owner?" Nick became concern with Anne's hesitancy to answer. "Having second thoughts?"

"Things have become complicated. I'm not sure what to think right now."

Nick was not happy with the vibes he was getting from Anne. He needed her to stay on course. "Why don't you come on over, and we can catch up."

"Thanks but I think I'll pass tonight. It's been a long day."

"Is it that it's been a long day or that you have other plans?"

Anne tilted her head in confusion at Nick's comment and the bitterness in his tone. "Wasn't that O'Keefe's truck I saw go speeding by? I hate to think I interrupted a budding relationship. Maybe that's why you are having second thoughts on selling this place."

"Nick, that's not fair and none of your damn business."

"Just keep this in mind, Anne. The person interested in this business is serious about getting it. If you need the money as bad as you say, then there is nothing to think about. They are not going to wait long on you to make a decision before taking matters in their own hands."

"Is that a threat, Nick?"

"Just a friendly warning. I'd hate to see you get hurt." Nick did not wait for a response. The small engine of the tow motor filled the night air. Nick continued with the task of putting the plane into the hangar.

ELEVEN

*T*he sight of Anne sitting behind the desk raised Maggie's defenses. She didn't have the energy to fight another battle. "What are you doing here this late at night? Why are you going through these files?"

"Paul came by earlier. He wanted to give you these and talk with you." Anne ignored the tone in Maggie's voice.

Maggie took the pages. "This is all of the activities in the business account." Her brows furrowed together as the impact of the information sank into her tired mind.

"Dad knew this the night he died. He met with Paul that night. Paul's been checking into Lynda's background."

Maggie did not miss Anne's referral to Mac as her dad. "This explains why she keeps everything locked up tight." Maggie laid the pages on the sofa beside her. "I didn't believe that story she gave about how Mac wanted the files locked up. Considering his cash register is an old cigar box kept in the flight instructor's desk. He has always run this place on the honor system." Maggie kicked her shoes off and wiggled her toes. "Has he found anything out?"

"Only that she left Florida after divorcing an abusive husband." Anne chose to leave the detail about Nick introducing her to herself.

"Things just keep getting better and better." Maggie stood and walked across the office to the coffee pot.

"I'm not sure what you mean."

"You know I had that meeting earlier with Jared and Kyle."

"Yeah, but I figured it went well since you flew them to St. Simons tonight." Maggie added two spoonful of hazelnut creamer to the coffee. "It was far from that. Dennis and Nick flew them last night. Neither one of them told Jared or Kyle about me and this place. Long story short, they offered Dennis a job as their pilot. Imagine their surprise when I showed up today." Maggie took a sip of the hot liquid welcoming the caffeine. "There were some intense moments. I was on my way out when Kyle asked me to come back. They asked me to fly them tonight. I guess when they couldn't find Nick or Dennis, I began to look a lot better to them."

"So was tonight a one-time deal?"

"No, we got things squared away. They are satisfied with me as their pilot. Although at first they put this stipulation that I had to have a copilot. "

"That's why you took Seth."

"Yeah, but their minds changed after they saw how well I handled the plane, especially after losing the left engine."

Anne moved to the edge of the chair. "What happened?"

"When I switched the fuel tanks, I lost the left engine. Luckily, I got it back. The mechanic in St. Simons is sure it was trash in the line."

Anne tried to imagine how intense those moments must have been for Maggie. "Why do I get the feeling there's more?"

"Yeah, Mac's account has been frozen for delinquency." Maggie took another sip of the coffee. "Also, Nick and Dennis were there, but I didn't see them."

"They returned an hour ago. I saw Nick briefly."

"Not trying to stir the pot, but where are you with Nick?"

"Not anywhere."

"I've never trusted Nick. He has always reminded me of a used car salesman."

"I guess both of us have seen different sides of him I remember he used to show up at the house for dinner." Anne leaned her head against the back of the chair. "Don't get me wrong, he's always liked chasing women, but he was committed to Dad and helping him around this place."

"I asked Mac one time about Nick, thinking he didn't have a family. Mac said Nick's stepfather is a prominent doctor in Atlanta."

"Nick has always been reserved about his relationship with his parents. The one time he really opened up with me was when he'd had too much to drink. He said that his stepfather had married his mom giving them both a home. Nick's mom doesn't know who his father is." Anne studied the picture of her parents. "I guess that is one thing Nick and I have in common."

"What's that?"

"Not knowing our fathers. His not by choice, but mine due to stupid pride."

"Something happen tonight."

"You could say that. Aunt Ethel opened my eyes to some things I didn't know." Anne looked at Maggie. "For years, I blamed this place and you for taking my dad away from me. But in truth, I'm the guilty one."

The emotions displayed in Anne mirrored the same ones Maggie felt. "I think we all carry some guilt once realizing the truth behind why things happen the way they do."

"I asked Aunt Ethel if the main reason Dad left the business to you was to block me from selling it. She said no there was more. She said that Dad left you the business as a way to make up for the way he hurt you." Anne felt that is was important for Maggie to understand that Mac pushed her away for her own safety. "It was to protect you Maggie. Remember Foots?"

"Yeah, he went missing and we never found out what happen to him." Maggie could not fathom why Mac would feel that she was in danger.

"That's not true. Dad found him in the tool room dead with a threatening note. He felt the person that killed Foots would hurt you."

"So, instead of telling me, he decided to banish me." Maggie sat the coffee cup down with a trembling hand. Anger welled within her.

"Maggie, he did it because…"

"Don't you dare say because he loved me. If he loved me, he would have been honest with me." Maggie remembered the day he told her it was time for her to leave. "I stood right here in this office and begged him to not make me go. I pleaded with him. I told him how much I loved him and that he was wrong. You know what he did? He turned his back on me and walked out that door." Maggie pointed to the door that led to the back hangar. "He left me standing here sobbing and pleading with him."

Anne wanted to comfort Maggie. She searched for words that would take away the feelings of hurt, betrayal, and anger. Unfortunately, those emotions were the same one's she'd held for her father for a long time. Instead, she decided to shift the subject. "When Paul was here, I noticed a picture on the desk that wasn't here yesterday."

"What picture?"

"It was me with my first show horse, Dapples."

"You mean the one with your face pressed against his muzzle." Maggie wiped her face with a tissue.

"Yeah." Anne's eyes widened, surprised Maggie recalled the image.

Maggie played back the previous day and the conversation over the pictures. "You're right. I didn't catch it was missing. Mac always kept it on his desk next to mine. Where is it now?"

"Paul took it." Anne's heart warmed at the knowledge that her father kept her picture on his desk.

"Why?"

"Mom took that picture the last day I was with her."

"I don't get the significance of that."

"Tonight, talking with Paul, I remembered him being at the accident. He said he didn't find Mom's camera in the truck."

"Maybe he missed it. Have you spoken to Aunt Ethel about it?"

"No, I plan to ask her tomorrow about it." A yawn escaped Anne. The hands on the wall clock approached two a.m. "When I woke up yesterday, I was hell bent on coming here and making your life miserable. I guess the joke's on me. I plan to call Lou and tell him that I'm not fighting Dad's will. This may be my last chance to get to know Dad, that is, if you are willing to let me continue to come here and be part of this place."

"You are welcome here. This was your father's business. You belong here as much as I do." Maggie sat the empty coffee cup on the side table and stood.

"No hard feelings?"

"No hard feelings."

Together they exited the office. Like Anne, when the day

started it was filled with worry. The old worries were no longer a threat, but there were new ones building.

"Well, at least you had a short walk home." Anne nodded toward the camper.

"I wish I had a guest room to invite you to stay. Are you going to be okay driving to Farmington?"

"I'll be fine. Don't expect me to show up here bright and early all bushy tailed like I did yesterday."

Maggie let out a hoot. "Think of the drama that will be missed."

TWELVE

Maggie tapped her fingers on the desk while waiting for her assistant to answer. Janice was always first to arrive in the office by seven a.m. sharp. She made sure everything for the day was organized and ready for whatever Maggie had on her calendar. "Good morning, Janice."

"I was getting worried about you." Janice had never known Maggie to take a day off from work. She didn't know much personally about her boss, except, she seemed dedicated to her job and left little time for a personal life.

"It has been an interesting three days. Anything I need to know about?"

"No, I was able to get all of your appointments rescheduled."

"Good, I need you to do me a favor." Maggie did not wait for Janice's reply. "Run a history on Keegan O'Keefe. I want a list of all his ratings and any incidents involving him."

"Sure. You want me to send it to your email?"

"No mail it. I don't have access to the Internet here. There isn't the first computer in this place." Maggie had put getting Internet service to the offices at the top of her list. One thing she planned to change was bringing Mac's Flying Service into the age of computers. Maggie grabbed her coffee cup and entered the lobby.

"Morning Maggie." Dennis sat at the flight instructor's desk. "I saw the four-fourteen last night at St. Simons."

"Yeah, I need to talk to you about that." Maggie filled her cup but decided to wait to put any creamer in it. She preferred the flavored one in she kept in Mac's office. "Do you have any students this morning?"

"No. What's up?" Dennis knew the second he saw the four-fourteen sitting on the ramp that things had changed for him. If Maggie Cosby thought he was going to continue in his current position, she had another thought coming. He'd watched her enter this hangar and root him out of opportunities. Mac pushed her, molded her, and made her his right arm. Then she left. There was no way he was letting her take this opportunity away from him.

"Let's go to Mac's office." Maggie knew their conversation was not going to be pleasant.

Dennis remained silent and followed her. He sat on the couch and avoided eye contact with her.

"Dennis, I have always had a lot of respect for you." Maggie spooned two heaping of creamer into her coffee. "This is why the purpose of this conversation is hard for me." Dennis listened while scraping at a non-existent spot on his jeans with his thumb nail. "I met with Jared and Kyle yesterday. I know about the offer they made to you."

"Maggie, I'm sorry. They asked me to be their pilot. We talked after Mac's funeral."

"You mean Nick talked to them. I'm aware of the conversation the four of you had the other night." Maggie waited for

Dennis to digest the full impact of her disclosure. "Voices carry well at night between the hangars. I was in the back hangar when ya'll returned. It was evident that you and Nick neglected to tell them about me."

"Jared and Kyle will never agree to you being their pilot." Dennis tried to control his anger. "They don't believe women should be flying. They only tolerated you because of Mac."

"Bottom line, Jared and Kyle's contract will remain with Mac's Flying Service and with me as the primary pilot." Maggie braced herself for the storm that was about to rain down on her.

"And I get whatever crumbs you decide to pass along to me just like Mac did." Dennis propelled off the sofa and towered over Maggie. "I have paid my dues to this place, pimping this business, bringing in students, and managing the flight school. It's my turn now to get one of the few gravy jobs on this airport."

"Dennis, I would have been willing to let you take more than your share of the flying for Jared and Kyle. Now, I'm not sure if I can trust you or even want you associated with this business. If you want to search for employment elsewhere, I'll be willing to give you a recommendation."

"I don't need your charity." Dennis put both hands on the edge of the desk and leaned closer to Maggie. "You'll not have to worry because I just quit. Let's see if you can handle the flight school and pilot services and manage this business before you run it into the ground to the point no one will give you a plug nickel it."

Dennis pushed the desk making it slide toward Maggie. He slammed the door behind him. Maggie took deep breaths, trying to regain control. She could not shake the violent display of Dennis' action and how threatened he had made her feel. Foots came to mind. Could Dennis have been the one behind Foots and the threats? Maybe he thought without her, Mac would have given him more opportunities.

Flipping through the rolodex on her desk, Maggie located Paul's number. Dialing it, she pulled Dennis' personal information from the filing cabinet. Her wait was not long before she heard Paul's voice on the line. "Good morning, Paul. This is Maggie."

"Hey girl, I came by last night to see you."

"I know. Anne was here when I got back from St. Simons."

"I have to admit I was surprised to see her there. I guess she filled you in."

"Yes, she did. Paul, I want you to add two more names to your list, Dennis and Nick."

"I already have Dennis. Mac gave it to me along with Keegan's. Why Nick?"

"Just a feeling." Maggie paused. "Paul, have you checked into Keegan?"

"Not yet. What's up?"

"There was an issue with the plane last night. I had the mechanic at St. Simons look at it. During our conversation, I mentioned Keegan. The man said Keegan worked at the FBO, and there was an incident. He also said he told Mac not to hire Keegan."

"What happened with the plane?"

"The left engine quit when I changed fuel tanks. Paul, Keegan was the one who fueled the plane last night. I'm checking his background on my side. Can you look and see if there's any criminal history?"

"Already on it. Did the mechanic give any details?"

"No. Keegan gets uncomfortable when his past is mentioned."

"I'm sure Mac would not have hired him if he was trouble."

"I would like to think so. Mac would have given the shirt off his back if he thought someone needed it."

"True."

"Dennis quit this morning."

"What brought that on?"

"He didn't like that Jared and Kyle agreed to let me take over their account. He stormed out of here."

"Sounds like you've already had a hell of a day and it's not even ten o'clock yet."

"And the day ain't over yet."

"Not sure I get your meaning?"

"I plan to speak with Lynda this morning about the accounts."

"Are you sure you don't want me to bring her in and talk to her?" Paul was not comfortable with the idea of Maggie confronting Lynda.

"No, I want to hear her side of the story first."

"At least let me be there when you speak to her."

"I appreciate the offer, Paul, but I'll be fine." Maggie did not give Paul time to object to her decision. "Anne said you took a picture of her with you last night."

"I'm having it checked. Why do you mention it?"

"Because that picture has always been on Mac's desk ever since the day it arrived."

"Do you remember who sent it?"

"It came in the mail with no return address. I opened it thinking it was junk mail." Maggie took a sip of her cold coffee. "Paul, you remember Foots?"

"Yeah. Why?"

"Anne said last night Mac found Foot's body in the tool

room with a threatening note. She said that was why Mac pushed me away."

"He never mentioned anything about it to me."

"Don't you think Mac's death is suspicious?'

Paul remained silent for a moment. "Maggie, I have my suspicions. I wish you'd let me be there when you talk to Lynda."

"Fine. She hasn't shown up this morning."

"Just give me a call when you are ready, and I'll be right over."

"Okay."

****

Maggie refreshed her cup of coffee added creamer. She continued to look over the report Anne had shown her last night and compared it with the one's she found in Mac's flight case. She recognized that it was the same report that Mac had given Paul. The exception was Mac's handwriting beside transactions to a DE Aviation.

Maggie flipped through the accounts payable file. She did not see a folder for DE Aviation or any information pertaining to the account. "That's odd. Why would an account receive a monthly payment and not have a file folder or any invoices?"

"They say those who talk to themselves show signs of early senility," Keegan answered Maggie while propping himself against the door frame.

"It is only if you answer yourself and begin a complete conversation that one should worry."

"I saw Dennis go storming out and squealing tires through the parking lot. Thought I'd check and see if you are okay."

"Thanks for the concern. Yes, I'm fine. Dennis quit this morning."

"Wow! That's a shocker. What set him off?"

"Not getting Jared and Kyle to hire him as their pilot. They are staying with us."

"Jeezz, I guess that is good, but what about the flight instruction?"

"I'm going to handle it until I can get another instructor."

"That's an awful lot on your plate." Keegan worried that Maggie was taking on too much. "I hate to be the bearer of more unhappy news. There's a gentleman out here who wants to see you. He said he's with the Airport Authority"

"Wonderful, just what else I need today."

"I can tell him you're not here."

"No, I might as well take this bull by the horns."

****

"Good morning, Gerald." Maggie shook the hand of her former student.

"Maggie."

"I guess you are here to tell me the Airport Authority is ready to tear this place down for the sake of modernization."

"You believe in getting to the point." Gerald gave a nervous chuckle. "We have a tentative agreement with a new tenant. After Mac's death everyone assumed Anne would sell the business."

"I guess that is what you get for counting your chickens before their eggs hatch." Anne walked into the office. "Seems like you and the Airport Commission have gotten yourselves in a bind, and now you want to make it our problem."

"We have the option of not renewing your lease."

Anne directed her attention to Maggie while still addressing Gerald. "I'm sure our attorney, Madison Barfield, will be pleased to hear this. Lawsuits have a way of getting drawn out."

Gerald's smile froze on his face. "The next meeting is

in two weeks. I just wanted you to know this hangar is the primary focus. You may want to start looking for another place if you plan to stay in business."

Anne waited until she was sure he was clear of the office. "Sorry, I didn't mean to barge in and take over."

"Thanks, I think you threw him off kilter. I didn't expect to see you this early."

"I wanted to get over to Lou's office. I thought I'd come by and see how things are going."

"Fine if you know how to flight instruct."

"I take it things didn't go well this morning with Dennis."

"Wow, you are smart."

"Easy girl, sarcasm is not a good bargaining chip." Anne spotted the plate that had held a slice of her Aunt's pound cake. "Tell me your breakfast was not coffee and pound cake."

"And if it was."

"I just figured you for a health food junkie."

"I've been a little busy." Maggie handed Anne the pages she'd been reviewing. "I found this in Mac's flight case. Notice how DE Aviation is circled and the amount of the checks."

"Are you familiar with them?"

"No. I can't find any files or invoices for them in Lynda's office."

"I bet Dad didn't know about these payments."

"That's what I'm thinking, too."

Anne looked at her watch. "I'd love to hang around longer today. Thankfully, I have a full schedule at the barn this afternoon. Why don't you come down this evening, get away from this place, and let's talk some more. Bring yourself a change of clothes and make it a sleep over. I can cook a mean steak, and don't take this the wrong way, but, Cosby, you ain't looking so good." Anne took a piece of paper from the desk and a pen. "Here's my cell phone and the number to the farm. Give me a call when you are on your way down. If you like to ride, come down early, and we'll go on one of the trails."

"Thanks. Let me see what's going on with the flight schedule today. I'll walk out with you. "

Anne and Maggie walked into Lynda's office and stopped in front of the picture window. Anne watched Keegan working on Doc's plane. He intrigued her, angered her, and made her imagine what his kisses would taste like.

"Be careful, Anne. Things aren't always what they seem."

"Is there something you're not telling me?"

"Just be careful." Maggie was not ready to share her suspicions about Keegan.

"Who said I was looking for anything in particular?" Anne pulled her truck keys from her jeans pocket. "I've got horses waiting to be ridden. See you this evening."

****

"Keegan, Maggie around?" Seth had spent the morning making adjustments to his flight schedules.

"She's in the office. It's been hell of a morning around here."

"How so?"

"To start off, Dennis stormed out after quitting."

"I guess he wasn't happy about Jared and Kyle's decision."

"To say the least. Not long after that, Gerald Mixon came by wanting to talk to Maggie about this place."

"Is he still here?"

No, this is where things get real interesting. Not long after I left him with Maggie, Anne showed up." Keegan watched Seth look to the office with concern. "Yeah, me too. I stood out here waiting for the fireworks to start again between those two."

"I take it there were no fireworks?"

Keegan shook his head. "No fireworks. Actually, Gerald was the one who walked out all red faced on his phone saying something about the two broads threatening a law suit."

"I wonder what's up."

"I'm not sure, but after Gerald left both Anne and Maggie stood in Lynda's office for a few minutes talking"

"Maybe I should check the weather forecast for snow today." Both men chuckled at Seth's comment.

"Hey, you got anything better to do than harass people?" Maggie shut the office door behind her and joined the two men.

"Is that how you treat your lunch date?" Seth did not miss how pale and tired she looked.

"I didn't know we had a date." Maggie enjoyed the play between them. It was like old times. "I'm waiting on Lynda to drag in. Aunt Ethel sent me enough food to last a month. I'll share."

"Okay. Keegan said it's been busy here today."

"That's an understatement." Maggie turned her attention to Keegan. "Can you take a look at the four-fourteen? We had some issues with the left engine."

"Sure. What happened?"

"It wouldn't run on the left tip tank. I had the mechanic at St. Simons look at it. He found some trash in the fuel. I mentioned I'd have you look at it." Maggie searched for any reaction from Keegan.

"You mean Raymond?" Keegan remained cool and did not allow his expression change. He was sure the man did not have anything good to say about him.

"I think so. That's where you worked before coming here." Maggie continued to watch for any response.

"I did." Keegan knew Maggie was fishing. He wondered if she had already pulled his records. "I'll take a look at it this afternoon." Keegan wiped his hands on a shop rag. "Right now, I'm gonna head out for some lunch."

****

Dennis punched the buttons on the phone. He hit the steering wheel out of frustration. Nick's answering machine was not what he wanted. "Nick, hey man, I'm headed your way. We need to talk."

Nick listened to the message. "I guess you'd better get out of here before he shows up."

"He sounded upset. I wonder what happened this morning."

"I bet it has something to do with last night."

Lynda grabbed her jeans. "I'd better get over to the hangar and see what's up."

****

Nick finished snapping the button of his jeans. He and Lynda had cut it close. Nick thought about how his doorbell had become the object for people to take out their anger. "Hey, man, you sounded pissed on the phone."

"To say the least." Dennis stopped inside the doorway. He thought he caught a whiff of Lynda's perfume. "You got a woman here?"

"Naw, just me. What has you in such a mood this morning?"

"Maggie was waiting on me when I got to the hangar." Dennis paced around the living room. "She didn't waste any time wanting to talk about Jared and Kyle."

Nick poured some juice into a glass. "Want some?"

"No thanks. Nick, she overheard us the other night when

118

we came back. She knew they offered me the position as their pilot, but she went ahead and met with them and convinced them to stay with Mac's."

Nick strangled on the juice. "You mean they are going to keep their account with her."

"Yes."

"What did you do?"

"I quit. Let's see if she can handle it all."

"What about your financial situation?" Nick knew about the debt Dennis' mother left him before she died.

"I've got some cash stached. Dennis thought about the account he used to squirrel money. Hopefully, I can get picked up soon with a commuter service."

"Let me see what I can do for you. I'll make some calls and find out if anyone is hiring right now."

"Thanks, man. I don't want to go back to the hangar. I guess I need to call Lynda and let her know what's up. Her damn phone keeps going to voice mail."

"I'll let you know something soon."

"Thanks." Dennis trusted that Nick would find a solution for him. He needed to find Lynda and give her a heads-up. Maybe she would quit and leave Maggie with Keegan. That would serve her right for taking what was his.

****

"Damn, what is this today, grand central station?" Nick's morning had taken a turn toward chaos. He hated it when other people's problems interfered with him.

"No, but you better start getting all your runaway trains back on track there Masden."

"I guess you've heard." Nick cringed at the sound of the voice on the other end of the phone.

"Yes, and my question is what do you plan to do? Time is money, and the longer that business is not for sale the more money I am losing. "

"I'm working on it now. Dennis quit this morning."

"I'm aware of that. You're going to tell him there's a job in Panama City flying charter. He needs to be kept on a short leash right now."

"Yes sir."

"Masden, I expect you to get this situation under control soon. I'm not a patient man."

"I understand."

"Oh, and start spending less time with my daughter and more with that daughter of Mac's. Keep her fire lit and not the one in her bed. Get my drift?" Before Nick could say anything more, the line went dead

THIRTEEN

Paul entered through the back hangar out of sight. He opened the door to Mac's office. "You ready for this?"

"As ready as I guess I can be." Maggie moved from behind the desk. "Let me go get her." Maggie stopped at Lynda's desk. "You got a minute. We haven't had a chance to talk one-on-one."

"Sure." Lynda put the pen down and followed Maggie. She tried to hide her initial surprise at the sight of Paul sitting on the couch.

"Close the door. I asked Paul to be here because of some discrepancies I've found with the books." Maggie handed the financial reports to Lynda. "Do you know anything about DE Aviation? Why isn't there a file for them or any invoices?"

Lynda stared blankly at the pages. The sound of her pounding heart filled her ears. She dropped her head averting Maggie's pointed stare. "Dennis is DE Aviation. The DE is for his name Dennis Edwards."

"It still does not explain why Mac was not aware of these transactions." Paul interjected enjoying the scene unfolding.

"I caught Dennis in my office late one night. He was sitting at my desk with the check book open. There was a check made out to DE Aviation. He was signing Mac's name to it. He said he felt Mac didn't appreciate how much he did for this place. He said if I said anything to Mac he'd kill me." Lynda wiped the tears from her face. "By then, we'd been involved for several months and I'd moved in with him. He knew about how abusive my first husband had been with me." Lynda looked at Maggie. "I tried to tell Mac, but Mac trusted Dennis. He never realized how much Dennis hated him. I think I am going to be sick" Lynda covered her mouth and ran out of the office.

Maggie mulled over what Lynda had told her and about Dennis' display earlier At one point, she'd been afraid he was going to hit her. He wasn't upset over losing the opportunity to fly for Jared and Kyle. He was scared that the truth was about to be revealed. "What do you think, Paul?"

"That somewhere in her theatrics there's some truth. It would explain Dennis' reaction this morning."

Lynda interrupted before Maggie could reply. "I guess I'm fired and arrested."

"I think the best thing is for you to take the rest of the day off." Maggie stated.

"I understand." Lynda turned to walk out of the office.

Paul spoke before Lynda made it to the door. "One more thing, Lynda. Make sure you don't decide to do any disappearing acts in the meantime."

Lynda did not respond but continued to exit the office.

*****

Lynda was glad Dennis was not home. She propped her feet on the coffee table. Taking a long draw from the cigarette, she welcomed the biting sting of nicotine across her tongue and smoke filling her lungs. Slowly exhaling, she closed her eyes and soaked in the stillness of the house. She gathered her thoughts before having to make her phone call. "Hey, dad. It's me."

"This is a surprise. I didn't expect to hear from you today. I hope you are calling with good news." The sound of silence on the line spoke volumes. "Ummmm, then there must be bad news."

"Maggie knows about the money. She called me into her office and asked me about DE Aviation. That cop Paul Anderson was there too."

"What did you tell them?

"That Dennis was stealing from Mac. I gave some tears and a sob story about how Dennis threatened to kill me and was abusive."

He was familiar with his step-daughter's theatrics. A smile crept across his face imagining her performance. "What was Maggie's reaction?"

"She became all compassionate. I asked if I was fired or under arrest. She said she'd let me know. Of course, I got the usual don't leave town speech from that cop."

"Did you tell Masden this?"

"No."

"Good. The less he knows the better." The old man was pleased with how well Lynda was handling things for him. "Dennis' tirade could not have been planned any better. Cheer up, pumpkin. This isn't bad news after all." Lynda exhaled with relief. "You still working on that other project?"

"Yes sir. It's going like clockwork."

"Good. You keep Masden on task with Anne. I knew I could count on you to handle things up there."

"Love you too, dad."

****

"Welcome to Harris Farms." Anne greeted Maggie at the front door.

"This place is beautiful from the ground." Maggie shut the car door. "Sorry, I tried to get away from the airport sooner.

We still have time for a ride?"

"Sure, let me put your bag inside the door." Anne was surprised by Maggie's enthusiasm. "I take it you've ridden before."

"I have to admit it's been a while." Maggie walked beside Anne to the barn. "I rode Tennessee Walkers at a stable over in Gallatin and fell in love with breed."

"Have you ever been to Shelbyville during the Celebration?"

"Yeah, it's funny watching the men. All dressed up like Al Capone Gangsters and the way they hunch forward bobbing their heads in rhythm with their horse." Maggie gave her best imitation.

Anne's laughter echoed through the barn. "Oh my God, you have it down perfect." She gave a loud whistle and pushed the gate open to the pasture. "During my college days at MTSU, I worked for a few of the farms around Murfreesboro. Here comes the gang."

"Wow, they all are beautiful." Maggie was awed by the herd racing toward them. A few kicked their back legs and others tried to gain the lead. Above the sound of pounding hooves, she heard them each answering their master's whistle with neighing and nickering.

Anne smiled with pride at the compliment. "I'll let you ride Chance. He likes the ladies and will be gentle enough for you."

"Which one is he?"

"He's the chestnut. MY big beautiful boy is the solid black stallion."

"What's his name?"

"PJ. He's a Hanoverian."

"What does PJ stand for?"

"Passion's Joy." Anne lowered her hand under PJ's nose.

The rush of heated breath met her palm. The feel of whiskers and velvet muzzle massaged the open hand. "Hey, big boy."

"Hey, Chance." Maggie held her hand out while speaking in soothing tones. Chance lowered his head, giving a short blow before inhaling her scent. Maggie rubbed her hand down his neck, scratching under his mane as she moved closer. With gentle ease, she slid the lead rope around his neck.

"Come on, let's get these boys saddled up. I'll put the others in the round pen until we get back." Anne was amazed at how natural Maggie was around the horses. "I thought we'd ride to the back side of the farm. Which do you prefer English or Western?"

"I better take Western." Maggie patted the top of her thighs. "I don't think these thigh muscles could handle English."

****

"They say we should get frost tonight." Anne urged PJ across the stream and up the hill to the open pasture.

"It would be a beautiful night to fly." Maggie admired the clear sky and how large the moon appeared. The evening twilight brought cooler temperatures and a slight chill. "Mac never talked much about growing up here."

"I think this was a part of Dad's life that he was glad to leave behind." Anne rode beside Maggie and was impressed at how well she handled Chance. "His dad was a farmer and enjoyed the land, but Dad didn't share Grandpa's love for it."

"It's easy to see you've done a lot with the place."

"It been a lot of years of hard work and sacrifice, but yes, I have." The day Anne asked her dad for the farm had been one of the few times she'd initiated any contact with him. "I'd come home from college, full of big ideas and dreams of having a breeding and training center for Hanoverians. I asked

Dad if he'd let me move down here and build the place up. He said he didn't care, that he'd been thinking of selling it. I figured he was trying to erase his past and anything to do with Mom. So I moved down and started fixing the place. First, I only gave lessons and competed in paying shows. I boarded horses. Over time, I built a reputation and a following. This place held a lot of my childhood memories. The last memories of my mother are here."

"Ya'll were on your way home from here when the accident happened."

"It'd been a long day. The horse show was over in Alabama. We'd left the arena late. I tried to talk Mom into letting us spend the night. She was insistent that we come home that night." Anne reflected on the conversation she'd had with her Aunt Ethel the previous night. "Some things Aunt Ethel said last night explained a lot about my mother's mood that day."

"What'd you mean?"

"During the day, Mom disappeared. I couldn't find her anywhere. Usually, between classes we were working with the horses, or she'd be taking pictures for my scrapbook. She showed up in time for her next class to begin. It was obvious she'd been crying." Anne loosened the reigns and let PJ continue at his own pace. "She was pregnant, and the baby wasn't Dad's."

"Is that what Aunt Ethel told you last night?"

"And more. Dad didn't know about the baby. He found out at the hospital when Doc told him Mom had died. Aunt Ethel said that he had been staying at the airport in the camper at night. He'd come home in the morning before I would get up."

"I always thought he got the camper to have a place to fix something to eat or get ready for a trip."

"You know all these years I blamed him for Mom's un-

126

happiness. I bought into the stories she told about how he neglected her. By the time I was a teenager, he wasn't home much. I thought he hated us. You know why he married her?" Maggie did not respond but listened. Her earlier suspicions about Anne's motives dissolved. "Because she got pregnant by his friend. The man refused to marry her, and Dad stepped up to the plate. You know how she repaid dad? She continued her affair with that man. Dad caught them in bed together."

"Anne, are you saying Mac was not your real father?"

"No, I thought that too when Aunt Ethel told me the truth about my parent's." Anne paused and thought about the previous evening. The way her aunt's resolve dissipated. "Aunt Ethel has known everything about my parent's marriage. But, she'd promised Dad not to say anything to me."

"It had to be hard learning the truth." Maggie had a better understanding of the Anne she'd seen in her office last night.

"It was, and I am still digesting all of it. But, I'm glad she told me." Anne would always be grateful for her aunt's honesty. Lou had been angry with her decision to not pursue contesting her father's will. He had accused her of wasting his time and making him look like a fool in front of the Judge. Anne did not care about the feelings of one lawyer.

"Anne, I don't mean to pry, but I noticed you don't have a lot of horses. Are things okay here?"

"No. I'm about thirty days from losing the farm."

"Selling the business was more than an act of spite for you." Maggie felt genuine concern for Anne. She also respected the courage it took for Anne to admit how close she was to losing the farm.

"It was my last hope." Anne patted PJ's neck. "As much as

it breaks my heart, I'm going to have to let my beautiful boy go. His sale will pay off my debts. I plan to call a horse broker tomorrow. At least, I'll have his last foal from Angel's Glory."

"No, Anne. There's got to be another way." Maggie could see how much Anne loved the horse. "You selling PJ would be like me selling the Bonanza."

"I don't see any other way." Anne had sat up until the early morning hours studying the financials for her farm. Her savings had been depleted over the past few months in trying to keep the farm operating. The only asset she had that would generate enough capital to pay off her debts was PJ. She felt like she was betraying her best friend.

"We're almost back to the barn." Anne gently pressed her heel to PJ's side, making the horse move ahead. "I'll get the gate."

Maggie passed through the opening and continued to the barn. Her knees buckled as her feet touched the ground. She grabbed Chance's mane and the back of the saddle for stability. In an attempt to fight the wave of nausea, she rested her head against the side of the horse. Chance sensing Maggie's distress stood still.

"Hey, you okay? You look like you're about ready to pass out." Alarmed at how all the color drained from Maggie's face brought instant concern to Anne.

"Let me just catch my breath for a minute and get my strength back in my legs." Maggie gave chuckle. "Guess that's what happens when it's been a while since I was on the back of horse."

"Maybe some red meat will help you." Anne started loosening PJ's saddle. "Why don't you sit down and rest. It won't take me long to get the horses in their stalls and fed."

"I'm sorry I'm such trouble." Maggie welcomed the relief of a hay bale. She pressed her back against the barn wall and closed her eyes. Her limbs felt like rubber, and her heart raced. The cool night air helped stave off the feeling of fainting.

"Don't worry about it. While I throw the steaks on the grill you can clean up."

****

"You were right about that shower." Maggie entered the kitchen.

"You look better." Anne turned from the sink and dried her hands. "There is color in your cheeks. You had me scared down there at the barn."

"I guess with everything at the airport and not being use to riding wore me out."

Anne handed Maggie a glass of wine. "Well, tonight is for just relaxing and taking it easy. How you like your steak?"

"Medium rare."

"Good, it won't be long before they are ready. You mind setting the table?" Anne pointed in the direction of the cabinets. "Plates are up there, silverware is over there. There's a salad in the fridge. Dig around in the fridge there should be some dressing. Instead of potatoes, I grilled some asparagus and mixed vegetables."

Maggie found everything she needed to complete setting the table. Anne returned with the steaks and vegetable. "Those look and smell great."

"Thanks. Your steak is this one right here." Anne pointed to the steak she'd prepared for Maggie. Both women bowed their heads as Anne gave thanks for the meal before them. "How'd things go with Lynda today?"

"Interesting. She said Dennis is the one behind DE Aviation. He threatened to kill her if she said anything to Mac. By the time she discovered what he was doing, they were living together. She indicated that he was abusive like her first husband."

"So he's behind this. Does Paul think Dennis may have had something to do with Dad's death?"

"He didn't say. Since there isn't anything to indicate foul play in Mac's death, there isn't a case."

"I doubt anyone makes Lynda do anything. Why didn't Paul arrest her?"

"It's up to me to press charges."

"Are you?"

"I'm not sure."

"Surely you fired her?"

"No, but she will not have access to the bank accounts. I called the bank this afternoon and spoke with the manager. Also, I had the locks changed on the filing cabinets and the door to Mac's office. I brought a set of keys for you."

"Did you tell Madison?"

"Not yet." Maggie knew that Madison would give her the same lecture Seth had at lunch.

"How do you to plan to handle not having a flight instructor, flying for Jared and Kyle, and managing the office?" Anne took a sip of wine. "Maggie, even I know when I'm over my head. This evening was a warning that you are doing too much."

"Seth is going to help with the flight instructing. He agreed to it over lunch today."

"What's up with you and Seth?" Anne did not miss the way Maggie's voice softened with Seth's name.

"What do you mean?"

"Were ya'll ever an item or what?"

Maggie laughed at the thought. "No, just friends."

"That's a beautiful ring." Anne had admired the ring several times.

"Thank you, it was a gift."

"Why do you wear it on your left hand? Is there someone special in your life back in Nashville?"

"No, no one in Nashville."

Anne shook her head. "Okay, I'm confused. Usually a ring on the left hand indicates a serious attachment. Come on, Cosby, quit holding out on the juicy details."

Maggie did not know how to answer Anne's curiosity. Clearing her throat, she said, "It was among the things Mac left me. He'd bought it with the intentions of asking me to marry him." Anne stopped chewing and took a long swallow of wine. "Yeah, and you thought me getting the business was big news. How'd you'd like the idea of a step-mother your age?"

"It would have been interesting." A few days ago this news would have infuriated Anne. Instead, it saddened her to know her father watched a woman who loved him walk out of his life. "I guess we know why he didn't ask. It has to hurt to find this out now."

"It makes me angry at him. Foots was just the final excuse he needed." Maggie pushed the empty plate to the side. "Mac could never get past the age difference. We had some heated arguments about it."

"Dad could be stubborn. So, why wear it on your left hand?"

"I wear it to remind me of my decision to put everything I have into making Mac's Flying Service stay the success it is."

"Maggie, I'm sorry for pressing the issue. You can't just close yourself off. Don't make his mistakes."

"This coming from a woman who defines relationships as a pastime of drive by sex with no entanglements."

Anne made a hissing sound and swiped the air with her hand.

Maggie chuckled at Anne's antics.

"I'm just saying what if someone like Seth came along. Who is handsome, shares the same interest as you, and is in love with you. Would you just let it slip away?"

"First of all, I don't agree that Seth is in love with me. He is just a friend. I couldn't see him as anything else."

"Honey, you need to take those blinders off because that man is in love with you. The way he is always coming by checking on you. He has rearranged his life to be with you and help at the airport."

Maggie sat in silence digesting Anne's words. She thought of the night standing on the pier next to him. How his arm had felt around her shoulder. "I just don't know. The thought of falling in love is too painful."

"I'm just saying don't go shutting doors until you've walked around in the room and gotten to know its contents first."

Maggie wanted to get away from the subject of Seth. She was not ready for the feelings his name created within her. "Well, Ms. Advice for the Lovelorn, what about you? Are you holding out that Nick Masden is going to give up chasing women to settle down with you? Better yet, are you betting on a wild Irishman to sweep you off your feet?"

Anne spewed wine. "What makes you say a crazy thing like that? First of all I accept Nick for who he is and don't expect anything from him. Secondly, Keegan O'Keeffe is too judgemental for me."

"That's not the vibe I got from you today at the hangar. If he doesn't mean anything, then why did you make it a point to speak to him before leaving? What's going on between the two of you? I haven't seen Keegan act rude to anyone like he did you today."

"That was nothing." Anne took a quick sip of wine. Keegan's rebuff of her still stung.

"For that to be nothing, you sure left like a scalded dog." Maggie knew to leave well enough alone. "Let me help you with the kitchen."

"You can wash while I put things away."

Together, they had the kitchen cleaned in a few minutes. Maggie folded the drying towel and draped it over the sink. "Thanks for this evening. I enjoyed the ride, dinner, and just being able to be a girl."

"Same here."

"Think I'm gonna turn in."

"Goodnight. I might be down at the barn when you get up in the morning. Just make yourself at home."

"Thanks, Anne." Maggie closed the door to the guest bedroom. The heat from the kitchen had made the room toasty. She climbed into the fresh made bed and wiggled deep into it. Sleep was immediate.

****

"You're not gonna believe my news." Dennis grabbed Lynda and pulled her into his arms. He swung her around before letting her feet touch the floor.

"You are in exceptional spirits to be someone unemployed."

"Was unemployed...past tense, my love."

"That must have been Maggie on the phone begging you to come back."

Dennis rolled his eyes. "No, that was a friend of Nick's down in Panama City. He just offered me a job flying for his company, Reynard Air."

"Dennis, that is great. See, things always work out for the best. Looks like you are getting your dream job after all."

"Yeah, he said they run a fleet of turbo-props. That will help getting on with the big boys. They want me down there by Monday."

"Wow that is fast."

"Why don't you go in tomorrow and tell Miss Maggie Cosby that you quit. Come with me. We can get a place on the beach. Just think, no more giving flying lessons." Dennis planted a kiss on Lynda. "The best part is selling this house will pay off momma's medical expenses."

"I don't want to burst your bubble." Lynda pushed away from Dennis. "Have you forgotten the reason I left that area? My ex-husband."

"Didn't you say he disappeared, and no one has heard from him?"

"Yes, but I just don't want to risk him finding me. Anyway, I've lived on the beach before. It's not all it's cracked up to be."

"Baby, it will be different with me. I promise to take care of you." Dennis put his hands on Lynda's shoulders. He looked in her eyes pleading that she'd change her mind. "We can live anywhere you want."

Lynda broke free from Dennis's embrace. She was glad to be getting rid of him. He was such a clinger. "Dennis, I don't want to move from here."

"Is it Nick? Is he why?'

"No nothing like that."

"Then what are you saying? You want a long distance relationship?"

"No, Dennis, I'm saying it's time we go our separate ways."

Dennis opened the refrigerator and grabbed a beer. The

cap made a thud against the bottom of the trash can. "Then I guess there is no changing your mind."

"I'm sorry but no."

"Well, why don't we start going our separate ways tonight? With you leaving now."

Without saying another word, Lynda took her coat and purse from the couch. "I wish you the best, Dennis."

Dennis' response was a loud belch.

FOURTEEN

$\mathcal{K}$eegan stifled a laugh at the smudged grease on Anne's forehead. In the past few weeks, he'd watched her dedicate herself to learning all aspects of the place. He didn't know how she managed the hours she put in around the hangar and at the horse farm. "Feel like going up?" he asked.

"Thanks for the offer, but I need to get back to the farm to take care of the horses." Anne put the screwdriver on the worktable. "PJ and I have a standing date tonight. The Conyers show is next week."

"I promise to get you there in time." Keegan grabbed a tow-bar from the table and attached it to the plane's nose wheel. "You watch the wings and tail section." Keegan tugged the tow-bar. The plane begin a slow crawl. He was pleased Anne had accepted his spontaneous invitation. Lately, he found himself looking for any excuse to have her close to him.

"I use to go up with dad when I was little." The tidbit of information bubbled from Anne. She wasn't sure why she felt the need to share it.

"So it's been a while since you've been in one of these things." Keegan removed the tow bar and placed it on the tool table. "You ready?"

"I guess." Anne placed a foot on the foot plate of the main wheel strut and lifted herself into the cramped interior. Keegan's muscular frame filled the remaining space.

"You never learned to fly?" Keegan taxied the plane to the runway and completed the pre-flight checklist.

"Dad would let me play with the controls some. By the time I was old enough to take lessons…" Anne could not finish the sentence.

"You ought to get Maggie to teach you." Keegan understood the reason for the unfinished sentence.

"She has a lot on her plate right now."

"I bet she would be honored if you asked."

"Let me think about it. Where did you learn to fly?"

"I got my private pilot license while stationed at Pensacola with the Navy. Figured if I was going to work on these things I needed to know how to fly them."

"What made you go into the Navy?"

"Being young and stupid. I was carrying a lot of anger toward life and the world for the loss of my parents."

"Sometimes we can be our own worst enemy."

"You want to take-off?"

"Do you have a death wish?"

"No, here, listen to me. I have the rudder pedals to keep her straight on the runway. Put your hand on the control wheel and the other one on the throttle. Look down the runway." Keegan announced to the area traffic they were departing and positioned the airplane on the runway. "The throttle is like your feet when you ride, if you apply abrupt pressure, the plane will react harshly. Just as it is important to stay out of the horse's mouth with too much pressure on the bit, the same holds true for the control wheel. All you need are light, gentle movements. The relationship between horse and rider is the same for plane and pilot. The two must move together in harmony."

Anne did not expect the feel of Keegan's hand over hers on

the throttle. She tried to concentrate on the runway and not the heat building within her.

"Remember I have the rudders. All you have to concentrate on is the control wheel." Keegan waited until the plane reached take-off speed. "Okay, now increase your back pressure."

The small plane broke free from the ground. The sensation of flight along with being close to Keegan sent an electrical charge through Anne. From the corner of her eye, she admired the strong features of his face. A truce had settled between them.

"You might want to pay attention to outside the plane." Keegan teased.

"I was looking at the instruments."

"If that's your tale, I'll sit on mine." Keegan gave a lopsided grin.

"That's my farm." Anne recognized her barn. Tiny specks in the pasture were her horses. The tin roof to her house was distinguishable among the oaks.

"I know."

"How often do you fly over here?"

"Every time I have to come up for a test flight."

"I would appreciate it if you did not jeopardize the safety of my animals."

"Never had one to fail on me yet." Keegan lowered the nose into a descent.

"What are you doing?" Anne became alarmed at Keegan's intentions. "Don't buzz my farm. I have a mare about to foal. Last thing I need is her to get spooked and start running."

"Not planning on it." Keegan reduced the power and added carburetor heat. The airspeed of the plane slowed into the white arc. Keegan reached over to Anne's side and lowered the flaps.

"What the hell are you doing, O'Keefe? If this is a joke, it's not funny."

"You might want to hold on tight, things are going to get a little bumpy." Anne opened her mouth to issue a demand that he stop fooling around but was cut-off when the plane made contact with the grassy surface of the pasture. Keegan kept the nose wheel off the ground until the plane had slowed to a walking speed. "Thought you said you need to feed your horses."

"You have lost your mind, O'Keefe! What is Maggie going to say once she learns you've landed this thing in a horse pasture?"

"Not a thing." Keegan stopped the plane close to the gate. "Looks like we've got some curious spectators coming our way."

"Seems like they are familiar with the plane." Anne unbuckled her seatbelt.

"Mac use to come down and check on them and the farm when you were out of town. He's the one who showed me where to land." Keegan opened his door and exited.

"Why doesn't that surprise me?" Anne walked up to the large animals while talking to them. She called each one by name while petting their muzzles. Keegan felt a stir in him seeing the way she relaxed around the horses. Gone were her barriers and guarded emotions.

"You coming or not? They say they're ready for supper." Anne walked to the gate and unlocked it.

"Sure. You need any halters or lead ropes for them?"

"No, the gate to the road is closed. They won't wander far." Anne stepped aside allowing the six horses to pass by her.

Keegan admired the fine horse flesh. "All of them yours?"

"All but two." Anne pointed to her stallion. "This one is PJ." She knew her days were limited to being able to call PJ hers. She'd placed a call to a horse broker and had some potential buyers.

"How long before that one over there foals?"

"Angel's Glory is due to drop sometime next month." Anne continued with her introductions. "The Quarter horse is Chance's Dream, my teaser horse. I also use him for giving lessons. Girl is the newest addition to the farm. She's a rescue horse. Her owners abandoned her when their farm went bankrupt."

"The other two horses are borders?"

"Yeah, they belong to Lou Holsenbeck's wife and daughters. The sorrel is Belle, and the other one is Mister." Anne closed the gate. "I let them graze while fixin' their feed."

"You have a nice place."

"Thanks." Anne opened the barn doors. Nails awoke from his from his spot on a hay bale. He stretched and yawned at the same time before hopping down. "This is Nails. Actually he runs the place. I just work for him."

"Why the name Nails?"

"I found him as a kitten in the drainage ditch at the entrance to the farm. The temps that night dipped down to the twenties. I told him he had to be tough as nails to have survived the cold temperatures."

Nails rubbed against Keegan's pants leg before reaching upward with an out stretched paw. "He wants you to pet him. Take it as a compliment. Nails doesn't take well to strangers."

Keegan scratched Nails behind the ears. The cat responded with a loud purr of approval. "What do you need me to do to help you?"

"You can check each stall to see if they need water. I cleaned them this morning. "

Anne went to the feed room. She busied herself with preparing each horse's feed for the evening. She listened to Keegan whistling an Irish tune. Anne daydreamed of a life with him, about what it would be like working side-by-side on the farm and at the airport. She could see herself settling down with him raising a family

"You think you got enough feed in that bucket?"

"Guess I need to take some out." Anne realized what she'd done and blushed.

"You have about twenty stalls in this barn. Is it normal that they are this empty?"

"No, up till two months ago, every stall was filled and we had a waiting list." Anne grabbed the handles of two buckets.

"What's happened?" Keegan followed suit taking the remaining two buckets.

"A lot of unexplained incidents—like stall doors and the main gate being left open for its occupant to wander out freely. There's been damaged equipment too." Anne stopped at the first stall. "The most severe was bread being left in one of the stalls. One of the horses found it. It was touch and go but my vet was able to get it back to good health. The bad side was word started getting out that this place was unsafe to board horses. So, one by one, I have watched my steady income leave in trailers. Lou's wife has remained loyal and supportive."

"Did you find out how bread was left in the barn?" Keegan understood the danger of a horse eating bread.

"No." Anne moved to the next stall and continued to swap empty feed buckets with filled ones.

"Do you know why anyone would want to ruin your farm's reputation?" Keegan did not like the idea of Anne being in danger.

"That is a question Paul and I are trying to find out." Anne finished putting feed in the last two stalls. "With everything that's been going on with Maggie and the business, we are concern that the two are related."

"You mean that stuff about the Airport Authority?" Keegan had noticed the frequent visits Paul made to the hangar. Anne's mention of trouble with the business was news to him. He had chalked Lynda's moodiness to Dennis' departure, and Seth had become a permanent fixture flying with students.

Anne hesitated, not sure how much she should share with Keegan. Maggie's words of caution lingered with her. Her gut instincts told her that Keegan was not a threat. "That and more. Dennis was embezzling from the business. Dad knew about it before he died. That was what Paul wanted the night he came by the hangar. To tell Maggie about the meeting he had with Dad the night he died."

"Lynda was part of it, wasn't she?" Keegan never trusted the woman. The word opportunist always came to mind when he thought of her.

"She says Dennis threatened her." Anne reached up and grabbed four lead ropes from a hook in the tack room.

"That's not Dennis. None of it." Keegan took two of the lead ropes from Anne. "When Lynda arrived, she wouldn't give him the time of day. She made fun of him when he wasn't around. About three months ago, she did a one-eighty and started chasing him. The poor boy didn't have a chance."

"That's about when money started missing." Anne made a mental note to tell Maggie.

"Does Aunt Ethel know about the trouble here at the farm?" Keegan followed Anne to where the horses were grazing.

"She does and has already expressed her concern about me being down here by myself." Anne clipped a lead rope to PJ and moved to Angel's Glory. "I can't abandon my horses and farm because someone is trying to scare me."

"You two ready for dinner and a clean stall?" Keegan clipped the lead ropes onto Chance and Girl. He followed Anne into the barn.

PJ looked back at Keegan and gave a snort. "He is very protective of me." Anne laughed at PJ's antics. She put Angel's Glory in her stall. PJ pawed the dirt with his hoof and shook his head up and down.

"I would be protective too, if you were my girl." Keegan commented. He shut the door to Chance's stall and put Girl in her stall next to Chance. "He is really rambunctious tonight."

"He knows it's time for his date with me. Do you mind waiting while I work him?" Anne thought about how these moments with PJ were numbered.

"No problem, glad to."

"Thanks. The show in Conyers will be our last one." Anne began to saddle PJ.

"Why's that?" Keegan was a good judge of horse flesh, and PJ was top of the line. The eighteen hand horse had a good constitution and had not reached his prime. There was no logical reason why Anne would be retiring him.

"Some potential buyers are coming to see him at the Conyer's show," Anne whispered, feeling that PJ would understand her words.

"You're selling him?" Keegan realized how serious the situation was for Anne and the future of the farm.

"Yes." Anne adjusted the chin strap of her helmet. "I feel like I'm betraying him. He has helped me build this place. Now, I have to let him go." She mounted the stallion and turned him to the indoor arena. For now, she had to focus on the present.

There would be time for heartache later.

Keegan walked beside Anne and PJ to the indoor arena. The rectangular ring was set up for Dressage and Hunter Jumper. "This is real nice. I can see why Mac was proud of you and this place. He always talked about how hard you worked down here."

"I wish he was here now. There are so many things I'd love to just share with him." Anne often found herself having imaginary conversations with her dad. At times when she was working in the barns or riding PJ, she'd pretend he was there watching.

Keegan remained silent. He understood the loneliness of missed relationships. There were times he wished his parents were still alive. It took years to come to terms with his anger over their loss. His narrow escape of serving time in prison and the Navy taught him that using one's fist was not a solution to life's regrets.

He took a seat and watched the two work together in unison. The magnitude of Anne's decision to sell PJ settled upon him. He knew that without PJ, the viability of the farm would not last. He focused on the woman and horse. They moved about the arena working together as one unit. The classical music created a backdrop for the beautiful dance unfolding before him, a relationship shared between two partners built on trust and love.

The loud scream brought Keegan's thoughts to the present. The sight of Anne's body flying in the air and impacting with the ground made him bolt. The horse's massive hooves pawned the ground around her limp body. Not wanting to further spook the horse, he approached with gentle movement. In low, soothing tones he called the horse's name. He was able to reach the loose reins and take control of PJ. He continued to talk in soothing tones to the animal. Confident PJ was safe, Keegan rushed to Anne. He let out a sigh of relief at the sight of her sitting up. "Anne, you okay?"

"Just got the wind knocked out of me."

"What happen?"

"I don't know. Everything was fine, and then he saw something in the dirt and shied away from it."

Keegan began looking around to see what could have spooked PJ. Within seconds he spotted a long black item in the dirt. With the toe of his boot he pushed the item, a rubber snake.

Anne's skin began to crawl at the sight of the snake. She hated any form of them, fake or real. "Someone put this here for this reason."

"Knowing you ride by yourself and that horses are afraid of snakes." The scenarios of what could have happened to Anne terrified him. "This is getting serious Anne. I don't think you should be riding or staying on this farm by yourself."

"What am I suppose to do, hire a babysitter to come and watch me ride? I can't afford that."

"You tell me when you are riding, and I will be here. It may have been a while since I've been on the back of a horse, but I don't want you riding alone, period. As for you staying by yourself, that's over too. I'll sleep in the barn. But I do not want you alone here."

"Yes sir, you planning to start tonight?" Anne did not like being bossed or having other's make decisions for her. She eased herself from the dirt. Her hip ached from the impact of the fall. She tried to not show how much pain she felt. All she needed was commander Keegan whisking her to an emergency room.

"As a matter of fact yes. I'll call Maggie and tell her where the plane is."

"Then you can take care of PJ while I go up to the house and start supper. There is a spare room you can use. You don't have to stay in the barn." Anne looked Keegan in his eyes. "Oh and one more thing, not a word of this to Aunt Ethel or anybody else."

Keegan knew by the slow movements Anne made she was hurt worse than she admitted. He wasn't going to push his luck about her getting checked. He'd won the important battle and that was making sure she was safe. He owed it to Mac.

****

Keegan walked up the concrete steps onto the front porch. Flower beds on both sides of the steps were dressed in fall colors with mums and pansies. The aroma of bacon and eggs wafting from the inside made his mouth water. He opened the screen door and let it slam behind him. "Honey I'm home."

"Funny. You can wash up in the bathroom in my room. The guest room is that door over there." Anne pointed to the room close to the kitchen.

"Yes ma'am. I'll go wash up for supper." Keegan returned in time to see a plate of homemade biscuits being put on the table. "This smells awesome."

"Thanks. I often cook breakfast for supper. It's quick and easy." Anne sat down and poured coffee into the mugs. "You want to give thanks."

Keegan bowed his head and made the sign of the cross before giving thanks. "What time do you get up to work the horses?"

"Usually start around five a.m. on the days I go to the airport."

146

"Damn, these are good." The hot buttered biscuit melted in his mouth.

"What did you expect from Ethel's niece? Do you think I grew up in her house and didn't learn to cook?"

"Didn't mean any offense. It's not often I get homemade biscuits."

"You get down home much?"

"Mainly holidays." Keegan enjoyed the last bite of biscuit. "This was awesome."

Anne surveyed the carnage of the meal. She began to collect empty dishes and take them to the sink.

Keegan notice the slow, stiff movements and knew Anne was hurting. "Let me clean the kitchen. You probably could use a hot shower and a good night's sleep."

"You've got a deal. See you at five." Anne's body did not disagree with the idea of a shower and sleep.

****

The house had become silent except for Keegan's movements in the kitchen. He poured a cup of coffee and walked to the front porch. The ground glistened with a light coating of frost. His breath formed in front of him. Keegan sat in the swing and listened to a lone whippoorwill.

Anne's fall had scared him more than he was willing to admit. He tried to push the what-if scenarios from his mind. The important thing was she was not seriously hurt. The woman had been a pain in the rear, but she'd managed to surprise him each day.

Keegan open the screen door and was cautious to not let it slam. He shut the wooden door and turned the deadbolt lock. A soft whimper came from Anne's room. Concerned, he cracked open her door to see her sit upright in the bed screaming.

Keegan rushed to her and pulled her into his arms. "Sssh, it's okay. You're having a bad dream." Anne buried her head into Keegan's chest finding safety in his embrace. "Do you want to talk about it?"

"It's the same one I've been having for the past few weeks. It me and Momma riding in the truck together. It's raining and dark. I'm scared because of the lightning and thunder. Then out of nowhere there are head lights coming at us. Momma screams and jerks the wheel. All I remember is the sound of the truck flipping."

"Do you want me to stay with you until you fall asleep?"

Anne nodded her head. She slid back under the covers and turned to her side. The bed shifted with the weight of Keegan spooning next to her. "I'm here now to keep you safe."

Keegan listened to Anne's soft, steady breathing. The fragrance of jasmine filled his nostrils. The weight of a wayward breast rested on his hand. Instinctively, he pulled her small form closer to him. He wished he could hide his building desire. His well-meaning intentions were taking a different course.

Anne turned and looked at him through half closed eyes. Her slender arms encompassed his neck. Keegan took her mouth into his. Anne's body pressed close against his. The heat of desire radiated through the thin material of her gown. Keegan slid his hand down the curve of her waist and over the rise of her round hips. His fingers locate the hem of her gown.

Anne met the urgency of the kiss with her own growing desire. Neither gave thought to the consequences of their actions. Only their hearts and emotions guided them.

Anne wanted to connect with Keegan. All of her hungered to touch, feel, and taste him. She was a stranger to the building emotions that threatened to rip through her. Each kiss, caresses, and breath was charged. More than her body hungered for the man.

Together, they moved in rhythm in sync with each other's needs. An act of comfort turned into a moment of rescue. Anne became aware of her nakedness and vulnerability. Hot tears stung the back of her eyes. She reached for the covers hiding her exposed body.

"Are you okay?" Keegan feared that he'd caused her more pain.

Anne shook her head unable to speak. She held her breath trying to not give away her tears.

Keegan moved her hair from her face surprised by the dampness on her cheeks. "Are you sure?" The tremble of her shoulders was all the answer he needed. Regret began to make its home with him. "Anne, I am sorry. I did not mean for this to happen. I promise you, it will not again." Keegan left Anne alone in the darkness.

Fifteen

*A*nne awoke to a stream of daylight coming through the bedroom window. She'd overslept. There were horses to be fed, stalls to clean, and Keegan. She was not sure where to go from last night. She wanted more of what she'd shared with him. His reaction had made her believe he wished it had never happened. She pulled on her robe.

Anne glanced into the guest bedroom to find the bed made and no sign of Keegan. She returned to her bedroom. Ignoring her body's stiffness, she rushed pulling on a pair of jeans, grabbed a fresh shirt from the laundry basket, and pulled her hair through the back of her ball cap. She had to find Keegan and make things right with him. It was important that he understand she didn't regret what they shared, and last night was more to her than physical.

The sight of the vacant spot where the one-fifty had been parked made her heart sink. Deflated from the possibility of talking to him, Anne entered the barn. All of the horses were out of their stalls. Fear ran through her at the thought something had happen to them. Breaking into a run, she passed the cork board. Standing at the gate, Anne shrilled her loudest whistle. The sound of thundering hooves answered her call. Relieved she recognized the herd coming over the rise from the stream. She waited at the fence for each horse's arrival. All were accounted for.

Anne returned to the barn to check the stalls. A note attached to the cork board caught her attention.

"Anne, fed and watered the horses. Let them out into the pasture. Their stalls are clean and with fresh bedding. I didn't want to disturb you this morning. Keegan."

Anne folded the note and slid it into the back pocket of her jeans. Sitting down on a bale of hay, she leaned against the wooden wall and closed her eyes. For the first time, there was someone who thought of her and her needs. The cynical side of her clouded her thought. "Harris, he feels guilty and regrets last night. If he cared about you, he would not have slinked off this morning to avoid you. Don't read too much into it."

****

"Morning Anne." Maggie exited the camper.

"Morning." Anne searched the hangar looking for Keegan.

"You okay? Keegan sounded upset when he called last night." Maggie noticed the frantic look on Anne's face. "He didn't go into details. Only said it was best if you weren't alone."

"I fell from PJ last night. It was stupid. I wasn't paying attention." Anne tried to downplay the whole incident. She didn't need everyone getting all up in arms about what happened. "Where's Keegan?"

"Oh, he flew over to Griffin to pick-up some parts." Maggie felt there was more to the previous night's events. Keegan's mood this morning was not his normal chipper one. He'd been surly.

"There's something I want to ask you." Anne put both hands in the back pockets of her jeans.

"Sure."

"Would it be possible for you to give me some lessons? I would like to get my private pilot's license."

"I would be honored to give you lessons." A large grin splayed across Maggie's face. The level of humility in the way

151

Anne asked indicated how important learning to fly was to her. "Want to start now?"

"You got time?"

"I can make time. Come on. Let's go have some fun."

****

The plane's engine shutting down broke Keegan's concentration. He recognized Anne's voice. There was laughter and excitement in it. His mood darkened with each lilt of her voice. He had no one but himself to blame. He knew her kind, yet he allowed himself to get sucked into her. The joke was on him. The idea of walking away from Anne Harris terrified him more than being used by her. The damn woman had wormed her way into his thoughts, soul, and heart.

Anne's hand, simulating flight, stopped in mid motion. The laughter in her voice and face evaporated. Keegan's expression was one she was too familiar with. The disapproving, judgmental stare had returned. She was positive he actually growled at one point.

"Not sure what happened last night, but I think he's in a worse mood than he was earlier. You gonna say anything to him?" Maggie hated that a happy occasion had been dampened.

"Better now than to let it fester." Anne wasn't sure what she'd done to make Keegan angry. "I'll see you in the office."

"Good luck." Maggie was confident that Anne could hold her own.

****

"You didn't have to take care of the horses this morning." Anne stood on the opposite side of the work table.

"Thought you'd appreciate a day off." Keegan muttered. He continued to work with the part on the table.

152

"You planning on staying at the farm tonight?" Anne shifted her weight onto the balls of her feet. "Because I now have two vehicles here."

"If you feel safe having me around." Keegan opened a drawer to the toolbox and searched for a screwdriver.

"Like you said last night, there won't be a repeat of what happen." Anne wanted to scream at him for his behavior. She didn't like the stilted polite conversation they were having. It was obvious she'd done something to upset him.

"Then I guess I am." Keegan took the part and turned his back to Anne. He wanted to pull her across the table and kiss her. His body betrayed him. Like an addict, he wanted her despite the after effects. Her laughter beckoned to him like a siren's song.

"Fine." Anne's cell phone began to ring. "Hello."

"You sound like you're in a mood this morning. Who put a burr under your saddle?"

"Just a lot on my mind, what's up?" Anne recognized Nick's voice.

"You've been scarce. I've missed your company. How about dinner tonight?"

Anne turned and looked at Keegan. "Tonight will be fine. Why don't you pick me up at the airport around seven?"

"Sounds good." Nick was pleased that he did not have to drive to the farm.

****

"You need any help?" Anne folded the phone and entered Maggie's office

"Not unless you have any extra cash lying around." Maggie pushed her glasses to the top of her head and rubbed her eyes. The insensitivity of her comment resounded with Maggie. "I'm sorry, Anne. I shouldn't have said that."

"The truth is what it is."

"You still planning on selling PJ?"

"Yeah, some potential buyers are going to be at the show next weekend."

"Anne, I wish there was something or another solution."

"Speaking of solutions, what's up with Lynda?"

"Paul still hasn't had a chance to talk to Dennis. Apparently, he's moved to Panama City and is flying for some company down there. Lynda should be here soon. You can just about set your watch to her. Couldn't ask for a more model employee."

"I'd be too if I'd just got caught with my hand in the cookie jar." Anne's phone began to ring. She looked at it to see it was her horse broker calling. "Better get this. Catcha later."

"See ya." Maggie opened the checkbook and stared at the invoices on the desk.

Lynda stuck her head in the doorway. "Excuse me. You said you needed me to get supplies today?"

Maggie smiled briefly. "Yes, I put a list on your desk this morning. If you don't mind, I put on there some hazelnut flavored coffee creamer."

"No problem. You want me to pick up a couple extra so you have some for the camper?"

"That would be nice." Sitting in the quiet of the office, Maggie drummed her fingers on the desk, looking at the stack of invoices and the green numbers on the calculator. "Where am I going to find that kind of money?" Maggie asked the calculator as if it had an answer.

"Talking to machines now?" Madison inquired as he leaned against the door frame.

Maggie let out a heavy sigh. "Guess I really didn't expect an answer. What brings you by?"

"I wanted to talk to Keegan about doing an oil change on my plane and to check on you."

"That's mighty nice of you."

"Things still going good with Anne?"

"She's really taken an interest in this place. I think it's growing on her. She asked me to teach her to fly this morning." Maggie let out a laugh as Madison's mouth dropped open. "You might want to take a breath there. You are beginning to look like a guppy out of water."

"Miracles can happen, I guess. What brought that on?"

"Keegan flew her down to her farm last night. I guess she liked it and has decided she wants her private pilot's license."

"Is he her newest toy?"

"I don't think so." Maggie felt protective of Anne. "She's really changed since Aunt Ethel talked to her. You'd be amazed at the person she is now."

"Sometimes, seeing is believing." Madison paused. "Lynda still working around here?"

"Yes."

"I'm not sure if I agree with your decision there."

"You are not the only one. Seth has been very vocal with me."

"Just be careful, Maggie."

"I will."

"Don't forget we have the Airport Authority meeting tomorrow night."

"I haven't."

"Oh, and I need to give you this." Madison reached inside his jacket and pulled out an envelope.

"What is this an eviction notice?"

"No, it's the title to the Bonanza. You are officially the new owner of 4JR." Maggie gave Madison a hug. He immediately noticed how thin she felt. "Start taking better care of yourself. Promise."

"I promise." Maggie took the square keychain with the keys to the Bonanza. "Think I'm gonna start now."

****

Maggie eased the single engine plane onto the runway. She held the brakes and applied full throttle, enjoying the feel of the two-hundred and eighty-five horse power engine straining to be set free. At the perfect moment when she felt that both she and machine could no longer stand the anticipation of breaking free from gravity, she released the brakes and allowed the plane to speed down the runway and climb over the city she loved, Athens.

Level at three thousand feet, she turned the volume down on the Unicom channel and its cluttered chatter of other pilots. Maggie eased the plane into a gentle bank and continued south of the airport. There was no specific destination or agenda, only the freedom to enjoy the feel of the plane. She dialed the local AM station into the Non-Directional Beacon navaid. The needle pointed in the direction of the station's tower. Tunes from the eighties played in her headset.

With a light grip on her partner's controls, she began to dance across the clear floor decorated with a brilliant blue blank sky. First, she rolled the plane into a ninety degree bank and allowed her partner to twirl her around the horizon. With perfect timing and coordinated steps on the rudder, she rolled level on the heading they started their dance.

They waltzed with chandelles and tangoed with figure

156

eights. Maggie felt giddy and in love with her partner. Together, they floated, turned, and soared to the different beats of the music in her headset.

Exhilarated and energized from the freedom to indulge in her whims, Maggie leveled the wings and trimmed the plane. She relaxed her hold on the control wheel and allowed the plane freedom to fly its course. Gone was the dull pain of grief, the frustration of arguing with Seth about her lack of care, worries about Anne selling the one thing that brought her peace, fear of losing Mac's to an unseen threat, and the web of lies created by those that surrounded her.

Maggie recognized the landmark below her. She'd wandered over Anne's farm. Horses grazed in the open pasture. A red truck drove from the barn. The driveway in front of the house was vacant. The place was no longer Mac's childhood home, but the home to a new friend. Maggie's life had been blessed with good friends. Most of those relationships had begun at the airport.

Then there was Seth. He could make her so mad at times she wanted to spit. Then in the next moment, she'd find herself wishing for his kiss. She greeted each day filled with anticipation of seeing him walk through the hangar door. Together, side-by-side they worked as a team. Meals were shared with casual conversations of days gone-by and thoughts of the future. Still, she kept him at a distance. Part of her was not ready to say goodbye to Mac.

****

Heels tapping across the concrete floor distracted Keegan. He had to do a double take to recognize the woman dressed in a print skirt, simple white blouse, and low heels. "You are awfully dressed up. Must have a hot date tonight."

"What concern of yours would it be?" The urge to grab Keegan and shake him until that chip on his shoulder flew off made Anne take a step toward him. She hated this state of confusion he created within her. Never in her life had she been unsure about herself. After one night at her farm, he had managed to be everywhere she turned during the day. His laughter echoed through the barn. The ease that he spoke to the horses whispered through her heart. She'd imagined him sitting across from her at the kitchen table during lunch. The haunting of all was his scent that lingered on her sheets and the feel of his lovemaking branded in her soul. He was the reason she'd spent extra time on her hair, make-up, and choice of clothes. She wanted him to see her feminine side. Instead, all he saw was a woman that used men.

"None." Jealousy fueled Keegan's sharp tongue. He'd spent the day trying to concentrate on work, but he could not forget how Anne had felt in his arms. He wanted to push aside the belief that to her he was only a passing fling. Anger followed jealousy, directed more on him for wanting her. He knew she was a heartache waiting to happen.

"Is that Maggie in the Bonanza?" Anne recognized the plane taxing to the back of the hangar.

"Yeah, she said she needed to clear her head." Keegan started to apologize for his brash behavior, but the apology died at the sight of Nick strutting into the hangar.

"Wow, aren't you all dressed up. Hope you didn't have to wait long." Nick placed his arm around Anne's waist.

"Guess he's not use to seeing you with your clothes on." Keegan muttered under his breath.

"I just got here, and thank you." Anne chose to ignore Keegan's comment but the sting of his words throbbed.

"Thanks for keeping her company for me." Nick pulled Anne closer to him, fueling the Irishman's jealousy.

Keegan tipped an imaginary hat. "Just call me Chance."

Anne shot a look of anger at Keegan.

****

"Hey, was that Nick and Anne leaving?" Maggie was surprised to see Anne with Nick.

"That it was." Keegan crawled under the airplane and loosen the oil plug.

"That's odd"

"What'd you mean?"

"Nothing. Have you by any chance seen my cell phone?"

"No, is it missing?"

"I can't find it anywhere. Are you working late?"

"Yeah. Madison wants his plane in the morning to go to St. Mary's." Keegan reached for a roll of paper towels to wipe the black oil from his hands. "Seth should be back soon."

"I heard him on the radio. I'm gonna go look for my phone."

"Good luck finding it." Keegan opened the box with the new oil filter and began to rub grease around the rubber seal. "Oh, Kyle called and wants you to take him down to Macon in the morning. Said the Bonanza would be fine."

"Thanks." Maggie entered the office searching for her phone. She'd been unable to find it for the past two days. The last place she remembered using it was the morning she called the Nashville office. In desperation, she knelt on her knees and searched under the desk. Luck had smiled on her. She reached and retrieved the small device, thankful she'd finally found it.

Sitting on the floor, she flipped the phone open and saw it still had a charge. There were numerous voicemails waiting for her. Maggie began to listen to each one. Many were from Seth, a few from Paul keeping her updated, and the one she'd been waiting for from Janice.

****

Aromas of Cajun cuisine wafted through the air whetting any appetite. New Orleans Jazz could be heard above the hum of conversations. The place was packed for a Tuesday. Harry Bissets was a local favorite.

"I'm glad you made reservations." Anne liked that they were seated in a corner under the atrium. It allowed a view of the stair case. Wait staff maneuvered the stairs to and from the kitchen. "It amazes me how well they are able to balance trays of food and not miss a step."

"It has happened on occasion." Nick unfolded his napkin. "That's how Mac and I met Maggie."

"How come?" Anne took a sip from her water glass.

"She literally came crashing into our lives because of that bottom step."

Anne looked at the stairs. "I never knew how they met."

"She came down the stairs with a tray of food and missed that step right there. I was sitting in this spot. Mac witnessed it all."

"What happen afterwards?"

"The manager came out yelling at her and fired her. But not before your dad had his say." Nick paused waiting for the waitress to place their drinks. He downed his in one swallow. "That was the first time I'd ever seen Mac come close to losing his temper. We helped her up. Mac was insistent on taking her home once he learned she'd walked from Five Points. As they say, the rest is history."

Anne thought about the scene Nick had described to her.

"Stories like that make me realize how little I knew about him. It's my fault for not having a relationship with him."

"How so?"

"I ate supper with Aunt Ethel a few weeks ago. She told me the truth about my mom, about how she and dad met and why he married her." Anne picked up the glass of wine and held it in her hand. "She said Mom had been unfaithful to Dad many times right to the night she died. She said Mom was pregnant."

Nick choked on his second drink. He began coughing. His sinuses felt like an inferno. "Sorry, that went down the wrong pipe. Mac never mentioned she was pregnant when she died."

"I guess since it wasn't his he didn't want people to know out of respect to her."

"Mac knew it wasn't his." Nick continued to struggle with catching his breath.

"Aunt Ethel said that he and Mom had stopped being intimate with each other. It was about the time he started sleeping at the airport." Anne took a sip of wine. "Anyway, Aunt Ethel said she knew that mom was seeing someone right before her death."

"Did she have any idea who it was?" Nick signaled the waitress for another bourbon.

"No. You were around a lot then helping dad with the business. Did he ever mention anything to you about Mom?"

"Mac would never have talked about that with me." Nick wanted to move Anne from the subject. "You and Maggie seem to be getting along. Lou said you decided not to contest the will."

"I did. This may be my last opportunity to really get to know him." Anne finished her wine. "I guess that means I'm not interested in any investors. So, should I be worried?"

"No, that person is no longer interested in Mac's Flying Service." Nick focused on the menu. "I hear that the hangar is the topic of the next Airport Authority meeting."

"It is. Gerald Mixon came by to let Maggie know." Anne was relieved that she didn't need to tell Maggie about the investor. "Madison has been reviewing the lease and will be there. He and Maggie are going to represent the business. I'll be along for moral support."

"I guess that is good."

Anne pushed the remaining bites of salad around on her plate. "Do you know why Dad pushed Maggie away from him?"

"Because he wanted her to do more with her life than he did with his."

"You remember Foots."

"If I remember correctly, he went missing and was never found."

"He was found dead with a threatening note. Dad got scared for Maggie's safety. That is why he made her leave."

Again, Nick found himself having difficulty eating without choking. "Damn, I never knew that. Does Maggie know?"

"Not until I told her." Anne leaned back for the waitress to take her salad plate. "Maggie thinks Dennis may have done it, especially after the way he quit. She thinks he was jealous of her and the way dad let her fly trips with him."

"Dennis did resent Maggie during that time. He complained several times that if it wasn't for her, he'd get more twin time." Nick polished off his third drink and did not have to ask for the fourth. It appeared in front of him like clockwork. "You tell Maggie about this the night she stayed at the farm?"

"No, the night she came back from the trip to St. Simons." Nick's knowledge of Maggie's visit surprised Anne.

"That must have been late. I figured you left while I was putting the plane in the hangar."

"I was going over some reports Paul had dropped off for Maggie."

"What kind of reports?"

"Dad met with Paul the night he died. He gave Paul some financial information about the business. They discussed the fact that someone was stealing from the business." Anne cut into the eggplant pirogue. "He also said the autopsy did not show any foul play."

"I didn't realize there was any question about Mac's death." Nick took a bite of his jambalaya before continuing. "What made Mac think someone was or is stealing from the business?"

"I'm not sure what got him suspicious, but on the reports Maggie found in his flight case, he had transactions circled involving DE Aviation."

"Does anyone know who is doing this?"

"She talked to Lynda who said it was Dennis."

"How do you feel about everything?"

"Uneasy, like there's a lot of unanswered questions. I agree with Paul and Maggie. Dad's death was too convenient. Then there are the incidents that have happen at the farm. The last one caused PJ to throw me."

"Are you okay?"

"Just a little bruised and sore. Thank goodness Keegan was there to pull him away before I got hurt worse than a few bruises."

The thought of Anne being harmed was unsettling to Nick.

He also did not miss the mention of Keegan's presence. "That explains Keegan's demeanor tonight when I picked you up."

"I'm not sure I get your point."

"He wasn't pleased that I showed up. What did he mean by just call him Chance?"

"Chance is my teaser horse I use to help bring a mare in season for breeding."

"I get it now. So, am I still your stallion?"

Anne studied the food on her plate before answering. "Things have changed for me. I want more than a fling."

Nick laid his fork down on his plate and propped his elbows on the table. "Anne Harris, are you saying you've gone and fallen in love with Keegan?" Anne continued to study the food on her plate. A slow blush formed at the base of her neck spreading to her face. "Well, I'll be damned if it isn't true. You don't have to say a word. Your face just told on you. I bet the fool doesn't even know how you feel."

"No, and that's the way I want to keep it."

Nick shook his head enjoying the last bite of his meal. "This place is always good." He picked up his fourth drink, holding it up to Anne. "Here's to good food, good company, and enough talk about Mac's Flying Service." Anne remained silent at the compliment, knowing it was the alcohol talking and Nick's way of changing topics.

Anne looked at her watch. "I really need to get home. I have to get an early start in the morning. Maggie and I are flying at eight."

"Don't tell me she's suckered you into learning to fly."

"No, she didn't sucker me into learning to fly. I decided on my own that it is something I want to do."

"Poor Anne, all work and no play. Who would have

thought you'd want to become an airport rat and fall in love with a grease monkey. "

"Nick, there's no need to become nasty."

"Sorry, guess I had too much to drink."

"Then I'd better drive. Do you want me to drop you off at your place?"

"Not unless you plan on being dessert." Nick swayed. "Oh, that's right, you're a one man woman now."

Anne ignored Nick's comment and continued through the crowded restaurant. Pride swelled within her at the concept of belonging to someone. She cursed that that person was a stubborn, opinionated, and sexy Irishman.

****

"I don't think you are capable of driving." Anne watched Nick steady himself next to the car. "Let me drive you home. I can get a taxi back here to get my truck."

"I'm okay." Nick rarely had more than two drinks with a meal. The topic of conversation made him want a steady flow. "Why don't you hand me the keys."

"At least let me follow you." Anne stood in front of Nick with her back to the hangar.

"Only if you promise to stay." Nick could not have timed Keegan's appearance on the porch. He pulled Anne into an embrace and planted a kiss on her. His hands glided down her body. The embrace tightened with the depth of the kiss.

Anne pushed away from him. "What the hell was that?"

"Take it that was a no." Nick was sober with satisfaction. The look of fury on Keegan's face was priceless.

"Good night Nick." Anne walked away relieved that Keegan's truck was still in the parking lot.

165

****

The scene in the parking lot scorched itself into Keegan's memory. The guilt for his previous actions evaporated. Jealousy seized his emotions and blinded him. The only vision he had was Anne ensconced in Nick's embrace. A greased credit card could not have passed between them. Someone really needed to explain to them the value of getting a room.

"I'm glad you're still here," Anne said, ignorant to the snare in which she was close to being entangled. "I forgot to leave you the keys to the farm truck."

"Sure, no problem. Where're the keys?" Keegan's back stiffened momentarily. He tossed the wrench in his hand onto the work table. The force of the landing made the wrench bounce off the table's surface and land on the concrete floor with a clang.

"Here." Anne stepped aside in time to keep the wrench from hitting her foot.

"I don't know what time I'll finish here." Keegan snatched the keys from her.

Anne could feel the well of anger and hurt brimming within her. She wanted to return his fire with hers. He'd been growling and grunting all day. The comment about Nick not use to seeing her with clothes on throbbed within her. She had made every effort to show him that she was not the woman he saw at her father's wake.

Her best defense at that moment was retreat. She knew if she spoke, the damage of her words would in essence be like gasoline on a raging fire. The drive home seemed shorter than usual. Anne slammed the door making the truck's body rock. She tossed her purse onto the couch and made a straight line to her liquor cabinet. Not bothering with a glass, Anne took a long drink from the bottle of scotch. Her feet ached from the shoes on her feet. In one swift movement, she kicked off the shoes. Each shoe making a thud as it landed on the other side of the room. She'd worn them along with the new outfit in hopes of seeing Keegan.

She tossed her head back and laughed. The joke was on her. Aggravated and exasperated with men overall, Anne decided to try to get good night's sleep. She stripped naked and slid into the bed. Naked. That was how she felt around Keegan. He could strip all her defenses and make her vulnerable to emotions she'd spent a lifetime avoiding.

She closed her eyes and allowed the heat created by the scotch to work its magic. Peaceful dreams began to turn dark with the sound of pouring rain and the steady rhythm of windshield wipers. She tried with all her might, but she could not get a clear image of the road. The smell her mother's perfume filled her senses. The darkness of the night became illuminated with blinding bright lights. The sound of her mother's scream filled her head.

Anne had been sound asleep when Keegan entered her room on his way to the bathroom. He tried to ignore her sleeping form under the sheet. The moonlight shinning through the window caressed exposed skin. Her hair spilled over the pillow, creating an illusion of a golden halo.

The shower washed away the day's grime of grease. His body was clean, but his emotions were gritty from the day's events. The first whimper came when he slid on his pajama bottoms. He'd started to towel dry his hair when he heard Anne's restlessness. Whimpers turned into cries. He approached her bed with intentions of waking her. Before he had a chance, Anne bolted upright and screamed.

"Nick!" Anne did not realize the name that she'd called. The sight of Keegan beside her bed brought security and comfort.

Keegan wanted to turn and leave, but the look of fear and sadness on her face made him stay.

"Please stay with me." The words came more as a plea. Anne did not want to be alone. She wanted the safety and security Keegan's embrace could give.

"No ma'am. I've told you before. I don't get involve with women who make sex a sporting event. I'm not a substitute for Nick Masden." Keegan stepped to the door. "Maybe, you should have let him finish what the two of you started in the parking lot."

Anne stared at the vacant spot Keegan had occupied. Confusion, anger, and hurt churned within her. She pulled the covers up to her chin and stared at the doorway. The fear of another nightmare made her fight sleep. She imagined Keegan asleep in the guest room. Part of her beckoned to go to him, but pride and fear of rejection made her stay.

Sixteen

Anne stared out the passenger window of the truck. It was a crisp, clear morning. Perfect for flying. She ignored the gloomy weather report. The cheery voice on the radio talked about how the brewing hurricane in the Gulf had made landfall. It was now a tropical storm and had its sights on Georgia. Anne thought about the hurricane's name, Karen. It should have been Keegan.

Keegan's scowl deepened. His grip on the steering wheel tightened until his knuckles glowed white. He tried to sleep after leaving Anne. Each passing hour greeted him, taunting him that he was fighting a losing battle. He'd thought about leaving Mac's and looking for a new job. He really didn't have any ties or commitments, but his guilt of abandoning Maggie prevailed.

But it was more than Maggie that kept him at Mac's. It didn't matter how many different ways he tried to rationalize it; truth remained. He stayed for the woman sitting next to him. There were times he wanted to wring her neck. Then there were those that he thought of kissing it, holding her, becoming lost in her. Damn it to hell, he was falling for this woman. No, he *had* fallen for her.

"What did you mean about Nick last night?" Anne decided she was not going to cower to Keegan.

"You two need to learn the importance of getting a room."

Keegan remained focused on the traffic. He didn't want to concentrate on the image that had kept him awake last night. The one with Nick's hands on Anne and his mouth covering hers.

"Nick was drunk." Anne began to understand the source of Keegan's hostility. "There's nothing between Nick and me."

"That's one way of putting it. From my viewpoint nothing could have gotten between the two of you last night." Keegan turned the truck into the parking lot.

"Is that all you think about?" Anne could feel her anger beginning to boil. "If I didn't know any better, I'd say you are jealous. But that couldn't be true because women like me repulse you. It must be a hell of a sacrifice to have to sleep under the same roof with me. You really don't have too. No one is making you. Matter of fact, I'd prefer you not stay at the farm."

The truck lurched forward at the abrupt application of brakes. Keegan snatched the keys from the ignition and exited the vehicle. The body of the truck rocked with the brute force of both doors being slammed shut.

****

"Maggie, have you seen the weather forecast for this evening? It is going to get rough around here. I wish you'd stay somewhere other than this hangar." Seth wanted to take her by her shoulders and shake some reasoning into her.

"Seth, I'll be fine. This place is more secure than any house." Maggie was past being tired of being told how to take care of herself. Seth's constant worry and concern about how many hours she worked, the amount of coffee she drank, and her living in the camper was beyond the point of friendly concern. She hated the resentment building inside her toward him.

"I don't like you being out here at night alone."

170

"And I appreciate your concern." Maggie welcomed the sight of Anne standing in the hangar. "Anne's here. I've got to go fly."

****

Seth's back was to the lobby door. The sound of it opening made him turn in time to see Lynda entering with her hands full. Seth had kept his distance from Lynda since Maggie's discovery of the missing money. He maintained a polite and cordial demeanor when it was necessary to speak to her. He didn't agree that she should still be an employee.

"Here, let me help you with some of those." Seth reached to take some of the shopping bags from Lynda.

"Thanks." The weight of the bags being removed was welcomed to the aching muscles in her arms. "You can put them on my desk. I stopped and picked up some supplies for the office and creamer for Maggie. I noticed she was low in the camper and her office yesterday."

"I can take the ones to the camper." Seth looked through the bags and recognized the familiar bottle of creamer.

"I can do it. I think your student was pulling into the parking lot." Lynda continued to take items out of the bags and place them on her desk.

"Then I need to check the one-seventy-two's fuel." Seth exited the office.

"Looks like it's gonna get rough around here tonight." Keegan closed the bottom drawer to the toolbox.

"It does. That's what I tried to get through to Maggie." Seth stopped at the tool table.

"She won't budge on staying in that camper."

"Nope. I'm worried about her." Seth used to never pay the camper any attention. Lately, he wished the thing did not exist. He refused to go inside it.

"The way she doesn't take care of herself. I've noticed, too."

"You have your hands full with Anne." Seth realized the different interpretations his statement carried. "I mean another strong-willed woman that refuses to listen to reason."

"I keep thinking about how serious she could have been hurt when that horse threw her." Keegan relaxed his shoulders once he understood Seth's comment. "She could have been there for God knows how long. Maggie tell you about the problems she's been having?"

"Some. She also said Anne went to dinner last night with Nick."

"He made quite a display of groping her in the parking lot when they returned." Keegan had assumed Anne was at Nick's when he left the hangar. He'd been surprised when he saw her truck in front of her house when he arrived. He'd lain in bed for hours listening for her in case her nightmares returned. The sounds of her tossing and turning told him she'd not found sleep easily. Several times he found himself wanting to go to her, but instead he remained in bed wishing for the first sign of daybreak.

"Not fun watching another man's hand on someone you have feelings for."

"You mean Mac and Maggie. How long have you been in love with her?"

"Since the first day I met her here. It was obvious that she loved Mac."

"You sound like he didn't feel the same way."

"No, he did. I just think he was a coward in making her leave. Now, she has this unreasonable sense of gratitude to him."

"And you're worried that she will never see you because of him."

"It's hard competing with a ghost and sanitized memories."

"Or living ones." Keegan dropped the screw he'd been working with. "Damn."

"Here let me get you another one." Seth started to pull the bottom drawer of the tool box to retrieve the container of screws.

"Don't worry about it. I need to get the Bonanza out of the hangar for Maggie."

"Sure. I was on my way to check the fuel in the one-seventy-two." Seth looked at the doorway. "Lynda said my student was here. It's taking them a long time to come in."

Seth walked over to the entrance door and looked to see if his student was in the parking lot. The only cars were his, Maggie's, and Anne's truck. He shrugged his shoulders before turning and walking to where the plane was tied-down on the flight line.

****

"Let's start back toward the airport and do some touch-n-go's." Maggie was pleased with how well Anne handled the plane.

"What was that about you and Seth this morning?"

"The same thing. 'You shouldn't be living in a camper; you don't take care of yourself.'"

"He's kinda got a point Maggie. You push yourself too hard." Anne adjusted the directional indicator to the compass' setting. "He's not gonna wait forever. You've got to let Dad go."

"Like you are with Nick?" Maggie was getting tired of everyone telling her how she should feel. "Looked like you two were real cozy last night. You must not have taken your foot off the peddle when you left the farm to meet him at the airport."

"What do you mean?"

"Yesterday, I saw you leaving the farm when I flew over. You beat me back to the airport."

"Maggie, I don't know what you are talking about. There wasn't any plane flying over the farm when I left."

"A red truck was driving from the barn. I assumed it was you."

"I don't own a red truck or know anyone that does. No one should have been around the barns yesterday."

"You didn't notice anything unusual did you?"

"No."

"Maybe it was nothing. What's up with you going out with Nick last night?"

"Bad decision making. He called right after Keegan pissed me off. I agreed to go to dinner and him picking me up at the airport."

"That's a lot of trouble to spite someone you don't care about."

"Whatever. It wasn't that bad. We went to Bissets. He told me the story of how you met Dad."

"Bless his heart, Nick almost wore his dinner that night. I sucked as a waitress."

"So it sounded."

"Easy, don't make me do something you'll regret—like lose an engine."

"Bring it on; I can handle it. Maggie, when did you know you loved Dad?"

"That night. He was like a warrior protecting me. He pretty much told my boss where to shove it. But it was how gentle he was with me. He didn't leave my apartment until he knew I was okay. I've never told anyone this, but he left some money on my kitchen table and his business card."

"Why'd he leave you money?"

"That was what brought me out to the airport the next day. I waltzed into that hangar set to tell him I wasn't a charity case. That he could keep his money. He said he knew I needed it and that my boss refused to pay me my tips. We argued some more, he offered me a job, and told me to consider it my first week's salary. Why?"

Anne hesitated trying to find the courage to open up to Maggie. "I've never allowed myself to become emotionally involved with anyone."

"Until Keegan." For Anne's sake, Maggie hoped that Paul would not find anything about Keegan. Janice had been brief saying that Keegan had been part of an investigation.

"The first night at the farm, the way he rushed to me and the relief in him that I wasn't hurt. He was scared for me. Later that night, another one of my nightmares about the accident came back. Again, he was there by my side taking care of me." Anne looked out the window and the ground passing under the main wheel. "For the first time in my life, I honestly understood what it meant to make love to someone. Not have sex for pleasure but to expose your soul to them." Maggie listened without interrupting. She knew Anne had reached a crossroad in understanding the vulnerable side of loving someone. "Then everything changed. His mood changed. He went from this caring person to an iceberg, apologizing and promising it would never happen again. Last night, Nick tried his damndest to get me to go home with him, but I felt dirty at the thought of it. I didn't want another man touching me the way Keegan did."

"Anne." Maggie spoke with a soft voice. "Have you tried to tell Keegan how you feel?"

"How credible would I be standing in front of him and saying, I love you? I have given him every reason to believe the worst in me."

"Then you have to give him reasons to believe otherwise."

****

"Keegan, Maggie around?" Paul walked into the hangar.

"No. She's up with Anne. You need a plane?" Keegan opened the box of parts.

"No. I just need to talk to her. Been trying to get her on her cell phone."

"She must of not found it. Said she lost it. You want me to tell her to call you?"

"I'll leave her a message on the board." Paul walked over to the dry erase board and wrote beside Maggie's name. He turned and studied Keegan before walking toward the exit door. "Catch you later."

****

Tropical Storm Karen shook the hangar doors announcing its arrival. A balmy breeze whipped through Maggie's hair. She struggled with the claw like prawns of the tow motor and the nose wheel of the plane. Thunder rumbled and the horizon ignited with Karen's fireworks.

The pregnancy of the pending storm intensified Maggie's urgency to secure the planes and prepare for its brutality. She tried not to count the seconds between the jagged streaks of lightening to the sonic boom of thunder, but her mind clicked the seconds. The trees' agitation against the strength of wind muffled Seth's presence. It was the startling tap on her shoulder that alerted her she was no longer alone.

"Will you please stop doing that!" Maggie was not surprised to see Seth. He was always there.

"Doing what?"

"Sneaking up on me and scaring the daylights out of me." A flash of lighting and crack of thunder caused Maggie to jump again. She hated storms. "What are you doing here anyway?"

"I was worried about you. Let me get this. You go and open the hangar doors." Seth took the tow motor and connected it to the plane's nose wheel.

The sky lit up again. The wind grew more impatient. Neither Maggie nor Seth escaped the down pour of rain.

Seth eased the plane into the hangar and helped close the doors.

"You are soaking wet." Maggie stepped back from the metal doors. She was glad to be away from them considering the lightening popping around them.

Seth wiped a strand of wet hair from the side of her face. "So are you. You have any towels."

"In the camper." Maggie opened the camper door.

Seth looked around the cramped interior and tried to control his frustration. It was obvious why Maggie chose to stay in the confined space. Everything was a lasting reminder of Mac. In the tiny bathroom, Mac's aftershave and personal items sat on the small sink. A blue oxford shirt that was his hung on the door's hook. The whole scene made him think of a tomb.

"Here. It's a good thing Aunt Ethel brought me my laundry today." She pulled a folded towel from the basket.

Seth took the towel from Maggie and began to wipe the rain from her face. The dark circles under her eyes again brought alarm to him. He felt her pulse racing as he lifted her hair from her throat and neck. "Maggie, you look tired. Why don't you come to my place tonight? Let me take care of you."

"I'm fine. I will take a good hot shower and get some rest as soon as this storm dies."

"You don't have to stay here. If not my place at least go to Aunt Ethel's. I would feel better if I knew you were somewhere other than here."

"Your concern is sweet, but I prefer to stay here."

Seth's anger exploded like a clap of thunder. "Maggie, have you looked at yourself lately? Besides looking like a raccoon with the dark circles under your eyes, your complexion is pale. When was the last time you ate a good meal? I'm not talking about frozen dinners or something requiring the use of a microwave. How many times have you skipped meals with nothing but a cup of coffee?"

"Who appointed you my keeper?" Maggie tried to control her anger. Seth had become her right arm in helping her with the business, but his constant worry about her made her feel suffocated.

"No one, Maggie." Seth felt that with each passing day he was losing her all over again.

"Then maybe you should mind your own business and let me take care of myself." Maggie did not expect to be whirled around. The sudden movement made her stomach lurch and her stability falter. Seth's firm grip steadied her.

Seth moved Maggie in front of the mirror on the bathroom door. "Look at yourself Maggie. Is this how you look when you take care of yourself? You are a living ghost who has buried themselves in the memory of a dead man. Do you think this is what Mac wanted for you?" He pointed to the bathroom. "How many times do you sneak in here to smell his cologne? I bet you sleep wearing his shirt." Seth yanked the shirt from the hook.

Maggie stripped the shirt from Seth's hands, "Get out! You have no right to judge me! Why do you care anyway?"

"Because I love you, Maggie Cosby. I have loved you ever since the first day you showed up here. But you were Mac's girl. I hated the way he pushed you at first, controlling your life. If Mac said jump, you asked how high. It didn't matter how much, you had to try. You'd jumped through any hoop he put in front of you."

"If it wasn't for Mac, I wouldn't be where I am today. Yes, he was demanding, but he always had my best interest at heart."

"Like when he made you leave the one place that was home to you?" Seth remembered the way she cried when she packed her office. They both had promised to keep in touch. He was leaving for Paris Island within the month. "And the people that you called family?"

"He had his reasons." Maggie had not shared the story about Foots with Seth.

"Mac always had his reasons, especially when they suited him." Seth could not understand Maggie's sense of loyalty to Mac. She refused to admit his faults. "Don't get me wrong. I will always consider him a great friend, but he could be selfish. He couldn't be man enough to marry you. Instead, he left you a ring, a note, and the knowledge that he was a coward."

"He also left me this business."

"And you are killing yourself trying to prove to him that he made a mistake in pushing you away." Seth took a step toward Maggie and kissed her. He allowed the kiss to blossom into the passion he had restricted himself from feeling. He savored the taste of her mouth, the play of her tongue, and the catch of her breath.

Seth released Maggie. "I love you, Maggie Cosby, but I

can't continue to watch you bury yourself in the memories of a man who didn't have the courage to fight for you. You have a choice. Accept the love of someone who has proven he will fight beside you and for you, or continue living in the memory of a ghost." As he stormed out into the hanger he looked back and whispered, "But understand that I will not wait forever."

Seth's words echoed in the quiet of the camper. Her heart ached at the pain in his voice. She knew he spoke the truth. Maggie exited the camper. Bare feet ran across the concrete floor and into the warm rain. The Jeep was still there. With all her might she screamed above the raging storm. "*SETH!*" Maggie ran toward the vehicle ignoring the pounding of her heart. Each step was an exhaustive effort. She had to reach him. It was Seth she wanted and not a ghost. He had to know. Her world turned black.

****

Seth pulled up to the Emergency Room doors and jumped out of the Jeep. With Maggie's unconscious body in his arms, he entered into the stark white waiting area. Like a drill sergeant he commanded. "I need some help!"

"Follow me." A nurse pushed the button beside the double wood doors. "Put her in this room."

Seth placed Maggie on the bed. The small room became overcrowded with nurses and equipment.

"Come with me. They will take care of her." Another nurse guided Seth from the room and back through the double doors.

Seth followed the young woman over to a small cubicle. He tried to remain patient at the multitude of questions. All he wanted was to be with Maggie. The image of her collapsing onto the wet pavement of the parking lot was burned into his soul. "When can I go back and be with her?"

"As soon as I can get all of her information entered into the computer."

Seth took a deep breath. "Look, I understand the importance of what you are doing. Can we please speed it up so I can be with her?"

The woman gave a tight smile, "We're almost finished. Do you know her date of birth?"

Seth answered without hesitation. "October 22, 1965."

"Are you the spouse?"

"No,"

"Does she have any next of kin?"

"Her parents are deceased. Killed in a trucking accident."

The young woman started to ask the next question but was not heard. Seth recognized the doctor in green scrubs who walked into the waiting area. "Doc, how is she?"

"We are getting her stable at this time. It's a good thing you got her here when you did. Come on back with me." Doc pressed his key card against the black pad on the wall. "Our first concern was getting her heartbeat and blood pressure under control. The nurses have put several warm blankets on her to help. She was on the verge of shock when you got her here. I've given her something to relax her."

Seth listened to Doc. The smell of disinfectants and the machines beeping reminded him of the last time he was in a hospital. He had been out on deployment when he received the call. His CO informed him his brother, John, was ill, and he was being rushed to the hospital. There was a flight waiting to take him home. Twenty-four hours later and still in his flight suit Seth walked into the waiting room of the Neurological ICU. He spotted his father holding his mother. His father did not have to speak a word. The look on his face told Seth he had not arrived in time. The chance to say goodbye had been stolen.

Seth was not prepared to see Maggie's frail body lying in the bed. The sight of IV's and machines hooked to her made him nauseated. Doc saw the color drain from Seth's face. "Take a deep breath. I know it can be a scary sight, but she's a fighter Seth. Tell me what happen."

"I was worried about her being at the hangar in this storm. When I got there, she was out trying to get the planes put up. I helped her, but we both got caught in the rain. I tried to convince her to come to my place or at least go to Aunt Ethel's, but she was adamant she'd stay in the camper. We had an argument over how she's been taking care of herself or the lack of it." Seth looked down at the floor staring at his shoes. "I was in my Jeep getting ready to leave. She came running out of the hangar toward me and collapsed before I could get to her."

"Maggie's had me concerned for a while. This is probably exhaustion." Doc patted Seth on the back. "Her labs should be back within the hour. You can sit here with her. Let me or one of the nurses know if she regains consciousness."

Seth pulled a chair next to the bed. He lifted Maggie's hand and enfolded it into his. He could not speak past the lump forming in his throat. He brought her hand to his lips kissing it. "Maggie, honey, wake up. Please open your eyes."

Maggie enveloped in the warm fuzzy cloud saw Mac standing at the doorway of her old apartment. "May I come in please?"

She stepped back, giving Mac room to enter into the kitchen. "Are you here to tell me I am fired? I realize that giving your boss ultimatums before walking out is not wise." Maggie held out her hand. "Here are the keys to the hangar"

"It's not necessary for you to do this, Maggie." Mac took the keys and placed them on the kitchen table. He wanted to pull her to him and never let her go. He expected the protest that began to form on her lips, lips that he loved kissing. "Since the night you literally crashed into my life at Harry Bissets, you have turned my world upside down. My head says I'm a fool and crazy. You make me want to take a chance on us. However, I do not want to rob you of your youth."

In the background Maggie could see a figure begin to emerge. Mac turned in the direction of the shadowy shape and handed him the keys. Mac looked at Maggie. "Here is someone that will give you a future of love, contentment, and children. He loves you."

Before Maggie could answer Mac disappeared. She could hear Seth's voice telling her he loved her and was sorry for causing her pain. Out of confusion and wanting to talk to Mac one more time, Maggie pleaded. "Mac, please don't go. I love you."

The words slashed through Seth's tattered emotions. He'd been telling her that he loved her. Words of apology became pleas for her to open her eyes. Still it was Mac who filled her dreams. It was Mac she loved. Seth removed his hand and stood. He looked at Maggie, drinking in her image. Like a drunk thirsting for a drop of whiskey, he leaned over and gently kissed her. It was time to accept reality. She would never love him.

He turned and walked out of the room with intentions of walking out her life.

****

Groggy from the medication and confused by her surroundings, Maggie surveyed the small room. She searched her memory for answers, but the only thing that returned were Seth's words and watching him leave her.

"So you're awake." The nurse entered and adjusted the setting on one of the machines. "You had all of us scared."

"Seth." Maggie asked in a hoarse whisper. "I need to talk to Seth."

"You talk'n about that fine young man who brought you in here?" Maggie nodded. The nurse located Maggie's pulse and studied the second hand on her watch. "He's gone."

Maggie scrunched her face and attempted to get out of bed. "Whoa now, Sugar. You gonna have to lay yourself back down. You ain't strong enough to go traipsing around in that hospital gown showing all of us your rear end."

"I've gotta find Seth." The urgency to find Seth made her ignore her body's objection to movement.

"All in due time. But, right now you need to rest." The nurse continued to check Maggie's vitals. "The doctor is admitting you for the night. You must be special because he doesn't usually take ER cases. You get some rest. I'll be back when they get you a room on the floor."

Maggie rolled to her side and pulled the covers over her shoulders. Seth had brought her here and left. It was her fault he was gone. Sleep pulled at her eyelids and sand formed in their corners. Her dreams went to a place where Seth no longer existed in her life.

SEVENTEEN

"Hey, Seth. Gotta a minute?" Doc was not surprised to see Seth staying close to Maggie.

"I was on my way home." Seth saw the papers in Doc's hands. "Those the lab results?"

"Yeah. Let's step in here." Doc pushed open the door to another room. "Paul, I thought it would be good to include Seth on this."

"Seth." Paul opened his can of dip and put a fresh pinch between his gum and cheek. Doc had caught him in the hallway and told him about Maggie being admitted. He had been called in on a homicide. Doc's request for him to hang around for Maggie's lab results dissipated the desire to return home and crawl back into bed.

"Her labs just came in. There are high levels of arsenic in her blood work." Doc gave time for the information sink into Seth and Paul. "It also explains why her heart and blood pressure was extremely high."

"How could she have arsenic?" Seth's mind swirled with the information. "Could this be what caused Mac's death?"

"Those are questions I plan to find answers for." Paul spit into the trash can.

"Didn't the toxicology reports on Mac not show arsenic?" Seth began to think of a list of people who would want to hurt Maggie. Nick was the first to come to mind, and the second was Dennis. Were the two of them working together to take over Mac's Flying Service? He was sure Nick was the one that helped Dennis find employment. Then there was Lynda. Seth had given up on persuading Maggie to fire the woman. Somehow, the three of them were thick as thieves. He was positive.

"Not if we did not know what to look for." Paul answered.

"Arsenic poisoning can be disguise as a heart attack if given at low dosages over a given time period, which would explain why it didn't show up in Mac's autopsy." Jim interjected as he entered into the small room. "Sorry, I was looking for Paul when the nurse said ya'll had stepped in here."

Seth looked at Paul and then to Jim. "Is there any way the existing toxicology report could indicate if Doc is right?"

"I doubt it." Jim replied while removing his pipe from coat pocket. "If cause of death is ruled natural, all samples are destroyed."

"Does this mean you'd have to exhume his body?" Seth cringed at the thought.

"Not necessarily." Jim sucked on the pipe stem wishing it was filled and fired. "With the technology we have today, all I need is a sample of Mac's hair to take to the crime lab."

Paul read the dial of his watch. "I'll call Ethel and see if she still has any of Mac's toiletries. If so, I'll get it to the GBI lab for testing."

"You don't need to do that." All three men stared at Seth not understanding. "Maggie still has Mac's toiletries in the camper."

Paul stopped in mid-stroke of entering the final digit of Ethel's phone number. "Then I need to get a search warrant written and rouse a judge out of bed to sign it." Paul half way out of the room turned looking at Seth. "You wanna come along?"

"Sure." Seth had exited Maggie's room intent on walking out of her life, but the information shared among the four men redirected his course. There was no way he could leave her with the knowledge that she was in danger. He rationalized that he'd stay until she was safe.

****

"You two search out here in the hangar." Paul directed his comments to the two officers. "Seth, you stay with me. We'll start in the camper." Paul entered the camper. He picked up the small hairbrush, placing it in a paper bag sealing the bag. "Seth, is there anything that Maggie consumes on a daily basis that could look like arsenic?"

"Yes, her coffee. She always drinks it with powdered creamer. She likes the one that is flavored with hazelnut."

Paul spotted a bottle of creamer and her coffee cup on the sink. He picked up the plastic bottle and opened the lid. Paul turned the bottle to the side looking at the contents. "Does she keep this stuff anywhere else?"

"She keeps another one in her office."

"What about the lobby?"

"No."

Paul bagged the bottle and cup before exiting the camper. The two uniformed officers met Paul and Seth. "What'd ya'll fine in there?"

One of the officer's spoke. "I got a bottle of Drambuie, creamer, and sugar." The officer held out several bags filled with the items.

"Hey, Captain, you might want to take a look at this." The other officer standing in front of the tool box held a clear bottle of white powder. "Found it pushed way back in the bottom drawer with some dirty shop towels over it."

Paul lifted the bottle up to the florescent light turning it while watching how the fine powder clung to the insides of the container. Not saying anything, he put the bottle with its contents into an evidence bag. "Keegan uses this toolbox?"

Seth knew Paul's find was not favorable for Keegan. It gnawed at him the way Keegan diverted him from getting the box of screws from the drawer earlier. "You don't think he's behind this?"

"Can't say right now." The discovery of the bottle and the information he'd gathered over the past week did not look good for Keegan. He'd noticed the message for Maggie to call him had been erased. They had spent the past few days playing phone tag. "I've got a friend at the State Crime Lab. She works the night shift. I'll drop you back at the hospital and get these things to her. You might want to call Anne and let her know about these developments."

"I'll give her a call on the way home." Seth had made the decision that he would enlist Anne's help.

****

Everyone exited oblivious to the person standing in the back hangar. Taking his phone from his pocket, he pressed speed dial. His wait was not long before the other party answered. "Masden, get your ass over to the hangar now." Not giving Nick time to respond he disconnected the line. In the darkness of the hangar, he lit up another cigar watching the glowing tip. He enjoyed the rich Cuban flavor of the tobacco.

****

The woman stirred next to Nick. "Who was that?"

"Your dad. He's at the hangar and wants me over there now."

"He's not supposed to be in town until tomorrow. Did he say why?"

188

"You know your old man ain't much on giving explanations, only orders." Nick pushed back the covers and grabbed his jeans from the floor. "Best not keep him waiting long. He didn't sound in a good mood."

"I'll be here when you get back." Linda rolled onto her back and allowed the sheet to fall.

****

Nick resented the fact that he had to dance to the tune of Linda's father. He pulled up to his hangar in case anyone saw him or his car. Nick walked across the ramp. He entered the back of Mac's hangar and was greeted with the smell of cigar smoke.

"Took you long enough. Bet it wasn't easy leaving that daughter of mine in bed. How's she anyway."

"She sends her regards. I'm sure you didn't summon me out here in the middle of the night to ask about Lynda's well being. Anyway, do you think it's wise for us to be here since Maggie is in the camper?"

"She's not here. You've got a situation on your hands, and you need to get it taken care of fast."

"What do you mean?"

"That cop and flyboy were out here earlier searching the place. It looks like someone's got people suspicious." The man re-lit the cigar.

"What do you mean?"

"That cop has been asking question about Lynda. He's talked to some boys over at the PD in Panama City." The man drew on the cigar. "The good thing is he's been checking into that mechanic also. Wouldn't be surprised if he's done a little investigating on you, too. Be amazing if he connected the dots between you..."

"Do you think it's wise you smoking those things in here. I damn near didn't get the scent out of Mac's office the last time you were here." Nick didn't want to hear anymore of the man's smug musings. "Be careful where you drop your ashes. You left them all over his office. It took me all night to get that office back right so no one would be suspicious."

"Look son you let me worry about myself, anyway, that's what I have you for, to clean up my messes." The man pointed his short stubby finger in Nick's chest. "You need to stop concentrating so much with your lower head and start thinking with your real brain. Fix this mess. I don't like what I've been hearing about how Maggie and Anne are getting chummy around here. Make sure they don't have any success at that meeting tomorrow. Tell that daughter of mine she better get her ass in gear with those accounts." The man took a long drag on the cigar, making it glow like embers before exhaling the smoke. "Just remember, I know your secrets, Masden." Without another word, the man walked away leaving Nick standing alone in the darkness.

Walking to Mac's office, he opened the door. He tried not to think about the last time he was in the office at this hour. He had tried to ignore Mac's body while cleaning the office to make it look like Mac had died alone. Nick looked around trying to see what was missing. The picture with the Anne and the horse was gone, along with the one of Mac and Dianne. He figured Anne had taken them with her to the farm. The empty spot that was home to the bottle of Drambuie caught his attention. It had been full the night he'd visited Maggie. The missing bottle of liqueur bothered him. Nick closed the door to the office and exited the hangar. He turned the engine on and allowed the heater to blow on his chilled body. The sound of his phone interrupted the silence of the car. "Hello."

"You still with Dad?'

"No, he's gone."

"You on your way home?"

"Yeah, I'm leaving the airport now."

"Wanna talk?"

"He's upset about how slow things are going. He said that Paul and Seth were out here earlier tonight searching the place"

"Where's Maggie?'

"I don't know. All he said was not here." Nick was met with silence on the line. "He's getting antsy and wants us to speed things up. Before I left, I checked Mac's office. A bottle of Drambuie was missing." Again, Nick was met with more silence on the line. "I'll see you in a few minutes, and we can talk more."

"See you then."

****

"Hello." Anne's groggy voice came through the phone. Two a.m. phone calls were never good news. Her first thought was Aunt Ethel.

"Anne, sorry to call this late." Seth stood outside the hospital entrance. "Seth. What's wrong?" Anne sat up in bed.

"It's Maggie. She's in the hospital."

"I'm on my way." Anne jumped out of the bed and grabbed a pair of jeans. "What happened?"

"She collapsed. You don't need to come." The fear and worry in Anne's voice matched the level of emotions he felt. "Doc is keeping her overnight. I need your help moving her out of that camper."

"It's about time. Is she agreeable to this?" Anne sat down on the bed and looked at the closed door to her room.

"No. Do you think Aunt Ethel will let her stay at the house with her?" Seth looked to the row of windows that marked the floor where Maggie was.

"Yes. You know Aunt Ethel loves Maggie like family." Anne looked at the digital dial of her clock. "She'll be up in a few hours. I'll call her then. Do you need me to meet you at the airport to get her things?"

"No. Call me after you talk to Aunt Ethel. We'll work out the details then." Seth wanted to tell Anne about the arsenic, Keegan's tool box, and Paul's suspicions. Everything had a time and place. His main concern was Maggie at the moment.

"I'll give you a call as soon as I talk with Aunt Ethel." Anne pulled the covers over her. "Seth, is she going to be okay?"

"Doc thinks so." Seth had to believe that to be the truth at the moment.

"Good. Get some rest. You sound wiped out." Anne placed the phone on her night stand. The worry in Seth's voice made her believe there was more than he was telling. She agreed that it was well past time in moving Maggie from the camper. For a moment, she thought of waking Keegan and telling him. The soft knock on her door caught her by surprise. "Yes."

"Anne, is everything okay? I heard you talking." Keegan had become a light sleeper since staying at the farm. He found himself listening for sounds coming from Anne's room. Her nightmares had become a nightly event.

"It was Seth. Maggie's in the hospital."

"Is she okay? What happened?" Keegan opened the bedroom door and sat on the edge of the bed.

"Seth said she collapsed. Doc is keeping her overnight." Anne studied the man sitting on her bed. She had often heard his footsteps during the night coming through her room. On occasions, they would pause before continuing. "I'm going to call Aunt Ethel to see if she'll let Maggie stay at the house."

"It's time she gets out of that camper. I never liked her staying in it."

"I think we all agree on that."

"Is she by herself at the hospital?"

"Seth's staying with her."

"Good." Keegan stood and looked at Anne before turning and leaving her.

EIGHTEEN

Sunlight filled the room and spilled across the floor. Maggie looked around the room. She did not remember being moved from the ER to her current location. Her body felt rested for the first time since the news of Mac's death. Memories of the previous evening reappeared. The harsh words exchanged, Seth's kiss, the strength of his arms carrying her, and his voice barking commands all played a montage.

She noticed a chair pulled close to her bed. The indention of someone sitting in it remained. Maggie reached to touch the cold leather, but her fingers could not make contact. Was it wishful thinking that Seth had been the one that had filled the chair? The creaking of the door made her hope it was him returning.

"How's my favorite girl today?" Doc entered Maggie's room and was immediately pleased with what he saw. Pink was in her cheeks, and the dark circles that had been present for the past weeks had disappeared.

Maggie gave a weak smile. "I bet you say that to all of your female patients. What happened?"

Doc did not like being dishonest. He had an obligation to his patient "You need to slow down and take better care of yourself is what happen. You collapsed from exhaustion.

194

I'm releasing you today under some strict conditions. One, you are going to stop living in the camper. Secondly, you are going to promise you will eat three well balance and healthy meals a day. That means no more living off coffee."

"I promise to take better care of myself, but I am not moving from the camper." Maggie's thoughts filled with the hassle of trying to find a place to live. The camper was perfect. "I don't have time to apartment hunt."

"That's why you are staying at my place." Aunt Ethel entered the room with Anne.

"The decision is made. We moved your items to Aunt Ethel's. She has plenty of room and needs someone to fuss over." Anne sat her purse on the chair and expected the rush of arguments.

"The camper is fine. I promise to slow down and take better care of myself." Maggie wondered who consisted of the "we."

"Honey, I have plenty of room at the house." Ethel moved to the foot of the bed. "Don't for one second think you are going to be a burden on me."

"I'm going to make sure you take care of yourself at the airport." Anne stood on the opposite side of the bed. Doc knew they had her surrounded.

"I'll be by daily to make sure you are following doctor's orders." Doc smiled knowing Maggie could not argue with either of the two women. "These are conditions of my discharge. I'll get a nurse to start making sure you can go to your new home."

****

"Anne will show you upstairs to your room." Ethel hung her purse and coat in the foyer closet. "I'll fix you some lunch."

"Thanks, Aunt Ethel. You shouldn't put yourself out for me." Maggie hated having people fuss over her.

"It's no problem." Aunt Ethel patted Maggie's arm.

Maggie waited until Ethel was out of hearing distance. "I want to get to the airport. We've got that meeting tonight with the Airport Authority. I need to be there."

Anne stared at Maggie before speaking. "I'm sorry, but what part of Doc's instructions did you not understand? Madison and I will handle the Airport Authority tonight." Anne pointed up the stairs. "March. Bed is the only place you're going. Doctor's orders." Anne did not give Maggie any space to turn back to the front door.

Maggie grabbed the banister. "Anyone tell you that you're a bossy bitch?"

"Stop talking and keep climbing." Anne tried to maintain a calm, confident exterior. The way her friend took each step and the labored breathing worried Anne. Seth's increased level of protectiveness of Maggie brought more questions. "You're staying in my old room." Anne entered the room and began to pull the covers back on the bed. You make yourself comfortable while I go and help Aunt Ethel."

Maggie leaned back on the pillows. She began to think about Seth's words of refusal to watch her live in Mac's memory. Maybe that explained his absence. Maggie rolled to her side and closed her eyes. Images of Seth filled her dreams.

****

"Did she raise a big stink about being moved?" Seth entered into the foyer of Aunt Ethel's.

"About the amount we expected." Anne closed the door. The deep lines of no sleep formed at Seth's eyes. She was sure his emotions were the source of fuel that kept him awake. "We pretty much had her surrounded and didn't give her much opening for argument."

"I'm glad she's out of that camper." Seth could already imagine the responses Maggie gave.

"She had the audacity to ask me to take her to the airport. She's worried about the meeting tonight." Anne took Seth's coat. "Watching her climb the stairs and how much it exhausted her, I'm worried Seth. Is Doc sure this is just exhaustion?"

"That's what he said." Seth looked up the stairs. "How is she?"

"Sound asleep. You can go up and check on her. Take a left at the top of the stairs then the first room on ..."

Seth was half way up the stairs before Anne could finish. He located the bedroom without any problem. He was greeted to the sounds of soft snores. Seth stood in the doorway watching Maggie's form on the bed. He'd watched every breath she took during the night.

She was safe. That single thought had kept him calm. She had people around her who would protect her. He had made sure. Aunt Ethel would care for her like a mother hen. Anne had promised to watch her at the airport. Doc and Paul would be there. She didn't need him. He'd made sure.

He reached into his pants pocket and grasped the blue topaz ring. The nurse had given it to him in the ER. He studied the ring before placing it on the night table. Maggie stirred. A strand of hair fell across her face. His hand moved it, and he studied her face. Brave. That was the way he would always see her. Fearless and determine to not let anyone or thing break her. "I'll always love you, but you're Mac's girl."

****

Anne busied herself in the kitchen. Her thoughts preoccupied with the two friends upstairs. They were more than friends. They were family. Maggie had become a sister. "How is she?"

"She's sound asleep." Seth wiped his face with his hands.

"I think she was out before her head hit the pillow." Anne placed a hand on Seth's arm, "The coffee's fresh. Want a cup?"

"Sure." Seth sat at the island. He studied the bottle of non-dairy creamer. How many times had he seen Maggie heaping the white powdery substance into her cup, innocent to the danger it contained?

"Do you want to talk?" Anne was sure the bottle of creamer was not the purpose of Seth's intense scrutiny.

"Where's Aunt Ethel?"

"She's gone on some errands. I told her I'd stay until she returned." Anne poured two cups of coffee. "Let's go to the living room. You look like you could use a friend."

Anne sat across from him. He looked worse for wear, as much as Maggie did. Seth closed his eyes trying to gather his thoughts. Where does one start explaining his actions, worries, and emotions?

Seth took a deep breath and slowly released it. "I went to the airport last night to check on her. I tried to convince her not to stay in that damn camper. She was stubborn as a mule refusing to listen to reason. She got caught in the downpour. We went into the camper to get some towels. The place was like a tomb with Mac's stuff. I lost it with her. We argued." Seth looked away from Anne. He wasn't sure if he could finish.

Anne saw the pain in Seth's face and eyes. "It's hard to care for someone and watch them destroy themselves."

"You are speaking of yourself." Seth did not expect the wisdom of Anne's words.

"Yes. Think of the last time the two of us were in this room. I was hell-bent on displaying my lack of grief over Dad. Now, I'm embarrassed by my actions."

"You are no longer the same person that I witnessed that day."

"That is because those who love me didn't give up on me. Mainly Aunt Ethel, even my dad." Anne reached out taking Seth's hand. "I have a new family in you and Maggie. I care about the two of you and hate seeing both of you unhappy. You love Maggie. It is easy to see, so don't give up on her. But it is plain as day that you are carrying a load of guilt right now."

"I pushed her last night." Seth saw Anne immediately stiffen as anger flashed across her face. "Not physically. Something inside me snapped when I went inside the camper. Have you been in there?"

"Not since the night I brought the food from Aunt Ethel. Why?"

"It's like a tomb. Mac was everywhere. From his toiletries on the sink to his shirt hanging on the door."

"The blue oxford."

"Yes. I bet she sleeps in the damn thing." Seth knew he was right by the way Anne refused to look at him. "I gave her an ultimatum. Choose Mac or me. I believe she ran out last night to tell me she didn't want me. Only, she didn't get the chance. Even in her unconscious state at the hospital she cried out for him." Seth stopped and gathered himself. "She doesn't want me, Anne. That is why I've made the decision to go back to the airline. I can't compete with a ghost."

"I never imagined you as a quitter." Anne knew her words stung. "You keep fighting because you are the living. You are here at this very moment, worrying and taking care of her. You keep showing up each and every day letting her know you care. You continue to love enough for the two of you."

Seth sat quietly letting Anne's words settle in his head and heart. The passion in which she spoke them took him by surprise. "Is that what you do with Keegan?"

"I've given him enough reason to doubt me. Going out with Nick didn't help either."

What did Doc tell Maggie was wrong with her?"

"Exhaustion, fatigue, bad diet. Why?" Anne didn't like the vibe she was getting. "There's more?"

"Yes. Paul was at the ER last night. Doc pulled him aside after he got Maggie's labs. Someone's been poisoning Maggie with arsenic."

Anne sat stunned at the news. "It has to be Lynda. I knew keeping her around was trouble." Images of her dad paraded through her mind. He looked haggard. "What about Dad? Did she kill my dad?"

"Paul got a search warrant for the hangar." Seth's lack of agreeing with the theory of Lynda made Anne nervous. "He believes the arsenic was being mixed with Maggie's coffee creamer. He took your dad's hairbrush from the camper."

"Seth what are you not telling me?"

"He found a vial of white powder in Keegan's toolbox."

"That doesn't mean Keegan did this. It means that Lynda put it there."

"Anne, has Maggie told you about the trip to St. Simons?"

"She lost the left engine, but it was trash. That's what the mechanic told her. She hasn't had any more problems with it since then." Anne remembered Maggie's warning about being careful and things not being as they appeared.

"Keegan ever mention his past to you."

"Not really. He's been sketchy about it. He said he grew up on a horse farm near Savannah. His parents died in a car accident when he was young. And his grandparents raised him." Anne listened to herself and realized she really didn't know much about Keegan.

200

"Don't you think it's convenient that he was there when PJ threw you? Have you had anymore incidents at the barn since he's been staying there?"

"Seth, I don't like what you're implying."

"He used to work at the F.B.O in St. Simons. The mechanic that worked on the plane for Maggie didn't have good things to say about Keegan. He said he warned Mac not to hire Keegan."

"Maggie tried to warn me about him, but I didn't listen."

"Anne, I've always liked Keegan and felt that he's a genuine person, but right now, things aren't looking good for him. Just like you, I don't want what I am thinking to be true."

The sound of the back door slamming announced Aunt Ethel's return. Anne reached over and gave Seth's hand a quick squeeze. "Same here. Are coming to the meeting?"

"Yes. Anne, be careful."

"I will." Anne walked to the front door with Seth and watched the man take the front steps with ease. He stopped, turned, and wave at her. Maggie was a lucky woman to have someone like him to love her. Anne wanted to go and ask Keegan if what Seth had told him was true. She couldn't believe he was the reason for the problems at the barn. The way he treated her horses made her positive he couldn't hurt anything living. He always spoke with respect toward Maggie and had expressed his own concerns about her well-being. She turned to go to the kitchen, but stopped at the sight of a red truck pulling in the driveway. Her heart recognized the driver while her mind screamed for it not to be true.

Carrying a vase of flowers, Keegan shut the door to the truck.

"That your truck?" Anne opened the door and stepped onto the porch. She did not give Keegan passage from the bottom step. "I've never seen it at the airport."

"I live in the trailer park across the road and walk to work." The tone in Anne's voice made him feel like he was at an inquisition. "I thought I'd come by and check on Maggie. Is she okay?'

"Just exhaustion and poor diet." As they talked, Anne's mind was replaying Maggie's warning and the conversation with Seth. She began to believe that all this time the fox had been living in the hen house. Everyone focused on Lynda and Dennis, making it easy for him to steal, and commit murder.

"We all know how she hasn't been taking care of herself."

"She has me and Seth to look after her now, so she'll be fine."

"Good." It was obvious Anne was not going invite him inside. "Here, I brought these for her. Oh, and this came in the mail for her. It's from her Nashville office. I thought it might be something important."

"Thanks. I'll put these in her room." Anne took the vase of flowers and envelope.

"You going to the meeting tonight with Madison?"

"That's the plan."

"See you there." Keegan turned to walk down the step.

"Keegan."

"Yes?" He stopped and turned.

"I think it best you don't stay at the farm."

"You plan on riding alone?" Keegan baffled by Anne's abruptness assumed that Nick was the reason behind her decision.

"I'll be okay." Anne did not give Keegan a chance for further conversation. She closed the front door and watched him walk to his truck.

"Who was that dear?" Aunt Ethel entered the foyer. "Oh,

aren't those just lovely. They must be for Maggie."

"It was Keegan, and yes, they are. I'm going to put these in her room." Anne climbed the stairs and entered her old bedroom. Maggie had not moved from her original position. In an attempt to not make any noise, Anne eased the vase of flowers on the night stand. She saw the blue topaz ring. Seth must have left it. She started to place the envelope under the ring. Curiosity made her pause. The contents of the envelope made her wonder if it was about Keegan and DE Aviation. Had Maggie been conducting her own investigation and remained quiet?

Maggie began to stir. Slowly, she rolled to her side and focused on Anne standing next to the bed. She rubbed her face with both hands. Perfumed fragrance of star gazer lilies permeated the air. "How long was I out?"

"At least two hours. I'm sorry I woke you."

"What's that?" Maggie looked at the envelope in Anne's hands.

"It's for you. Keegan stopped by with the flowers and said this came in the mail. It's from your office in Nashville."

"Oh, it's some paperwork about my leave of absence. I'll look at it later." Maggie took the envelope and laid it next to the vase of flowers. Her hand touched the ring. She studied it before putting it on her left hand. "Where's my phone. I need to talk to Seth."

"Your phone is in a safe place. He stopped by to check on you." Anne wanted to talk to Maggie about Keegan, St Simons, and the red truck, but she knew the time was not right.

"He told you about last night." Memories of the previ-

COMING HOME—A SECOND CHANCE AT GOODBYE

ous night became clear. "I went after him Anne. I was going to tell him I chose him."

"You need to tell him that and the sooner the better." Anne reached in her back pocket for her phone. "That's my horse broker. We have a second offer on PJ."

"I still hate that your selling him. Are things better since Keegan's been staying at the farm?" Maggie pushed herself up and leaned against the headboard.

"It has, and he isn't staying at the farm anymore." Anne decided to let the call go to voicemail. "I'll let you know how things go tonight." She started to walk out of the room but paused. "If you mean what you say about Seth, it would be wise to stop wearing Dad's ring."

Maggie glanced at the ring and the empty space where Anne had stood. In her heart, she knew it was time to remove the ring from her left hand. Slowly, she removed the ring and put it back on the night stand. Her hand brushed the envelope. Fatigue made another appearance bringing the inability to keep her eyes open.

****

Anne tugged at the hem of the blazer. The palms of her hands felt like a rain forest. She swallowed trying to get past the knot in her throat. "You'll be fine. Just stop fidgeting, Madison whispered as they sat in the audience. The six men seated behind the large desk droned on about topics involving the airport. Anne turned to see who was seated in the audience. She spotted Seth. He gave a brief wave and smile. The mention of Mac's Flying Service caused her to turn her attention back to the front. Madison tapped Anne. He stood up and walked to the podium. Anne followed behind with her hands shoved in the blazer pockets. Madison spoke into the microphone, "Madison

204

Barfield and Anne Harris present representing Mac's Flying Service."

Anne recognized Gerald Mixon. "Where is Maggie Cosby? Isn't she the new owner of Mac's Flying Service?"

"She will be once the estate of Mac Harris has been probated and settled. For now, I am the executor of that estate." Madison opened the folder in front of him.

Gerald looked at Anne. "It is to our understanding that Mr. Harris' estate is being contested by his daughter."

Anne cleared her throat trying to settle her nervousness. "That is no longer true. I support my dad's wishes to leave Mac's Flying Service to Maggie Cosby."

"Which still leaves the question of where Ms. Cosby is tonight? Shouldn't she be here instead of you, Ms. Harris?"

"Ms. Cosby is unable to attend due to health reasons." Madison was sure the airport grapevine had been humming about Maggie's collapse. Men could be busy bodies more than any group of blue hairs.

Gerald frowned at the comment and muttered before continuing, "The subject at hand is the future of hangar that Mac's Flying Service operates. The lease agreement for that building ends the first of next month. The authority has been approached by another Fixed Base Operation that is willing to lease the property and build a more modern facility. Have you reviewed the current lease agreement?"

"I have." Madison pulled the lease agreement from the large folder.

"If I may speak?" Anne moved toward the podium. "In the past month, I've had the opportunity to become acquainted with my dad's business. This is not just some old building. This hangar is the last remaining one from when this airport trained

Navy pilots during WWII. It's a statement of how the hard work of one man built a small business. People of all walks of life enter my dad's business looking for one common interest. The love of flying. Together friendships and partnerships are formed. Learning to fly at Mac's Flying Service has become a tradition for many families. The employees that come to work every day are dedicated to these people and more importantly to this airport. I am not one to object to progress. At the same time we also can't just throw away our past for something more modern, shiny and new. I ask each of you not to close the door on this piece of history and tradition. Thank You."

Anne stepped from the podium. She slid her palms down the front of her skirt. Silence exploded into applause. Anne turned. Everyone was on their feet clapping. A few whistles shrilled, and "Way to go Anne" was shouted. She spotted Nick against the back wall. He nodded at her before turning and exiting. A short heavy set man followed him through the side door.

The constant pounding of a wooden gavel and Gerald Mixon's raised voice was muffled. Slowly, the applause waned. "Thank you, Ms. Harris, for you words. At this time the board will vote on the renewal of the lease for Mac's Flying Service. All those in favor raise your hand." One by one each person raised their hand until five out of the six seated members were accounted. Gerald Mixon's hand remained flat on the desk. "Then let the record stand that the lease has been approved with five in favor and one opposed. This concludes the agenda for this meeting. Meeting is adjourned."

Madison turned to Anne. "Your father would have been proud of you tonight."

"Anne, hon, you were awesome in what you said. I'm so

proud of you." Aunt Ethel grabbed Anne into a motherly hug.

Anne welcomed the embrace, "Thank you, Aunt Ethel. I was so nervous."

"It didn't show." Keegan eyes met Anne's. She was surprised at the warmth they held.

Anne released her embrace from Aunt Ethel. "There's one person missing from this celebration."

"How was Maggie when ya'll left her?" Seth asked.

"She was still sound asleep." Aunt Ethel answered as the group began to move outside. "Why don't ya'll come on over to the house? I have a German Chocolate cake just waiting to be cut." There was no delay in accepting the invitation from the group.

Anne spotted Nick near his car. She noticed a figure move away from him and into the darkness. It was unnerving how one second the figure was there and in a blink gone. "I'll meet up with you at the house."

Keegan watched Anne join Nick. The way he reached up touching her face, followed by holding of hands and then an embrace, he tried to not let his jealousy get the better of his mood. She had made it clear this afternoon that he was not needed.

"Are you going over to Aunt Ethel's?" Seth knew the scene of Anne with Nick did not sit well with Keegan.

"No. I'm going home." Keegan opened the door to his truck.

"You're not staying at the farm with Anne?"

"Nope. She said she didn't need me." Keegan could not take his eyes away from Anne and Nick. "It's for the best anyway."

"Probably." Seth left Keegan and walked to his own vehicle.

*****

"Masden, do I need to remind you what is at stake here?"

207

The man spat in disgust.

"No, you don't." Nick hated the sound of the man's voice, the stench of cigar smoke, and the way he felt trapped by the man in front of him.

"Then how the hell did you let this happen?" The old man chewed the end of an unlit cigar. "You make sure that Gerald Mixon understands the significance of losing that vote. I believe you have a packet of compromising photos of him."

"Enough. I refuse to be a part of your scheme. I want out." Nick regretted the day he'd ever met him. Most of all, he regretted sharing his deepest secret during a drunken stupor.

"Listen to me, son. It's too late to start growing a conscious. There is no getting out." The man turned spotting the group that had formed around Anne. "You once asked what Mac Harris did to me. He destroyed my family. Women are like street cars. One on every corner waiting to be jumped on. Even you agree to that. But children, they're a different story. They are our legacy. Wives can be replaced, but a man's children can't. Mac Harris took my son, David Eugene Reynard, from me."

A chill crept down Nick's spine. He spotted Anne looking at him. "You didn't say anything about anyone getting hurt. You said you wanted his business destroyed. That was all."

"Guess I lied." The man disappeared into the shadows.

Nick watched Anne's group laughing and talking. He envied the comradely they shared. Each of them disbursed except for Anne. He started to open his car door. Anne calling his name stopped him. If anything happened to her, it would be because of him and his selfishness to protect himself.

"Hi, Nick." Anne smiled and put her hand on his arm.

"You were awesome in there."

208

"Thanks. Who was that man talking to you? Was he the person interested in the business?" Anne turned and looked into the darkness trying to spot the figure she'd seen.

"You could say that."

"I guess he got his answer tonight."

"I guess so."

"You sure are short on words tonight."

"Sorry. I don't mean to be a spoil sport. You should be proud of yourself. What you said about Mac's was perfect."

"Again, thanks." Anne looked at Nick. There was a sadness about him that tugged at her. The carefree laid back attitude and his quick with a joke seemed strangely absent. "You look like you've got the weight of the world on your shoulders. Are you okay?"

"Yeah." Nick smiled. He touched the side of her face. "Don't worry yourself about me. I'll be fine. I always am."

"Despite how things have gone between us, I'm still here if you need a friend. I don't regret our relationship. It's just…"

"That you've found yourself a family and someone to love. You don't need an alley cat like me."

"I don't see you as an alley cat, Nick."

Nick stared at Anne. She had grown into a beautiful woman. "Promise me you'll be careful."

Anne was not sure what prompted Nick's statement. "Should I be worried?"

"No. How's Maggie?"

Anne felt Nick was not being honest with her. "She's fine. She's staying at Aunt Ethel's house now."

"I'm glad. She doesn't need to be living in that camper."

"That's what all of us have been trying to convince her. I just wanted to come over and say hello."

"I'm glad you did."

"Just remember I'm here if you need me." Anne embraced Nick. She felt a loss like she was saying goodbye

"Don't be silly. But thanks." Nick returned the embrace.

****

Maggie unlocked the hangar door. The news of the Airport Authority's decision to renew the lease lifted the last weight off her shoulders about the future of the business. She passed the camper and did not think about going inside to visit Mac's ghost. Maggie stopped, picked up an empty box next to the trash can, and continued to her office. She stood in the doorway and looked around the room. Every corner spoke of its last occupant. It was time that she put her personality into the room. The first thing was placing the flowers Keegan had given her on the desk. One by one, she filled the box with reminders of Mac. She was sure Anne would like the pictures. The empty spot where the bottle of Dram sat gave her pause. Next to it was another empty spot where she kept her coffee creamer. There were more important things to worry about than missing bottles of liqueur and coffee creamer. The last of Mac's items carefully packed, Maggie sat the box on the floor. She would give them to Anne.

She sat behind the desk and opened her purse. She pulled the envelope from her Nashville office out and began to review its contents. Her eyes scanned over the list of licenses and certifications. She flipped to the page with findings of any past investigations. She was not surprised to see comments on the page. A plane Keegan had worked on crashed. The preliminary query indicated he had been negligent in securing a fuel line. One witness stated they saw Keegan as the last mechanic to work on the plane. The witness observed the plane leaking fuel on the ground after Keegan had completed working on it.

The Inspector's notes indicated Keegan stated he had secured the line and re-checked it. There were no signs of fuel leaking, and the line was in new condition. However, no one was able to support or contradict either Keegan's or the witness' accounts. The Inspector closed the case stating the cause of the crash was mechanical. No disciplinary actions were taken against Keegan.

Maggie could not help but wonder if Keegan had anything to do with the four-fourteen's fuel problem during her flight to St. Simons. She moved to the last page with Janice's hand written note, "No record of DE Aviation on file."

"Well, it is good to see you back." Keegan stood in the doorway of the office.

"Thanks, Keegan, and thanks for the flowers. That was thoughtful of you." Maggie folded the papers and slid them under a stack of papers.

"Just wanted to do something to help cheer you up and speed your recovery. It was lonesome not having you around here."

Lynda entered behind Keegan. "You look like you feel better. There is actually color in your cheeks. Everyone was concerned about you, but I told them you were fine. Anne was awesome last night at the meeting. Guess you both are excited about the lease."

"Thanks." The sound of voices inside the hangar caught Maggie's attention. She recognized Seth's voice. "I need to speak with Seth. Excuse me."

****

Paul quietly continued the conversation that had started outside on the porch with Seth. "The contents in the bottle tested positive for arsenic. The labs also showed arsenic in Maggie's coffee cup and the bottle of Dram. Mac's hair samples also had high levels of arsenic."

Seth glanced over at Keegan's tool box. "Do you think Keegan has something to do with this?"

"Right now anyone is a possibility. Is Keegan still staying down at the farm with Anne?"

"No."

"You need to convince Maggie to fire Lynda." Paul glanced toward the office seeing the two women.

"Would you like me to negotiate for world peace, too?" Seth knew there was no way of getting Maggie to fire her without telling her the truth. "Paul, I told Anne."

"With Keegan staying at the farm, it is for the best she knows."

"Have you been able to get in contact with Dennis?" Seth was relieved that Paul was not upset with his decision.

"No. I've left several messages for him to call me. Right now, I don't have enough to issue an arrest warrant. I'm still waiting for the bank to provide Maggie with copies of the checks that were made out to D. E. Aviation. Then I can get account numbers the money was deposited in." Paul turned, glancing at the office.

"Hey, ya'll having an awful serious conversation." Maggie approached the duo. It was the first time she'd seen Seth since the storm. She tried calling him but always received his voice mail. Anne assured her that he was busy with students and flying Jared and Kyle.

Seth was pleased with how well she looked. Aunt Ethel's nurturing had been what she needed. "Just talking about flying."

"Paul, I'm glad you stopped by. I was about to give you a

call. Can we talk in my office?" Maggie sensed the topic of conversation was not flying.

"We can talk later." Seth did not miss the reference to Mac's office being hers.

"Sure thing." Paul followed Maggie into her office. Maggie shut the door before sitting on the couch next to Paul. He noticed the box. "That had to be hard to do."

"It's time I moved forward. I will never forget Mac and will always be grateful for him being a part of my life." Maggie sighed and tried to fight the misty feeling in her eyes. She reached for the papers from her Nashville office. "My assistant mailed me these. Also, DE Aviation doesn't exist." Maggie stood and reached across the desk for another envelope. "Here are copies of cancelled checks.""

"Do you have anything with Keegan's signature?" Paul studied the scrawled signature on the back of the checks.

"Yes, right here." Maggie pulled some pages from a stack on the desk.

"I think I need to have a talk with Mr. O'Keefe. Is it okay if I keep these?"

"Sure." Maggie stood with Paul.

****

Keegan and Lynda were laughing at a shared joke. The look on Paul's face sobered Keegan. "Hey Paul."

"Keegan."

Keegan was familiar with the tone of Paul's voice. He'd heard it before many times in his youth. "Take it this is an official visit and not a friendly one."

"You mind riding over to the Police Department with me?"

"Do I have a choice?"

"It would be in your best interest."

"Then I guess I don't." Keegan tried to hide his embarrassment from those he'd considered friends. Thankful that Paul had not made a big display, he walked out the office and attempted to remain casual and quiet.

"Wonder what that's all about?" Lynda had been positive that Paul was there for her. She tried to control her relief when it was Keegan that had found himself in the cross-hairs. "Were he and Dennis working together?"

Maggie could not believe the audacity or the words coming from Lynda. "Paul just needed to talk to Keegan about some things." Maggie turned to Seth to ask if they could speak in private. Anne's arrival interrupted the opportunity.

"Did Paul arrest Keegan?" Anne's voice trembled at the vocalization of the words. The sight of Keegan riding in the back seat of the unmarked car had confirmed her worst thoughts. "Seth, is it true?"

"Is what true?" Maggie felt that she'd been left out of a secret.

Seth did not like that Lynda was being witness to this. He also knew he had two females on his hand that were on the brink of demanding answers. "Can we talk in private?"

"Let's go to my office." Maggie turned on her heels and headed into her office. Seth and Anne were stunned at the changes in the room. "What are you two not telling me?"

Seth closed the door and kept his voice low. "Maggie, there's more to why you collapsed the other night. Someone has been putting arsenic in your coffee creamer."

Maggie swayed a bit but remained rooted in her stance. "Keegan?"

"Paul searched the place and found a bottle or arsenic in his toolbox. It was in the bottom drawer." Seth continued. "He also took some of Mac's items from the camper and his bottle of Dram."

"Anne, you knew this?" Maggie wanted to be angry.

"Not until Seth told me when he came by to check on you." Anne could understand Maggie's sense of betrayal. "You remember the red truck you saw at my barn? Keegan drives a red truck."

"What are you two talking about?" Seth realized that he was the one in the dark with regard to the conversation.

"The day I flew the Bonanza, I saw a red truck leaving Anne's barn." Maggie began to explain.

"She thought it was me because that was the night I met Nick here to go to dinner." Anne continued.

"He was here working on Madison's plane." Seth had talked with Keegan before going to fly with a student.

"That's right." A small glimmer of hope began to build in Anne. Maybe, there was a logical explanation.

"Even so, that still doesn't explain everything else." Maggie reminded Seth and Anne.

"What do you mean?" Anne did not want to hear any more negative things about Keegan.

"I had my office in Nashville to do a background check on Keegan's records. Looks like he was under investigation for a plane crash eight months ago. The cause of the crash was a faulty fuel line."

Seth sucked in his breath. "Like what could have been wrong with the four-fourteen?"

"All this time we thought our biggest problem was Lynda's stealing. Could all three of them be in this? She, Dennis, and Keegan?" Maggie's mind swirled with information and theories. "They killed Mac."

"Paul still hasn't been able to talk to Dennis." Seth didn't want to add to speculation. "I think it's best if we wait and see what Paul finds out."

"Maggie, you need to let Lynda go." Seth felt the best way to get Maggie to understand the seriousness of the situation was to be honest. "Stop and think about how she's always making sure you have coffee creamer. Until Paul has enough to arrest her, she doesn't need to be here."

"What if she disappears? We'll never find her." Maggie sat down before her knees buckled. "What if all three of them were in cahoots? Am I about to be without a mechanic? I can manage without Lynda. But without Keegan?"

"Maggie has a point. If she fires Lynda it's going to alert her that we are on to her." Anne worried about how pale Maggie was becoming. The bead of sweat on her brow was not a good sign.

"Somehow, we will manage." Seth tried to assure her.

"We?" Maggie swallowed the bile burning the back of her throat. "Considering our last conversation, I believe you said you weren't sticking around."

"Is that what you want?" Seth was afraid of her answer.

"Hey. Before we start tearing at each other or saying anything anyone will regret, let's take a breath." Anne could feel the level of tension building. "If Seth was going to leave, he would not have spent every waking moment flying with students, taking care of Jared and Kyle, and worrying about you."

****

"Take a seat. I need to take care of a few things before we get started."

"Sure." Keegan sat in a metal chair. He'd had been in these rooms before. Time inched by before Paul returned. Keegan tried to remain calm but knew his past continued to haunt him.

"You dip?" He sat back taking a can of dip from his pants front pocket.

"No, never got into the habit."

Paul opened the folder lying on the table land looked at a few of the pages. "It seems like you aren't a stranger to this situation."

Keegan with arms crossed over his chest, sat as far back into the chair as he could. "No."

"Do you have any idea why I ask you to come here today?"

"Not a clue."

Paul spit into the trash can. "What can you tell me about the incident in St. Simons?"

Keegan pursed his lips as he ran a hand through his hair. "A plane I worked on crashed. There were some issues raised about the fuel line, if I had been negligent in securing it. I was cleared of that investigation, but I lost my job."

"Do you know who the witness was?"

"No"

"It was the other mechanic at St. Simons, Raymond. I just spoke with him on the phone about what he saw. He told me something interesting that this report doesn't." Keegan crossed his arms tighter over his chest and looked past Paul, "Raymond said you and the owner of the plane had a nasty argument. He was afraid it was going to get physical. It concerned him to the point he felt he needed to step in between the two of you."

"I am familiar with the incident. Raymond wasn't shy about making sure the investigators and FAA knew about the argument."

"Care to explain what upset you?"

"The man was insistent on making sure I knew what I was doing to his plane. You've seen the type around the hangar, the weekend warriors who want to work on their planes themselves. They want to micromanage everything that you do. I tried to be patient with him at first, giving him easy things to do. He saw one of the fittings on the fuel line had a little rust on it. I told him I had looked at it, and the fitting was fine. He wasn't happy with my answer and kept at the issue. Finally, I told him that unless he had the licenses to sign off his own annual that he needed to leave and not come back until his plane was ready."

Paul leaned over the trash, spitting before sitting back. He used the sleeve of his shirt to wipe his mouth. Paul opened the desk drawer. He reached inside and took out the bottle of arsenic. "Do you recognize this?"

Keegan picked up the bottle and opened the lid. "No, what's in it?"

"That doesn't matter right now. What matters is where it was found. It was discovered in the bottom drawer of your tool box, pushed to the back and covered with shop rags."

"Like I said I don't recognize it or its contents."

"You don't keep your box locked."

"No."

Keegan looked Paul in the eye and said, "Do you mind telling me what is going on here?"

"Tell me about you and Anne."

Keegan's nostrils flared as he tightened his lips and said, "There's nothing to tell."

"She told me about the incident at the riding arena the day you were there. She's also mention the trouble before that day.

The thing that gets me is since you've been staying there her trouble has stopped."

Keegan's abrupt movement made his chair slide across the floor. He stood in front of the two way glass and watched Paul in the reflection before turning around. "Why don't you get to the point? You think I'm involved with Anne's problems at the farm. You are also thinking I had something to do with the four-fourteen."

"Should I think differently? You tell me."

"Seems like you've got your mind set."

"Your past isn't helpful. Most of all, finding this in your tool box has created some concern."

Keegan picked up the bottle, "I don't know how much plainer I can get. I don't know nothing about this damn bottle." Keegan slammed the container back onto the table.

"Look, I've known you since you came to work for Mac. The things in this file don't fit the person I've seen around the hangar. But right now I need you to sit down. Tell me anything about you and your past even if it seems unimportant."

Keegan sat on the edge of the chair resting his arms on his legs. He stared at the white tile floor between them. "I had a hell of a temper as a youth, drank a lot, got into any type of fight at the drop of a hat. Put my grandparents through hell. One night, I almost killed a man. The judge was friends with my grandparents, and out of respect for them, instead of sending me to prison, he sent me to the Navy. The Navy taught me how to control my anger and to put it to productive use. After leaving, I moved back to St Simons to be close to my family in Savannah. I was able to get a job with the FBO at St. Simons as a mechanic. Shortly afterwards the business sold to a new company. Raymond came to work as lead mechanic. I didn't care much for him and tried to stay out of his way."

"Tell me about you and Mac."

Keegan slid back in the chair, a smile came across his face. "I liked Mac the first time I met him. He would always walk out into the shop and talk with me. We'd swap stories about planes and flying. He was likeable, nothing pretentious about him. One day after his visit, Raymond came over saying he didn't like Mac hanging around in the shop. It wasn't long after that the incident with the plane happened. I came to Mac and asked him for a job. He knew about the crash but hired me anyway. To this day, I am thankful for his generosity and taking a chance on me. So, why don't you tell me why I'm here and what's with that bottle."

"The content in this bottle is arsenic. The cause of Mac's death and almost Maggie's." Paul paused letting his words sink in and watching Keegan's reaction. "What I need to know is who wants you to take the fall for their actions?"

Keegan sat in stun silence staring at the bottle before looking at Paul. "You mean Mac was murdered?" Anger filled Keegan. The image of Mac's body on the floor still haunted him.

"That's the answer I am trying to find out."

Keegan stared at the bottle. "Did you check it for prints?"

"Yes, and it was clean."

"Do you have any idea who would want to hurt Mac or Maggie?" Keegan asked.

"I have my suspicions."

****

Keegan did not waste any time finding Maggie in the back hangar. "Maggie, can we talk?"

"Sure come on in." Keegan made his way up the small steps and down the narrow aisle to the cockpit. "Jared and Kyle want me to take them up to the Kentucky game tomorrow. Thought I'd come out here and check the plane." Maggie read the seriousness in Keegan's face.

"Maggie, I want to let you hear from me what happen in St. Simon."

Maggie placed her hand on Keegan's knee patting it, "You don't need to explain. Paul called me before ya'll left the station."

"Maggie, I would never do anything to bring trouble to you, this place, and Anne."

"Speaking of Anne, where are you with her?"

"I'd rather answer why's the sky blue." Keegan pondered for a moment. "She has this way of ticking me off one moment and the next wanting to protect her. I worry about her, but then I see her with Nick and think, why bother."

"Anne isn't seeing Nick anymore."

"What about the other night when they were groping each other in the parking lot and after the meeting, he was the first one she sought to speak to."

"The only reason she agreed to that dinner was because she was mad at you. I can't speak for the other night after the meeting, but I can assure you Nick is not the one who holds Anne's heart."

Keegan did not have to be the smartest tool in the shed to understand the meaning behind Maggie's statement. "She's been having nightmares about her mother's death. She always screams Nick's name."

"Does she know that?"

"I'm not sure. I didn't give her much of a chance to talk about it."

"Keegan, letting go of the past is hard. I think for the first time Anne is facing some truths instead of self-created myths. I also think she is learning new emotions, such as taking chances on loving and caring for people."

"You know the same could be said for you." Keegan looked at the ring on Maggie's hand. "For example, why you wear that ring on your left hand. Aren't you too busy looking for answers such as why Mac didn't love you enough. Why are you trying to prove to a ghost that you are worthy of this place? What about Seth? You know he has turned his life upside down to be here with you."

Maggie looked out the windshield down the long narrow nose of the plane and then at her hand with the ring, "My head understands that I have got to let Mac go, but my heart is not ready. But it's more than just letting go of the memory of Mac." Maggie stared out the windshield. "The last man I let take care of me discarded me like yesterday's trash."

Keegan reached over touching Maggie's hand. "Trust is a hard thing when it has been damaged. But if you continue to punish Seth for another person's mistakes, then no one walks away healed. You have got to forgive Mac."

"I know." Maggie sighed.

"Maggie, thanks for not firing me." Keegan moved from the co-pilot seat. "I need to find Anne."

"Keegan, if you can, convince her to let you stay at the farm again."

"I plan on it." Keegan patted Maggie on the shoulder and left her.

****

Keegan walked to the barn where he was sure he'd find Anne. She was brushing PJ and talking to him. He hated the thought of her selling the stallion. It was a topic he avoided with her.

222

"Keegan." Anne wondered what made Nails jump from the hay bale.

"You got a moment?" Keegan put both hands in his back pockets.

"Sure. What's up?" Anne put the brush in the caddy of grooming tools.

"I imagine seeing me in the back of a police car needs some explaining." Keegan leaned against the door frame. "My choice to go into the Navy was not a voluntary one. I almost killed a man one night in a fight. Instead of prison, the judge ordered I join the military. After the Navy, I worked at St. Simons."

"Where you met Dad." Anne held to PJ's lead rope.

"Yes. There was an incident with a plane I worked on. It crashed. No one was hurt, but because I worked on the plane, I was the focus of the investigation. The FAA cleared me, but I was fired."

"That when Dad hired you?"

"Yes." Keegan shifted his weight. "Paul told me about the arsenic. I would never do anything to hurt Mac or Maggie. I consider Mac's place home and Maggie family."

Anne wanted to ask, "What about me?" but she remained silent.

"I understand your decision about me staying here. But Anne, until Paul knows who is behind poisoning Mac and Maggie, the problems you've had here at the farm, and stealing from the business, I still don't think you are safe."

Anne thought about the red truck Maggie had seen. She'd checked every inch of the barn and horses but did not find anything tampered with. As much as she liked believing she didn't need anyone and wasn't scared, she was. "I agree."

"Good." Keegan had not expected Anne's reaction. He'd expected her to argue that she was capable of taking care of herself. "You getting him ready for Saturday?"

"I'm not sure. There's a second offer." Anne took PJ and led him into his stall.

"Oh." Keegan took the lead rope from Anne while she latched the stall door.

"I don't want to think about it." Anne stroked PJ's nose. "I only want to focus on good things, like getting to solo tomorrow."

"So, you think Maggie is gonna let you?" Keegan hung the lead rope on the hook next to PJ's stall. "Anne..." Keegan thoughts were on what Maggie had said about Nick. He wanted to apologize for his behavior, but Anne's phone interrupted his chance.

"That's the horse broker. I'll meet you at the house." Anne turned and walked outside the barn and to the practice ring.

NINETEEN

Madison walked into the hangar and watched the foursome around the Cessna, each of them talking and laughing. It made him feel good to see Anne and Maggie in good spirits. The place felt like it used to with people coming and going. He knew that Mac's spirit and legacy were being continued through these four people.

Maggie was the first to spot Madison standing in the hangar. "Hey, you missed seeing Anne solo."

"From the sounds of it, she did an awesome job." Madison tipped an imaginary hat to Anne. "Congratulations."

"Thank you."

"What brings you out here in the middle of the afternoon?" Maggie gave Madison a quick hug.

"To give you this and bring good news." Madison held out an envelope.

Maggie took the envelope. "What's this?"

"Open it."

"Oh, my goodness." Maggie's hand flew to her mouth.

Seth, Keegan, and Anne all three in unison asked, "What is it?"

Maggie looked up. "I am the official legal owner of Mac's Flying Service." Again the trio began chattering and offering their congratulations. Maggie held up her hand. "It gets better." She held up another document. "This is the lease agreement on this hangar. It states that as long as Mac's Flying Service is in business on this field it is to remain in this hangar indefinitely."

"I thought you would be pleased with this." Madison gave a wink at Maggie. He was still baffled by the terms of the lease. Gerald Mixon had been short on words when he dropped the document by Madison's office. Gerald had also informed Madison that he was resigning as chairman and moving his plane.

Maggie wrapped her arms around his neck. "This is the best birthday present anyone could give me."

Keegan and Anne asked in unison, "When's your birthday?"

Seth answered without hesitation, "Today." Maggie eyes widen with surprise that Seth remembered or even knew the significance of this date. Seth looked at Keegan, "I believe these two ladies deserve to be taken out for a celebration. Where would you ladies like to go?"

"The Fifty–Seventh and in the Bonanza." Maggie loved going to the restaurant located on PDK's airfield.

Madison laughed "Looks like you two boys better dig deep into your wallets tonight because these ladies have champagne taste." He took another look at the group in front of him, "I'd better get going." He gave Maggie a short hug and said, "Happy Birthday."

****

The flicker of the candlelight accompanied with the music and warmth of the restaurant made the night feel magical. The décor of the restaurant transported time back to World War II. Memorabilia from the Army Air Corp adorned the walls. A long row of windows allowed a view to Peachtree DeKalb's airport and one of it taxiways. For a moment, Anne felt as if Keegan was her dashing hero going off to war, taking with him her promise to wait for his safe return, all the while sending him scented love letters from home to help him through the lonely nights.

Keegan seeing Anne lost in her own world took advantage of the moment. Just looking at her took his breath away. How beautiful her face lit up when she laughed or smiled. The way her upturn nose crinkled. He thought about how her mouth tasted of sweetness like an over ripe peach when he kissed her. Even in the face of danger and worry, she carried herself with a strong resolve to not be defeated.

Looking over at Seth and Maggie, Keegan thought of how well the two complimented each other. Keegan knew if Maggie did not let go of Mac soon, she'd lose Seth. He had overheard Seth's phone conversation earlier with the airlines. It was apparent Seth was making arrangements to go back to work.

As the waitress brought out coffee and desert consisting of two cakes with candles in them, Seth picked up his cup. "Unfortunately, we are not able to toast this event with a glass of bubbly. I lift this cup to you Maggie in recognition of your birthday. Here's to you Ms. Cosby and the future of Mac's Flying service."

Keegan cleared his throat, "This is to celebrate the accomplishment made today by Anne who has shown that she can not only get a plane off the ground but also safely bring it back without creating any major damage needing to be repaired."

Everyone laughed as Anne glared at Keegan before taking a sip of her coffee. Keegan placed a small wrapped box in front of Anne. Surprised and more than a little curious, she asked, "What's this?"

"Something to help you remember this day." A gasp escaped when she looked at the contents. Picking up the necklace, Anne held it by the delicate chain. The gold pendant with an airplane on the front turned to reveal her name and the date on the back.

"Here let me help you." Maggie helped Anne with the necklace.

Anne reached up and fingered the pendant, "Thank you so much."

Seth turned to Maggie handing her a turquoise box with white ribbon and a bow, "Happy Birthday."

Maggie took the box with trembling hands. Inside sat a pair of emerald earrings surrounded by diamonds. She removed her earrings and replaced them with the emeralds. "Thank you so much." Then looking at Anne and Keegan, "I could not have spent this evening with anyone more important that those sitting with me around this table."

Maggie raised her cup, "Here's to friendship and new beginnings."

Anne's voice quivered. "Speaking of new beginnings, I have some news."

"You're pregnant." Seth teased. The sip of coffee became a scalding mouthful for Keegan. He immediately grabbed his napkin. "You okay, man? You'd think you were responsible."

Anne's face paled and she looked away. The thought of being pregnant had never entered her mind. She imagined the first flutter of life moving inside her. The joy of sharing the news and the anticipation of arrival created excitement. It would not matter if it was boy or girl, only that they knew they were a living testament to her love for the baby's father, Keegan. "No. That's not it. I sold PJ."

"Anne. I'm sorry." Maggie touched Anne's hand.

"Beatha Farms bought him."

"Were they the one's coming to the horse show?"

"No, they bought him sight unseen and gave me my asking price."

"Where is his new home going to be?" Maggie asked.

"At the same barn he's sleeping in tonight, mine." Anne smiled. "They want me to continue to show him and stable him at my place. They are paying me more than what I normally get to board and it will get the farm back in the black again."

"Have you ever heard of Beatha Farms?" Maggie was happy that Anne seemed at peace with the situation although it saddened her that she no longer owned PJ.

"They're from south Georgia around Dublin."

"Keegan, are you familiar with them?" Anne thought maybe he might know the people who now owned PJ.

"No. I've been out of the loop for several years." Keegan continued to sip on the glass of ice water to sooth his burning mouth.

Maggie cleared her throat and shifted the subject for Anne's sake. "I've been thinking that we ought to have a fall party at the hangar. Invite all of the pilots and people who have stood by us to show our appreciation of their loyalty."

"Are you sure that's a good idea?" Seth immediately did not like the idea of the hangar full of people and a party.

"I'm with Seth." Keegan hated to be a party spoiler.

"We all know how the airport grapevine travels. I don't want people to start thinking that Mac's is not going to survive." Maggie had been kicking the idea around since she'd gotten whiff of some of the rumors. "I think if we act like all is well, then people will keep their confidence in us."

"She's got a point." Anne understood Seth's and Keegan's concerns but also agreed with Maggie. "When were you thinking?"

"Georgia has an open weekend next weekend." Maggie knew that Jared and Kyle would not need her to fly them. That week was a break for everyone to take a breath from football season and enjoy the fall.

****

The flight back to Athens was smooth as glass. The evening air continued to cool from the temperatures of blackberry summer. In the distance south of Athens, Maggie spotted the towering plume of black smoke.

Anne studied the smoke. "Wonder what's on fire over there?"

Keegan joining Anne to see the location of the smoke felt a sinking feeling in his stomach. "Maybe it's the forestry doing a control burn."

Seth and Maggie exchanged glances hoping Keegan's assessment was correct. Maggie turned the plane in the direction of the smoke. As they approach the area it became evident that the source of the fire was coming from Anne's farm.

"Oh my God, my horses! That's my barn!" Anne cried out, feeling trapped inside the interior of the plane.

Maggie reduced the power and began a descent lining up with the pasture. She prayed that she'd have enough space to land and stop the plane. She'd only taken the one-fifties in and out of the pasture. Seth saw the concern on Maggie's face. He touched her hand, giving it a squeeze of confidence.

"Honey, put your seat belt on." Keegan tried to calm Anne.

Anne secured her seat belt. She closed her eyes and tried not to think about her frightened horses. The plane began to bounce across the rough surface of the pasture. Anne opened her eyes. In horror she watched the line of trees grow larger. For a fleeting moment, Anne felt that Maggie was not going to get the plane stopped in time. The nose of the plane touched the ground. Seeing Maggie release the back pressure on the control wheel, Anne knew they were okay.

Opening the door, Seth hopped out onto the ground. He turned around in time to catch Anne as she exited the plane. Keegan followed behind her. In the distance, sirens screaming could be heard.

Flames shot from the roof of the riding arena. Keegan reached the entrance to the darkened barn. Heavy black smoke billowed through the hallway of the stables. The frantic screams of frighten horses pawing and kicking could be heard. Keegan turned to Anne and ordered, "Stay outside."

Before Anne could reply, Keegan disappeared into the darkness surrounded by smoke. Within minutes, Anne could hear the thundering sounds of hooves coming toward her. She moved out of the way in time for PJ to gallop past her. All she could see was the whites of his frightened eyes. Behind him came the remaining horses: Chance, Girl, and Angel's Glory with her colt, Angel's Hope. Anne was thankful Joan and the girls had taken their horses on an overnight trail ride.

"Keegan!" Anne yelled into the darken abyss of the smoke filled barn. Seconds became hours. Panic controlled her thoughts. Anne took a step into the opening of the barn. A hand on her shoulder pulled her back. Anne turned to see Maggie and Seth. Together they moved her out of the way of the firemen and their equipment. Anne could not take her eyes away from the opening of the barn in fear she would miss seeing Keegan. She stood oblivious to the fine mist of water falling from the fire hoses. She watched men dressed in full turn out gear with their breathing apparatuses rush into the barn.

Anne held her breath. She could see the reflective yellow of a fireman emerging from the barn with Keegan's limp body. Another fireman followed holding a ball of black fur in his arms. "Keegan!" Maggie and Seth both tighten their grips on Anne.

"Anne, let the paramedics do what they need to help him." All three watched Keegan's unconscious body being laid to the ground. Paramedics rushed with their gear and knelt beside him. Again Anne tried to break free as Seth tried to calm her.

Anne did not take her eyes from Keegan. The Battalion Chief walked over to the trio with Nails in his arms. "This cat and that man over there must have nine lives because we had to dig them from under some debris. Seems like he was hell bent on saving this ball of fur." Maggie took Nails and cradled him in her arms.

"Where are you taking him?" Anne looked past the Battalion Chief to where Keegan was being loaded into the back of an ambulance.

"St. Mary's. Are you his wife?" Anne nodded her head without realizing the full intent of the question. "Then you can ride with him. Get in front."

Anne did not waste time getting into the passenger seat of the ambulance. She tried to turn and see Keegan. Her view was blocked by the two paramedics. A fireman slid into the driver's seat. "Ma'am you need to buckle your seatbelt." Anne turned and did as she was told. The wailing of the sirens deafened any conversation about Keegan's status.

****

Keegan opened his eyes and tried to focus them. The smell of smoke filled his nostrils. His hand moved and touched hair. Slowly, he tilted his head to see its source. He'd recognize the mass of blond hair anywhere. A face began to appear from the strand. A pair of blue eyes met his.

Anne sat up in the chair. She had not moved from his

bedside since he'd been brought in the night before. "Look who's awake."

Keegan's throat was sore and felt as if someone had poured hot acid down it. He tried to sit, but felt Anne's gentle touch on his shoulder pushing him back down. "Easy, you've got a few broken ribs."

She kissed him. A simple brush of the lips, one that left lingering effects on his soul. With the palm of her hand, Anne stroked his cheek while looking in his eyes. She eased herself onto the edge of the bed. Clasping his hand in hers, she kissed its palm before placing it over her heart. "I love you. You foolish, stubborn, pigheaded Irishman. You are here in my heart with every beat."

TWENTY

Dennis could not believe the purpose of Paul's phone call. He was needed for questioning about stealing money from Mac's Flying Service. Dennis paced around the apartment counting the number of rings to Nick's phone and hoping to not get voicemail. "Hey man, we need to talk."

"Can't right now." Nick looked at Lynda sitting next to him. "How about I get with you tomorrow?"

"Are you coming down here?"

"Yeah, say around two p.m."

"At my place?"

"Sure that's fine. See you then."

Lynda laid her head on Nick's shoulder, "Who was that, babe?"

"The new pilot. He wants to get together about the plane. We may go flying so he can get some time."

"That's nice"

****

Next day Nick did not have to knock on Dennis' door, "What's on your mind?"

"I got an interesting phone call yesterday from Paul."

Nick sat on the couch and propped his feet on the coffee table. "What about."

"He was asking if I could come up to Athens and talk to him. He said it's about some missing money from Mac's. He wants me up there the day after tomorrow."

"What'd you tell him?"

"I told him I didn't know what he was talking about and hung up on him." Dennis paced in front of the coffee table. "Nick, what the hell is going on up there? Is Maggie telling people I stole from Mac's?"

"Calm down. I'm sure there's a reasonable explanation."

"What is Lynda saying? I'm sure you've been talking to her."

"She hasn't said much of anything about Mac's."

"I just don't want anything to mess up this new job for me."

"So, things are working out well with Reynard Air."

"Yeah, I stay in the air a lot, and everyone is real nice. I can't say much for the owner because I've never seen him."

"Look, I think you are over reacting. I'll ask Lynda if she knows anything and let you know." Nick stood and patted Dennis on the shoulder. "I'm sure everything is fine, and there's no need to get all worked up."

"Call me as soon as you know something."

"I will." Nick hated that Dennis was an innocent pawn in the twisted web of deceit and greed. If only he had better control of his tongue when drinking. He thought Sam's offer the night he had to lay over due to weather was just one pilot looking out for another. Nick had accepted the offer to stay at Sam's condo instead of a hotel room. He'd always been friendly when they saw each other at the airport.

After a fifth of bourbon, Sam started asking him questions about Mac and his business. Nick cringed at how freely he talked about everything, telling details, details that led to his darkest secrets he'd never shared with anyone before.

*****

Chattanooga, Tennessee

Dennis, glad not to have any passengers aboard, released the brakes and increased the throttles. The past month he had been living in a dream, getting to fly all over the country. He liked the way people looked at him in his pilot's uniform. Women gave him a second glance.

Life could not get any better. The airplane shuddered as the right engine blew smoke followed by flames. He was four hundred feet off the ground, too low to turn back to the airport.

Dennis performed the necessary emergency procedures that had been drilled in him. He tried to control the plane. Time and space did not lend the needed resources. The twin engine burst into flames with the impact into the side of the mountain.

****

Athens, Georgia

"Maggie, there's someone on the phone for you." Lynda opened the office door and stuck her head out interrupting the conversation.

"Hopefully, Dennis will be here soon. Let me go and see who this is." Maggie walked into the office picking up the phone. "This is Maggie."

"Maggie, didn't you have a guy by the name of Dennis Edwards flying for you?"

Recognizing the voice of her boss in Nashville, Maggie asked, "Yeah, why?"

"Sorry to tell you this, but he died in a crash this morning outside of Chattanooga."

Maggie grabbed the edge of the desk. "No, not Dennis. Do you know anything?"

"We're still in the preliminary investigation. It looks like he lost an engine right after takeoff."

"Thanks for letting me know." With a trembling hand Maggie hung up the phone. Looking at Lynda, "Dennis was killed this morning in a plane crash."

The woman dropped her head. "He called last night saying he was stopping here today. He wanted to know if we could go to lunch."

"Lynda, I'm sorry I didn't know you were talking to him, considering everything."

"We weren't. That was the first I'd heard from him since he left."

Maggie looked at Paul who was pacing and checking his watch. With a heavy heart, she approached him. "I just got some bad news?"

"What?" Seth asked as he joined the group.

"Dennis Edwards died this morning in a plane crash outside Chattanooga." Maggie knew the impact of the news was not good for all of them.

"I need to make some calls." Paul was convinced that someone made sure Dennis did not make their meeting. "I may need you to take me to Panama City."

"Sure. Let me go check the weather and make a flight plan."

"If you don't mind, can I tag along?" Seth did not wait to be invited.

****

Panama City, Florida
Paul greeted the blonde man wearing a brown deputy uni-

form. "Hey man, good to see you. I wish it was because we were going scuba diving."

"Likewise. Two of my zone units are standing by at the apartment." The deputy squinted against the bright sunlight before putting on his sunglasses. "There hasn't been any movement in or around it."

"You got the warrant?" Paul buckled his seatbelt.

"I got it as soon as I got off the phone with you. Here it is." The deputy reached above the sun visor that looked like a filing cabinet of folded paper.

"Good. This kid was supposed to meet with me today about a case I'm working on."

"Convenient timing for him to die." The deputy parked in front of the apartment.

"A little too convenient." Paul hoped that Dennis' apartment would give him some answers. "Let's go see what's inside."

The interior of the apartment was pretty much the same as any other single bedroom bachelor pad. Except this one was neat and clean. Paul took a deep breath in disgust knowing someone had gotten there before they did. He recognized a familiar scent. The same scent he'd encountered in Mac's office the morning of his death.

"Looks like someone got here before us. Everything has been cleaned out, clothes, personal effects, papers, everything." The deputy walked around opening cabinets and drawers.

"That doesn't make sense." Paul opened the bedroom closet.

"What do you mean?"

"If you wanted someone to think Dennis is the person stealing money, then wouldn't you leave evidence laying around to implicate him?" Paul tried to control his frustration. He was not any step closer to the answers that eluded him. In his gut, he was positive Lynda was at the center of all of the events that had occurred, starting with embezzlement and ending with murder, but without Dennis, he didn't have anything to back up his suspicions.

"Unless it would place suspicion on someone you wanted to protect."

"True, but who?" Paul stepped outside and inhaled the coastal air. It made him homesick. He pulled out his can of dip. He placed a pinch of tobacco between his gum and cheek. "There's a girl working for Maggie by the name of Lynda Mercer. She said she lived down here but had to leave because of her ex being abusive. Funny thing is, no one has heard from him."

"Are you talking about Tom Mercer? The reason you haven't heard from him is because his body washed up on the beach a few years ago. We've never been able to solve his murder."

"Amazing, isn't it."

"Come to think of it, she's Sam Reynard's step-daughter. The deputy closed the driver's side door and put the car in reverse. "He owns the FBO."

****

Nick finished the last swallow of bourbon. News of Dennis' death had reached him through another pilot. It was hard to believe that less than twenty-four hours ago he'd been standing in Dennis' apartment. Throwing the empty bottle against the brick fire place, he felt like the glass shattering in millions of pieces against the hard surface. His life was like the room, spinning out of control, and he did not know how to stop it.

Nicked picked up a picture of Mac and him standing at the nose of the Navajo. He turned it over on the coffee table so he could not see Mac's smiling face. Mac was proud for Nick getting the job flying for the firm. A wave of nausea from too much bourbon made him heave over the arm of the chair. How could he have betrayed the one man who had been more of a father to him than an employer? More than any man his mother had brought into their lives.

Mac had taught him more about life than how to fly a plane. Nick had been allowed into his home and made part of Mac's family. Wanting the room to stop spinning along with the thoughts in his head, Nick lay back on the couch and closed his eyes. He did not know Lynda was in the room until she spoke.

"What the hell is going on in here, and why is there glass all over the floor?"

Nick opened his bloodshot eyes and focused on the woman standing over him, "Just doing some soul searching, something you ought to try."

"Is this about Dennis?" Lynda did not hide the disgust in her voice. "Where were you yesterday? Uncle Lou called here looking for you. I thought you said you were going flying with a new pilot."

"Uncle Lou...you talking about Lou Holsenbeck with the firm?" Nick's eyes snapped open.

"Yes." Lynda realized her slip.

"Lou Holsenbeck is your uncle?"

"Are you freakin' deaf? Yeah what about it? He's my mother's brother."

"This is unbelievable. Are you telling me Lou has been in on this thing too?"

"Pretty much, but no need to get all upset about it. Do you think Dad would put all of his trust in a two bit pilot, especially one who thinks he's God's answer to the female population?"

For the first time in his life, Nick felt like hitting a woman. "Dennis' death wasn't an accident, was it?"

"You're a smart man. You went to see him yesterday, didn't you? You don't have to answer. I already know you flew into Pensacola and rented a car. Thought you were being slick there, like you did by using Dad's leverage against Gerald Mixon to help Maggie get a sweet deal with that new lease, didn't you. You may have helped give Mac's Flying Service an indefinite home, but too bad your trip didn't save Dennis."

"*GET OUT...GET OUT* of my house now before I am no longer able to control my actions of wanting to choke the life out of your cold black heart."

Lynda neared Nick and got into his face, "Be careful, Masden. You have too much to lose. You don't want to wind up like Dennis."

Nick not moving spoke through clenched teeth. "I have already lost everything that was ever important to me. Now get the hell out of my house."

Lynda snatched her purse from the couch and left Nick standing alone. He listened to the sound of her car driving away. Picking up his cell phone, he dialed the number to the one person who could stop all the madness.

****

"Maggie, I appreciate you getting me down there. Just send me a bill." Paul had kept the information about Lynda and Sam to himself.

"I will, Paul." Maggie waited until Paul was gone. "Seth, I need to talk to you somewhere private."

Seth looked at his watch. "Maggie, I'd love to, but I've got to go."

"How long are we going to do this?"

"Do what?"

"This dance of polite existence?"

Seth took Maggie's hand off his arm and held up her hand. "As long as you continue to wear his ring. It's obvious you made your choice." Letting Maggie's hand drop, Seth briskly walked away.

"Go ahead, leave. That's one maneuver you have down pat." Maggie regretted her words as soon as they left her lips.

Seth stopped at the doorway and turned. "If that what you want." He turned and exited the hangar.

Maggie stared at the vacant space. Deep in her soul she knew that she'd pushed Seth away for the last time. She looked around the hangar, the offices, planes, and the place that was home to her. Everywhere were images of Seth. It was Seth's voice she heard, his thoughts that mattered to her, and him for whom her heart ached.

She ran to the doorway. Images of another time that she'd ran for Seth flooded her. How many chances does one person get to correct her mistakes? Maggie stepped onto the porch in time to see Seth's Jeep becoming a tiny speck while he drove away. Tears streamed down her face. It was too late. He was gone.

TWENTY ONE

"Aunt Ethel, are you okay? You're white as a sheet?" Anne reached out and touched her Aunt; she could feel her trembling, "Lord, what has you shaking? Where's Maggie?"

"Don't say anything. Just act natural and follow me to Mac's office." Aunt Ethel wished a million times over that she'd not opened the door to Maggie's office. The voices had piqued her curiosity. The person she found on the other side of the door with Nick and Maggie made her blood run cold.

Anne nodded and put the containers inside the door of the camper. She followed Ethel into the offices. Anne turned looking for Keegan. He was busy unloading hay bales from the truck for the weekend's party.

"Is it Maggie?" Anne had been worried about Maggie since Seth's departure.

"Little Anne, nice of you to join us. I was sure you didn't want to miss this little home coming."

Anne froze at the sight of the man pressing a gun into Maggie's rib cage. She looked from Maggie toward Nick. "Nick, who is this man, and what's going on?"

"Now that we have everyone together, I guess all of you would like to know the special occasion of this party." Sam walked over to Mac's desk and ran his finger across the frame with Anne's picture. "You sure do look like your ma. Nick you picked a nice frame to replace the one I broke."

243

"You knew my mother?" Anne turned her attention to Nick. "What does he mean?"

"Remember the man I mention that was your dad's friend at school? This is him, Sam Reynard." Aunt Ethel had met Sam twice during her visits to her cousins in South Georgia.

"So, you told her the whole little story of me and Diane. I hope you included how Mac killed my wife and son in revenge."

"It was an accident, Sam. Mac had nothing to do with Louise's death. She lost control of the plane on landing." Ethel moved closer to Anne and Maggie.

"That's because the the nose wheel collapsed, and who was it that was the last to work on that plane? Non-other than Mac Harris. It was just after he caught me in bed with his wife." Sam looked over at Anne to see her reaction. He could see she was not shocked by his words. "Seems like you told her everything about her whoring ma. I'm surprised that you had it in you to destroy a girl's image of her sweet mother."

"My mother was not a whore." Anne spat in disgust.

"That's a matter of opinion." Sam focused his attention on Nick. "Bet no one has ever bothered to tell you the truth about her death and who was responsible."

"Nick, what he is saying?" Anne looked at Nick. He turned his head away from her stare.

"Yeah, Masden what am I saying?" Sam removed the picture from the desk and shoved it in front of Nick. "I understand this picture has caused a lot of questions over the past month. Like how did it come into existence? Why don't you tell her?"

"It isn't important." Nick looked at Anne wishing that she never have to know the truth, not for his sake but hers.

"The hell it isn't. I want to know." Anne looked at Nick.

"Since he can't find the courage in his spineless body to tell you, I will."

"You see Nick here was entertaining your lonely, neglected ma while Mac was busy making this place stay alive. Unfortunately, Diane always had a way of taking seriously things poked in fun. She had to be the most fertile female I've ever known in my life time. All a man had to do was just wink, and she'd find herself pregnant. That's just what she did with Nick here, found herself pregnant with his bastard child." Sam laughed. "A bastard fathering a bastard. Amazing how history repeats itself."

"You slept with my mother?" Anne felt dirty and in need of a shower from the realization that she'd slept with the same man as her mother.

"Seems like Diane was going to tell Mac the truth when she returned home from your horse show. But Nick didn't want that to happen, did you, Nick? You knew if Mac found out that you'd been playing house while he was out of town, your gravy train would end right there."

Images of the night of the accident flashed in front of Anne's eyes, "You were there that night."

Nick closed his eyes, not wanting to see Anne's face. The events of Diane's last day alive replayed in his memory. "I came to the horse show to try and convince her not to tell Mac about us and that she was pregnant. She refused to listen to any reasoning. She said she had to get back to you and left me. I returned home and started drinking and trying to figure out what to do. Night had settled in, and I knew ya'll would be back from the show. I had to give it one more try to convince her not to say anything. I started toward Whitehall and drove by the house, but I didn't see the truck." Nick paused. He knew that his words were destroying the one person that believed in him. "As I turned onto the road to the farm, the rain began to pour. I was still reeling from the liquor. All I remember seeing were headlights coming toward me as I crossed the centerline. I swerved back in my lane in time to hear tires squealing and the sound of metal tearing." Nick stopped talking. He opened his eyes, which were filled with terror and regret. He hated what he saw as he looked at Anne. "I slammed on brakes and turned around. The carnage before me was the truck that your mom drove. I walked to the vehicle and looked inside. You were unconscious in the passenger seat still in your seatbelt. When I looked at Diane there was blood coming from head where she hit the windshield. She opened her eyes..."

"And said your name." Anne completed Nick's sentence for him. She realized that was the part of her nightmares that she could not remember, only that she would wake up screaming his name. "How could you just walk away and leave like you did?"

"At that point, I was stone cold sober. I got in my car and drove. When Mac said you had no recollection of the accident, and the sheriff department did not have any clues as to who had left the scene, I felt relieved." Nick picked up the picture. "Before leaving I grabbed your mom's camera bag in fear there were pictures on it with me. She was always shooting pictures of me. I would often tell her to be careful that you'd never know whose hands the photos could fall into." Nick looked at Sam, "I was right because one day this photo showed up here on Mac's desk."

"It was my way of telling you that you'd better stay on

246

task of what I wanted." Sam looked at Anne, "You see Nick's meeting you at that birthday party for Joan was no accident. I made sure that the two of you were sent an invitation. Both of you were nothing but pawns being moved across a chessboard for me. Everything was working great, even up to the point that Mac had the misfortune of leaving this earth." Sam looked at Maggie and Anne who now stood on either side of Ethel. "I had to give it to him. Considering his condition, he went down fighting for your honor Anne." Sam turned the second picture of Maggie around. "Yours and Maggie's pictures were the last images he saw before his poor heart gave out on him."

"Did you kill Mac?" Maggie asked trying to control her anger.

"Kinda, but I had some help." The three women looked over at Nick. "Oh, no, Nick is innocent in this part. I owe my debt of gratitude to my lovely step-daughter, Lynda." Sam enjoyed the surprise on the three women's face. "Lynda should have been my own flesh and blood. We are both from the same cut of cloth."

"She's the one that put the arsenic in my creamer and Mac's Drambuie? Where's the money, Sam?" Maggie did not care that her tone was confrontational.

"Was she the one behind all my problems at the farm and the barn fire that almost killed Keegan?" Anne restrained the urge to lunge for Sam.

"I have to give her credit for the arsenic and money, but I had some help with the farm." Sam allowed a grin to crawl across his face and reveal his yellowing teeth. "Then there was that poor sweet little cat. That was my first move. I knew Mac would send his precious Maggie packing to protect her."

Sam leered at Maggie. "With you out of the way, that made room for Lynda to take your place."

"Nick. No. Not you." Anne did not think she could bear anymore heartache.

"Nick's hands are clean on that. I believe the owner of a red truck is responsible."

"If you are implying Keegan. We know it wasn't him."

"Foolish girl. Of course, it was." Sam enjoyed the way Anne's confidence deflated like a leaking balloon. "Like your ma, you have poor judgment in men."

"Don't believe him, Anne." Nick pleaded. "It wasn't Keegan."

Anne lunged for Sam. She did not expect the force that slammed into her, knocking her to the floor. The sound of a gun firing and the acrid smell of gun powder filled the room. For a moment, she was sure she'd been shot but was confused at the lack of pain.

She moved in time to see Nick falling to the floor in front of her. A bright red stain began to appear on the front of his shirt. Gasping for breath, Nick looked at Anne and tried to speak. His words faltered as his eyes glazed over.

Maggie realized that no sound was coming from Aunt Ethel's direction. She looked up in time to see Ethel standing, holding the gun and pointing it at Sam. Before anyone could move or speak, the office door swung open. Paul stepped into the room with his gun drawn. Madison and Keegan followed. Sam sneered at Ethel. "Come on, old woman, pull the trigger. You ain't got the guts to do it."

Paul saw the gun in Ethel's hand. She moved her finger onto the trigger. "Ethel, don't. Taking another human beings life is something that will remain with you the rest of yours.

I've got it now. You are okay. Just lower the gun and hand it to me."

Madison took the gun from her hand and gave it to Paul. "Come on, let's go outside."

Keegan looked at Anne, her huddled body cradling Nick's. He could not stomach the scene. He turned and exited.

"Anne, come on, let's go outside." Maggie's first concern was Anne.

Anne gently laid Nick's head on the floor and accepted Maggie's hand.

"I thought I'd lost you." Ethel still shaken from the events embraced Anne. She was oblivious to the uniformed officers who walked passed her or the sound of Paul's voice reading Sam his rights.

"Where's Keegan?" Anne asked in a hushed whisper.

Maggie spotted Keegan standing in the hangar. Keegan turned at the sound of the closing door to see Maggie walking toward him.

"Anne is asking for you." Maggie tried to control her disappointment in Keegan's reaction

"Why, to replace her dead lover?"

"You don't understand Keegan." Maggie was taken aback by the venom in Keegan's tone

"I think I got a clear picture."

"Do you?" Maggie's anger snapped. She stood in front of Keegan. "What you thought you saw is not the reality. Yes, you saw Anne holding another man's lifeless body, but it is you that she has allowed herself to love. And if you are so ignorant not to realize that, then I pity you." Maggie's voice reached an hysterical pitch and echoed through the hangar. "She was almost killed in there trying to save me. If it had not been for Nick, she could be dead right now. So, instead of standing out here licking your injured male pride and ego, you need to have your ass in there taking care of her." Maggie's body trembled. "Or are you going to be another man in her life to disappoint her?"

"You're a good one to give advice about love." Keegan matched the fire in Maggie's eyes. "Did you know Seth is leaving tonight? He's going back to the airlines and has accepted a transfer away from here and you." Maggie rocked backwards at the news. "He came by yesterday and cleared his stuff from the flight instructor's desk. Instead of giving me lectures about how I should love someone, maybe you should practice what you preach."

"What's going on here? Why's there so many cop cars in the parking lot?" The handful of shopping bags fell to the floor when Lynda saw her father in handcuffs. "Dad!"

"I'm so glad you made it back in time." Paul walked over to her. "Lynda Mercer, you have the right to remain silent. Anything you say…"

"Are you arresting me? On what grounds?"

"…can and will be held against you in a court of law. You have the right to an attorney."

"I can't believe this. I know my rights. And you have to tell me what I am being charged with."

"If you can't afford an attorney one will be appointed for you. Do you understand these rights as I have explained them to you?"

"Yes, for the last time, what the hell is this about?"

"Please turn around for me and place your hands behind your back." Lynda turned around doing as she was told. The feel of cold metal touching her wrists made her shiver. "Lynda Mercer, you are being charged with murder and embezzlement for starters. And I think there're some folks down in Panama City that'd like to discuss the death of your late husband, Tom Mercer." Paul turned to one of the officer's standing next to him. "You can transport her."

"That was Sam Reynard. Lynda is his daughter." Keegan was still trying to digest what he'd just witnessed and heard.

"Yes. Lou Holsenbeck is her uncle." Paul took a package from one of the officers who had exited the office. "This is a wire that Nick was wearing."

"Nick was wearing a wire?" Maggie tried to understand how the pieces fit together. "Why?"

"He called me after we returned from Panama City. Dennis' death rattled him. He told me everything. How Sam was black-mailing him. Lynda's involvement. We've been able to locate the accounts she was funneling the money into."

"What about my farm?" Anne stood outside the lobby door. She looked at Keegan. All of them wanted to believe that Nick had told the truth about Keegan.

"We arrested the person responsible for the problems at the farm, including the barn fire." Paul noticed Seth's absence. "The man worked for Lou Holsenbeck."

"He saved us. Nick. He saw me reach for the gun. He shoved me to the floor." Anne needed everyone to know that Nick was not all bad. "He told me that Sam was lying about you, Keegan. He wanted me to know that you weren't responsible."

Keegan moved toward Anne in time to catch her in his arms. Another wave of sobs convulsed through her body. "Come on, Anne. Why don't we get away from here?"

Anne allowed Keegan to lead her out of the hangar and into his truck. She leaned her head back and stared at the roof. Every time she closed her eyes, the image of Nick's body on the floor filled them. Anne reached over and placed her hand on Keegan's thigh.

The grip on his thigh told him that Anne was still not in a safe place emotionally. He placed his hand over hers. From the corner of his eye, he could see tears sliding down her face.

Keegan turned the truck onto the road to the farm. He'd driven the stretch of road multiple times. No thought had been given to the fact that it was this same road that Anne had lost her mother—until now. Sobs shook Anne's body while she stared out the truck's passenger window. He did not need to ask the significance of the stretch of road they were traveling. It was where the accident had occurred. Her grip on his thigh tightened, and he accelerated the truck.

He parked the truck in the driveway and tried not to focus on the charred remains of the barn. Keegan squeezed Anne's hand before opening the door and exiting. "Stay here." He hopped out of the truck and did not waste time getting to the passenger's side. Keegan opened the door and reached inside. He gathered Anne into his arms and carried her inside the house. He gently placed her on the bed. She'd worn a skirt and simple blouse. Both were stained with blood and would need to be thrown away. There was a smear of blood on the side of her face and remnants on her hands. The assessment of Anne made a wave of nausea course through Keegan.

He turned and walked away. With all his strength, he tried to control the thoughts running through him. Reality of how close he came to losing Anne crushed down on him and made his knees weak. He grabbed the sideboard where she stored her liquor. His intentions had been to pour a glass of scotch for her. He downed the fiery liquid and reined in his emotions. Focus he told himself. She's alive and okay. The rest isn't important.

Keegan poured more of the amber liquid into the highball glass. He carried it into the bedroom. Anne's was curled in a fetal position. Strands of her hair covered her face. He noticed her fingering the pendant on her necklace. It was the one he'd given her. "Here this will help you."

Anne reached up and took the glass. In one quick swallow, she drained the glass of its contents. Keegan sat down and pulled her close to him. He tried not to focus on the blood that covered her. Guilt set in for not taking care of her. Maggie's words echoed about how all the men in Anne's life had failed her. His name now joined that list.

Anne closed her eyes and allowed herself to relax into the warmth of his body. Taking a deep breath, she tried to breathe in as much of his masculine scent. The events in her dad's office seemed like a bad dream, but she knew that it had been a cold hard reality.

In a hushed slow rhythmic tone, Anne began to tell of the events. "Nick was responsible for my mother's death. He'd gotten her pregnant and was scared of losing everything when Dad found out. He was the driver of car that came at us that night. I remembered tonight that he was there. It was his name Mom said before she died."

A sinking feeling began to form in the pit of Keegan's stomach. He had allowed himself to be blinded by jealousy. It was he who Anne turned to for comfort. Despite her words of love he refused to believe their truth. He had held back his emotions from her.

"Sam blamed my dad for his family's death and wanted to destroy anything associated with Dad." A shudder ran through Anne, "Somehow, Sam found out about Nick and my mom. He used it to blackmail Nick into helping him destroy the business. The picture on dad's desk was sent by Sam as a warning to Nick." Anne paused and listen to Keegan's strong, steady heartbeat. Her thoughts went to Nick and his final moments. "He tried to say something before he died. All I could think sitting on that floor holding him, was despite all the things he'd admitted, he saved our lives in the end."

Keegan cringed as he thought about what Anne had said to him. How the two people he had once considered the most selfish had risked their lives to save another person's. All he could do was hold on to her as tight as he could.

"You are quiet."

"I can't get over how close I came to losing you tonight. I love you, Anne Harris."

TWENTY TWO

M aggie parked her car behind Seth's Jeep. Her feet barely touched the ground until she found herself at his door. Frantic fingers pushed the doorbell creating a continuous chime of music. Impatient at the lack of response, she began pounding on the door with her fist.

"Maggie, what is going on?" Seth, breathless, stood in the doorway. He'd been showering when the insistent chiming of his doorbell created alarm for him.

"May I come in?" Maggie did not miss the luggage by the door and Seth's scarcity of clothing. The clean scent of masculine soap surrounded him. It was obvious he'd not taken time to dry from the form of water droplets on his chiseled chest.

"Is everything okay?" His concern continued to grow.

"I know I am probably too late, but before you leave, I wanted you to know I love you. The night of the storm I chose you. I didn't want you to leave." She moved forward and kissed him.

Seth placed his arms around her waist pulling her closer to him. His hands move downward over her body cupping her behind, lifting her off the floor. Maggie wrapped her legs around Seth's waist. Her body trembled with anticipation of his lovemaking. No longer did she want to imagine the feel of his body, to crave his kisses, and yearn for his love. "Make love to me Seth."

The husky plea was like a magnet drawing him to her. Seth

COMING HOME—A SECOND CHANCE AT GOODBYE

lowered his body over hers. He allowed his touch and kisses to express the love exploding inside him. His hands wanted to touch all of her at one time.

Her soul blossomed with life at his touch. She could feel the strong beat of Seth's heart against his chest under her hands. The taste of his mouth was intoxicating. She felt alive.

In the fading rays of daylight, their two bodies became one. Maggie did not close her eyes but held Seth's gaze. The emotions in his eyes spoke of the love that she too felt. The strength of his embrace brought the security she'd longed for. His kisses calmed her fears, giving serenity to her soul. Words were not needed as their bodies spoke the language of love.

****

Maggie woke to the sound of Seth's breathing. She liked the weight of his arm around her mid-section. Thoughts of the passion they'd shared reignited her desire for him. She tried not to think about the luggage sitting next to the door and his leaving.

"You're quiet." Seth knew she was awake. He had been in a half doze when he heard her breathing change.

"I was thinking about you leaving." Maggie rolled over and faced him.

"Do you want me to leave?" Seth pushed her hair from her face.

"No." Maggie traced his lips with her finger.

"Then I will stay." Seth leaned over and kissed her. "Did Keegan tell you?"

"More or less." Maggie placed a hand on his chest.

"That sounds ominous." Seth liked the feel of Maggie's fingers playing with the hairs on his chest.

"I'm surprise no one has called you about today's events."

"Maggie, what are not telling me?" Seth became serious.

"Let's just say it was an exciting day around the hangar."

Maggie began to tell Seth of the events. "…and then Anne reached for Sam's gun but Nick pushed her aside. Seth, Nick's dead. He saved Anne and me."

Seth did not move. Images of the scene Maggie described brought a chill. The realization of how close Maggie came to being harmed made him pull her closer to him. Neither of them moved but allowed the weight of the moment to pass.

"Keegan came in and saw Anne holding Nick's body. He lost it and stormed out. We had words about how he didn't understand what he'd seen. He told me you were leaving tonight." Maggie's voice caught in her throat. "All I could think about while there were police, the coroner's office, and other people milling in and out of the hangar was you. Mac's Flying Service did not matter to me without you."

Seth caressed Maggie's cheek before leaning in to kiss her. A kiss that began slowly and grew with intensity. He could lie with her in his arms for eternity.

EPILOGUE

*T*he house was a flurry of people moving about in a hurried pace to and from the large vans parked outside. People carrying clipboards shouted orders at those scurrying with loaded arms of everything needed to make this day special.

Inside was just as much a calamity of organized chaos, especially in the kitchen. Ovens exuded intense heat and aromatic smells of their contents. Above the hum stood one woman in control, like a Sergeant Major, over looking, inspecting, and directing, but not in a gruff military voice. She used a soft spoken voice filled with a deep southern drawl like sorghum syrup on a cold winter's morning. Her uniform was formal but not to the strict standards of an officer's dress uniform. It was of soft flowing chiffon. With each turn, she enjoyed allowing its hem swirl as if she was gliding and twirling to the music of the house.

This day had meaning for her on many levels. Her family was together, including her two sons. Both were always busy with their lives. Upstairs, she could hear the frantic footsteps of the two women as they prepared to embark upon the journey of marriage. For them and their eager grooms, this day had to be perfect.

Her feet floated up the stairs as if they were cushioned by clouds of excitement. Ethel knocked on the bedroom door before pushing it open. The bright yellow room bathed in sunlight illuminated the two women covered in white. Both of them turned around smiling and giggling like school girls.

With tears of joy in her eyes, Aunt Ethel looked at Anne and then to Maggie, "You girls are beautiful." Ethel stepped in front of Anne, "Every bride needs something old, something new, something borrowed, and something blue." Holding out a strand of pearls, she said, "These were your mother's. I wish she and Mac could be here today."

Anne turned her back and fingered the strand of pearls while Ethel secured the clasp. Looking into the mirror at the pearls, she turned giving her aunt a tight hug, "Thank you, Aunt Ethel. I love you."

"I love you too." Ethel turned to Maggie, "Seth wanted you to have this today." Ethel opened the box causing Maggie to gasp. "He knew how much the ring Mac gave you meant to you, so he had it cleaned and wanted you to wear it today."

Maggie took the box. Since the night she declared her love to Seth, Maggie had put the ring in her jewelry box. She slid the ring onto her right hand.

"That gives you something blue, but you don't have something borrowed." Ethel took Maggie's arm and placed a diamond bracelet around it closing the clasp. "This was a gift to me from my parents. Today, I am giving it to you."

Maggie held the woman close to her. "Thank you, Aunt Ethel."

A soft knock on the door interrupted the scene. All three women watched an older woman with streaks of gray highlighting her red hair enter the room. She moved with grace and confidence. "I hope I'm not intruding. A nice young man said I could find Anne in here."

"Yes ma'am. That would be me." Anne did not recognize the woman.

A well-manicured hand extended forward. "I'm Mary Katherine Finnegan."

"PJ's owner. Why are you here on my wedding day?" Anne wasn't sure if the smiling woman was friend or foe. She was about to tell the woman where she could go in not pleasant terms.

"My grandson asked me to give you this." Mary Katherine handed Anne a white envelope. "I've traveled a long ways to get here today to see this moment."

Anne looked at Maggie and then Aunt Ethel. She licked her sudden dry lips and tried to swallow. The time had come for her to say goodbye to her barn's pride. With trembling hands she opened the envelope and began to read the folded pages. "Oh my." Tears flowed.

"Anne, what is it?" Maggie and Aunt Ethel moved around Anne.

"This is Keegan's grandmother and part owner of Beatha Farms."

"Keegan owns the other half. It was part of his inheritance after his grandpa passed. He called me several months ago and asked me to discreetly handle the purchase of a Hanoverian Stallion. So I made the purchase using my maiden name. I sensed there was a lot more behind this horse than good breeding and training. I can see I was right." Mary Katherine stepped forward and took Anne's hands. "I've spent many nights worrying about that grandson of mine. He's had a hard life, and his stubbornness can get in his way. I knew it would take someone special to break him and settle him down."

"Thank you Ms. Finnegan." Anne accepted the woman's hug.

"Please, Mary Kate or Ma'am maw. You're about to be family." Mary Kate liked what she saw in Anne and knew that her grandson had chosen well. "I'd better get to my seat."

"You girls have kept those two boys waiting long enough." Aunt Ethel dabbed her eyes with a tissue. "Madison should be here soon for you."

"Speaking of keeping someone waiting, how long are you going to keep Madison waiting before you say yes to a date?" Anne sniffled and teased her aunt.

"I've got too much on my plate to think about that." Aunt Ethel blushed. The thought of Madison made her feel like a young girl.

Madison knocked on the door before opening it. "It's time girls." He admired the oldest of the three women. The blue chiffon dress accentuated her in the right places. He gave her a quick wink before escorting Anne and Maggie out of the room.

Thank you for reading *Coming Home—A Second Change at Goodbye* I hope that you enjoyed meeting the characters and their journey.

Here is a sneak peek at the second book in the Coming Home series, *Ethel's Song*.

Tori

ETHEL'S SONG

The crying sound of a baby increased Howard's already agitated state. For the past three nights, the little writhing bastard would not sleep for more than two hours waking him up. He didn't want this kid anymore than he did the first one. Throwing the covers back and muttering under his breath the uselessness of trying to get a decent night's sleep, Howard wandered into the kitchen.

The light of the stove cast enough light in the dark kitchen for him to see Ethel's figure sitting at the kitchen table. She was huddled with their infant son, who refused to latch onto the exposed nipple. "Can't you do something to shut that thing up? This is the third night in a row he has kept this whole house up." Stumbling across the orange linoleum floor, Howard pulled the silver handle on the fridge door, took out a gallon of milk, opened the top, and drank straight from the jug. Wiping his mouth with the back of his hand, he propped one arm up on the open door of the fridge looking. He could feel the resentment and contempt building toward the mousy, brown haired woman. The woman that he was shackled to in a marriage he did not want. Everything about his life was her fault.

Without having to look up, Ethel felt the heat of Howard's stare. Ever since the birth of Mathias, Howard had become meaner and more hateful to her and both of the boys. "Howard, I'm sorry we woke you. I'd hope by bringing him down here it wouldn't bother you."

Slamming the door of the fridge, Howard said, "Freaking

thing could wake the dead with all that shrilling he's doing."

Ethel ducked her head down over the infant while making shushing sounds and wishing Mathias would cooperate before Howard lost his temper. "I'm sorry."

"Sorry just isn't going to cut it, Ethel. I can't live this way. I begged you not to have this brat. You could have had an abortion."

"That is not the way to speak of your son, Howard. You know I could not have agreed to killing something that God created."

Howard's bellowing caused Mathias to increase the volume of his cries, "You and your religion. You didn't want to use birth control because of your religion. Selfish that is what you are, a selfish, stupid, fat bitch. I can't stand the sight of you. You should be thankful that someone like me was willing to marry you." Towering over Ethel, Howard watched as Ethel cradled the howling infant in her arms, hovering over it like a precious piece of porcelain. "Let's see how well you can raise this brat along with the one upstairs by yourself without me around."

Ethel closed her eyes as tight as she could to the point of seeing spots in their darkness as she rocked back and forth with Mathias against her chest. Silently, she prayed Howard would not hit her this time. She could already feel the disturbance in the air of his arm swinging back before coming down full force, backhanding her. The muscles in her body became rigid with anticipation of the pain that had become all too familiar.

Tick, tick, tick, the second hand of the wall clock counted down before another beating would begin. The front door slamming was her reprieve. The gunning of the car's engine followed by the squealing of tires created relief in her. It was not unusual for Howard to disappear. She didn't care where or who he went to when he left.

The muscles in her arms begin to quiver from being taunt for too long. Mathias had quieted down and was no longer screaming at the top of his lungs. For a moment, she was afraid she'd suffocated him. Slowly sitting up, she looked into the face of her infant son and was met with grayish blue eyes before a sleepy yawn was released.

The gentle touch of the small hand on her shoulder startled her. Fresh tears began to flow at the sight of her oldest son Thomas, dressed in footed pajamas, his head full of brown curls matching hers. A brown teddy bear with floppy arms and legs dangled from his other hand. In his small voice, Thomas tried to sound grown up for his tender eight years. "It's going to be okay, Momma. I will take care of you and Mathias. I don't care what Daddy says. You are smart and pretty, and I love you more than he does."

Ethel, reaching out and pulling her son close to her, could not speak past the lump in her throat. To her horror, she realized Thomas had heard the bitter, hateful words Howard spoke before leaving. Scared by the fact that she was now alone with two young boys to raise, Ethel was also relieved by the realization that Howard was gone and would no longer hurt her or her sons again.

Please Visit Us at: www.readtoribailey.com

Social Media
Facebook: ToriBaileyInk
Twitter: @readtoribailey
Pinterest: ReadToriBailey

CPSIA information can be obtained
at www.ICGtesting.com
Printed in the USA
LVHW08s1724020718
582346LV00005B/21/P